HOW TO MURDER A BOYBAND

JASON ROCHE

CRANTHORPE
— MILLNER —
PUBLISHERS

First published by Cranthorpe Millner Publishers (2022)

ISBN 978-1-912964-99-4 (Paperback)

www.cranthorpemillner.com

Cranthorpe Millner Publishers

LONDON

2001

CHAPTER 1

BIG FaT ARSe

So there's this big fat arse in front of me, blocking the path and turning an already depressing morning into one that makes you want to turn around, flip your umbrella the correct way and go home. But you don't. And there the arse looms, dominating the width of the concrete walkway, the seam on the worn denim moments away from a symphonic tear. With each stride it takes on another impossible dimension, percolating beneath the faded material, the unsymmetrical ovals buckling into an angry felled eight. There should be a law against this sort of thing; a code or something which prevents people like this ruining other people's mornings. And not because they're fat (oh no, that would be too easy to categorise and scorn them with that) but because they're taking up the whole pavement, maliciously blocking it so that hard-working, decent people like me are prevented from passing; so that our pursuant arses are all bunched together behind the one that momentarily holds the power.

I need to get past as the 'alarm didn't go off' excuse is getting way too stale and my umbrella's impotence means I'll look a complete state after another unforgiving downpour. And it's Monday, what a bonus. A WeightWatchers advert catches my eye and I momentarily forget that I'm late. Obscured by a lamppost and damaged by the relentless rain and glue from old posters, a distorted picture of a happy fat person with what looks like a tape measure lassoed around her waist seems to grimace back at me. Her thumb is raised towards me.

I force myself to relax and slow down a little, letting the rain pelt my forehead, trying not to wince from the stinging sensation. Someone impolitely coughs behind me and I'm not sure whether they're hinting for me to move or the Arse. More fruitless coughs follow and everyone's now jamming into my back like discarded trolleys in a supermarket loading bay.

The pressure behind me becomes too much so I make a desperate break for it, spotting a gap above his left love handle as he raises his hand towards his mouth, but it's like I'm a pebble on a bouncy castle as I get shunted backwards, relegated to the back of the 'arse-passing' queue, a swathe of burbled discontent scolding my feeble attempt. I'm at the back of the queue when my replacement at the front attempts another Kamikaze surge, this time making it through, turning towards the man with the arse and shaking her head as she speeds forward into the throng ahead.

The man finally comprehends that the sole reason for the jam is him and tries to press himself to one side against a chipped rail as the professional mob gush through the opening. His embarrassment is clear and the crimson appearing in his already rosy cheeks makes me stop, offer some sort of indecisive benevolent gesture and proceed through the diagonal shower. He smiles as I leave.

This is where I work: a large angular silver building in the City's kernel; a plethora of pink ties and mismatched thick pin striped suits and funny hairdos planted atop both male and female brains. Like a rabbit warren, everyone's bustling and scraping and gnawing to get somewhere or be somewhere or do something.

I make it to my desk in the open plan office with absolutely no view and people I'm hesitant to say I really know. The other usual: "Buses!" I say, shaking my head and logging on, ready for a day of staring into the bowels of my computer and making it produce something disproportionate to the amount of effort I'm willing to expend. At least I made it, soaked so that everything is uncomfortably damp for at least the first two hours. Thankfully I've not planned any meetings in the morning, but I wouldn't do that anyway – I'm not a morning person. I struggle; I mean really struggle with mornings – getting out of bed must be the single most soul-destroying exercise I embark upon. And I perform this heinous activity at least once a day. I've tried everything: jumping up as soon as I hear the alarm, peppermint soap for an awakening tingle; even putting my alarm clock on the other side of the room. But nothing works – it always spirals south into me counting backwards from twenty, dozing off at about eleven and then waking up in a panic half an hour later, having missed my bus and wishing I were dead. But I'm not; I'm at work, late.

I sit facing a girl named Christie who seems to know everything. She's very considerate because she always helps me finish my sentences especially when we're in meetings with senior management. Sometimes, usually in the afternoon, she stares at me for a couple of minutes shaking her head. That's all she does and then busily resumes showing everyone how stressed and involved she is. Whenever she has the opportunity to berate what she calls 'people like me' she takes it with open steaming palms, relishing each second of proving how much better she is than me. I think she's even resorted to spreading untrue rumours about my sexual orientation.

My desk has scrape marks beneath it from all the people I have to deal with. People like Christie. Also my pens are all destroyed, chewed to the hilt. Shattered bits of plastic adorn the bin, the edge of my lips and my stomach. A week ago I was engrossed in a fantasy about slapping Christie to death with a mackerel when the pressure of a frantic pen chewing episode sent a fragment flying through the air to embed itself in her hostile eyeball. It was an accident but you'd think a human rights violation had occurred – blood, tears, false concern, profuse apologies, but the best part was the silence, the beautiful silence. No more of her whining, nasal, dictatorial anecdotes. It was only brief resolve though; she was back to her usual form a day later with an over-the-top bandage and a few cheap 'Get Well Soon' gifts. All because of me and my pen chewing fetish.

The day at the office is so uneventful that I'm hesitant to even donate a full thought to it, so I won't. Getting home to my minimalist yet satisfyingly stark one bedroom flat is about as predictable as diarrhoea after a 4am kebab. Even though I should, I don't even greet Her anymore; I just dump my coat in the bedroom and retire to the television set where I can hibernate for a while. But the nagging starts the second I enter and I try to revisit the splinter of affection we once held for each other, taking Her hands in mine and begging for a peaceful evening. She hiccups, dropping a pile of dirty laundry at my feet and I can tell She's just got home because She's still in Her work clothes and hasn't had time to shower.

Usually I'm home first and She returns with the smell of strong cologne on Her throat after a 'work function', the customary emergency shower following to wash away God knows what. I sometimes wonder if I'm making this up or hoping it up; or perhaps I'm even content to be the aggrieved helpless victim, too afraid to talk about it and too numbed by the organisation of an average day. I always go to bed after Her, hopeful that She'll be well into Her wispy snoring and far away from my side of the bed. I sneak in, careful not to create an air pocket under the duvet, turn over and try to fall asleep while the weight of my world transcends through my conscious. I don't sleep well. Ever. Every night is a constant battle fuelled by the imminent lack of desire to get out of my warm sanctuary. She goes to work before me, which is a bonus because it means I can knock one off in peace. But then I fall asleep again and when I do eventually make it up and out, there's invariably some big fat rosy-cheeked arse toddling down the street ahead of me, waiting to block my way.

CHAPTER 2
LONDON TRAVEL

Morning time, complete with arctic ceramic floors and a shower that refuses to mix the hot and cold, so my skin is tingling like I've got a rash all over my body and my head itches. The cereal's good though, really good. I do live for how the raisins and oats blend to scrape the top of my raw morning palate while still making sure to let my body know that an exceptional bowel movement is just around the corner. Save it for the office, that's what I say. Rather get paid to embrace the hostile workings of a spotlessly Harpic power-cleaned digestive tract than pay to embrace the hostile workings of a spotlessly Harpic power-cleaned digestive tract.

I'm alone in the apartment, armed with a spoon and an iron, and determined to remain positive even though She forgot to take Her gym bag despite insisting that the later than normal Pilates class was going to 'burn, burn, burn! like never before'. And she forgot to flush which is probably worse. And inexcusable. And more pre-meditated.

The cereal's done, my shoes are shined and my shirt is almost ironed – good enough for a day that holds promise. I'm optimistic today: there's a glimmer of sunshine hopping through the balcony window and I slept reasonably well without any destructive interruptions of foul-mouthed women cursing their lovers or police sirens that seem to only circle my block. A television insert catches my attention because it's about the Beatles – old black and white images drawing me into a time of matching hairdos and pioneering music. But the news story is far more sinister; far more dire and disastrous for mankind. It reflects how we, as a species, have embraced all that is not real; licked the lid of all that is superficial. I can barely believe my ears when I hear it – like a plague creeping up on our shores leaving us gasping for air where there used to be plenty. The Beatles' record of number ones in the UK has been broken! By whom? Don't play coy – you know because they represent the very debris that destroys our society. A manufactured, talentless, tone-deaf bunch of dreamy eyed twenty-somethings with no looks, no brains, no height and too much hair. A boyband.

The last dregs of my early optimism slowly seep away leaving the usual numbness when I'm on the bus. Three hooded men-teens are hassling an old lady as the remaining passengers pretend not to notice, running out of places to stare apart from their feet. They taunt her by prodding with extended crooked fingers and persist by looping their arms around her, breathing down her slight blouse. I'm scared to the point of exhaustion and can feel the sweat draining into my semi-ironed shirt, but I must do something. I can't just stand by and let these criminals get away with it. I reach down into my broken jacket pocket and rest my fingers on the sturdy handle of my umbrella. I always like to carry it with me as protection. The hole in the bottom corner of the pocket creates a long bulge that I like to imagine serves to look like something more brutal than protection against the rain. To look as though it could do some damage.

But of course I don't use it. I don't really do anything except motion towards the opening door with a pathetic flick of the wrist for them to leave her alone. One grabs my neck and pushes me flat against the coarse material of the seat, my head clanking on the metal bar above the seat, and I sit pinned to the spot as they mock her and cuss at her and extend their corporal supremacy. I turn a blind eye as they rip the bag from her grasp, fish through it and throw it back at her. And I hate myself for it as they kick my freshly polished shoe on their way off the bus as if to say, 'Get the fuck out of my way white boy'. It is this injustice that makes my day worthless; this injustice that makes me want to learn how to use a gun, put it in one of their mouths and make them apologise to that old woman and fetch her paper and pay for her grandkids to go to school.

The Tube's not a whole lot better. I avoid the Tube whenever I can because no matter which line you're on, that same slightly fermented, slightly radiant piss smell fills the carriage, with the consistency of a Big Mac, and leaches into every exposed pore on my being. But today's commute is even worse than normal.

Three young girls looking as though they've crawled up from a sewer huddle together in the doorway of the carriage: a group of insurgents set oddly at place against a backdrop of pinstripes and raincoats, their paltry skirts straining to cover the puppy fat encircling their upper thighs. They're obviously on their way home from the night before, their noses raw and red from sucking cocaine off the toilet seat of some unhealthy nightclub. They look at me and giggle, their metal braces glinting in the stark artificial light. They giggle again seeking to renew eye contact. One runs her tongue along the metal tracks adorning the ladders of yellowed teeth. There's gum somewhere, ravaged between the metal wires like a snared pink mink. The other starts sucking her finger then slowly drops her hand towards her meagre chest, moistens the outer material of her white vest, feeding off my obvious discomfort. They notice me shifting uneasily on the bluemaroon seat with bright yellow arm rest. From the corner of my eye I try not to see them continue taunting me as I retrieve a Metro from the shelf behind me and open the pages to form a barrier between us. Children should be innocent; untouched.

I puke once I'm out of the Tube station, adding to the rainwater that feebly washes away the remnants of my partly digested breakfast. A woman throws me a coin while I'm hunched in the gutter and a bus hoots spraying a fine film of grimy street water across my flank. Her face is strewn with disassociation, like everyone else, yet somewhere tucked in her diminutive frown I notice a yearning to slap me twice with the back of her hand and tell me to pull it together. For me, squatting in my own fluids, I see that tiny glimmer of wanting to make a difference, and it represents hope. Everything will be the same again. Everything will be as it used to be. Before the boybands or cheap cologne; before the gangs of aggressive hoodies, before the taunting teenage girls. Before the boybands. Ruined everything.

CHAPTER 3

JOB

Violence consumed my weekend. Not intentionally but there's nothing better than accidental self-infliction to sharpen the senses. After my first gym workout in over a hundred years I decided to slice small slivers of wood for the cupboard I will never get around to building. For lack of the correct utensils the exercise involved a sharp blade, a hammer and a stray finger.

The initial burst of blood flowed with more shock than pain and my first reaction to shake it better meant that I was consigned to cleaning the kitchen ceiling for the next hour. Note: blood is not easy to clean off a white painted surface. This seemingly trivial injury, which almost saw future insults half an inch shorter, left me feeling as though I needed surgery and a 'Get Well

Soon' card. Upside-down, perched on a ladder, my resilient nail throbbing bizarrely to the theme from Magnum and wiping the congealing blood with a damp sponge, I took a moment to contemplate the notion of inflicting true pain. How the brutality of the world fills a single column of the morning paper and another beating, another child abuse case, another murder is no more than a raised eyebrow between a political scandal and a vacuous celebrity quote. Yet small pain seems to be the real torture; how the truly unaffected reflect on a stuttering none-dimensional existence while the affected suffer true pain: death, loved ones gone, torture, loneliness. And me all wounded, my finger swelled up and hidden, unlike my self-pity, in a tight protective plaster for weeks until I was ready to see if it had grown back.

When I was about eleven I shot a bird during a makeshift hunting excursion on a friend's uncle's pig breeding farm and, as I watched the helpless creature try to drag itself forward with sticky blood and hundreds of miniature polystyrene-looking white balls oozing from its neck, I decided never to kill again. For the remainder of the day and indeed future excursions, no one could understand why I was such a poor shot with a pellet gun. There is a notion that says try everything once and that philosophy certainly dispels varying levels of fear associated with particular activities. Killing is something to try but without any duress or aggression. There must be a definite purpose.

I had a haircut during my lunch break today. Walked into a cheap Italian hairdresser and demanded a short back and sides. After we had supposedly established the task at hand the balding barber proceeded to slice straight through the centre of my head. I watched as my gold spikes descended to the floor in a flurry of machine induced snipping. It was like a depressing hair-snow storm. I was a bald eagle. A boyband member always has perfect hair. It substitutes for their lack of ability, I suppose. That's in the first season though, when they go through the clean-cut stage; when they've just been 'discovered'. Then it descends into probably what they think of as cool: dreadlocks, exaggerated curls, a shaven scalp like mine. Some would say I've become obsessed by this phenomenon called Boybands but I merely call it research.

Most of my research takes place by accident: I'm casually strolling home and a boyband billboard assaults me, so contrived that I can only stand and stare; I'm minding my own business watching an engrossing programme on nothing and the art of discussing / feeling / hoping for / crying about nothing when a boyband documentary flares up like a case of tonsillitis. I try to stay away but inevitably, as though lady fate herself is pulling me nearer, I transgress back to the boybands. So instead of running from it and hiding behind the couch when there's nothing else to watch on a Saturday morning, I've begun to embrace them.

The Internet is also a wonderful place to gather

information although surfing at work amidst a host of inaction and missed deadlines can be as dangerous as it is unfulfilling. If I were ever discovered perusing a website on boybands the scandal would not only kill my ultra-fulfilling career but fuel Christie's rumours to such an extent that her compact eyebrows would levitate off her face as they almost do when she gets excited.

In line with my new fitness regime I now fetch coffee for the entire team and jog up the stairs without spilling a drop every day. The one person I don't fetch for is my boss, the person in the world I feel the most desperately sorry for. He never looks anyone directly in the face, in particular me, and spends his spare hours gazing out his window, lost in an obscurity of bored anticipation. I seldom exchange anything with him let alone words, occasionally partaking in brief dialogue about his wife and kids, whose names he frequently gets wrong.

I suppose this is an opportune moment to mention something else about my boss. This was one of those situations that seemed like a weird dream but one which further amplifies how he remains one of those hopeless individuals where societal norms have forced him into a solitude of unhappiness.

He regularly sits on his own in his office thinking. One night he was thinking. Intently. So intently that I stumbled into his office without knocking. I know I shouldn't have but it was late and the lack of personnel meant that I didn't know where the big stapler was; the one with the lethal staples that can fasten even the most formidable document, and his office seemed the most logical destination. It was late. Who works late on a Monday night?

He was facing the computer screen, his head awkwardly tilted down and twitching. At first I thought he might be admiring a specimen of the increasingly trendy genre of 1920s porno sites, complete with black and brown photos of orderly sex. But oh how the world became a plethora of possibilities. There between his legs, belligerently bobbling up and down and around his groin was the mailroom boy complete with duty cap and letters still scrunched in his left hand. My timing could not have been any worse: maybe it was the fright of my figure in the doorway; maybe it was just meant to happen; maybe he nibbled down on the sensitive bit in the front. He sent the team forth, so to speak. Everywhere; the boy barely escaping the rapid fire and scrambling sideways, attempting to get away and still holding the undelivered mail. I froze, feeling slightly nauseated (I've never seen another man do that in real life, let alone onto an auxiliary man) so I left as fast as was humanly possible, but not before our eyes met.

He wasn't at work the next day but I will surely keep you informed as to how he will play a most pivotal role in my destiny. I still didn't get to staple my document though and had to present it in one of those tacky orange sleeves which always end up curling at the corners.

A new girl joined today and we all made a relentless effort to make her feel welcome and settled, as we always do in these situations. She appears to be a nice girl: life-size smile, dainty gestures and a genial smell almost like cooking mustard. But something about the way she finishes her sentences, the tone raising an octave, leads me to believe she's not the sharpest steak knife in the overpriced steak house. So we all falsely warm to her, Christie in particular, whose smile quickly deteriorates to rolled eyeballs once the new girl's back is turned, although the one eyeball now doesn't seem to be able to roll as high as the other one, making her look slightly mongoloid.

The department makes a weak attempt at team building and decides to go for a drink at the local pub. My boss opts not to join us. I nod towards him as we shuffle in the general direction of the lift although I think he blocks it out or maybe I block him not noticing out. We're at this pub and it's pretty trendy and happening and full of power-dressing women and smooth-domed men. Everyone makes polite conversation for an hour talking about partners and unfinished work and kids and good places to eat and the recession and bin Laden and bullshit and blah blah and blah and more bullshit and everything that could possibly be ticked off on the top ten most boring list as well as the top ten most topical list until the boredom is concentrated onto one person.

I'm listening. So intently that my head aches and all I can think about is how wrong I was and how her dainty gestures have become finger wagging rhetorical questions about life, love and everything else that matters to her. Everyone has gone and it's just the two of us and in two hours I know everything about her family and her over possessive and violent and jealous and abusive boyfriend and how she can't understand why he doesn't want children. I'm the proverbial shoulder and it's soaked.

I can't think of anything to relieve myself from the situation, even contemplating going to the toilet and never returning. I think I innocently raise the topic of affairs and immediately there's a subtle suggestion somewhere that we have one, although I'm at the point where the origins of any conversation are hazy. The alcohol is turning both our sentences into ridiculously suggestive B-movie lines. She says, "Why don't we have an affair at the office; low key; bit of fun; no harm?" When I don't decline straight away there's suddenly a new possibility in her life and not because she believes what she said about me being cute but because she now has a weapon to use against her boyfriend. Or perhaps a safety net. A reserve parachute. A lifeline or a cushion.

We're back at the office, deserted in the middle of the night, and she's on her knees tugging at my trousers. But I can't because I have a sudden attack of morality and she's crying again as I pull her back to her wobbly feet. And I'm trying to hide the obtrusive bulge in my trousers and get out of there. And I've got to see her the next morning. It's the 'Let's not jeopardise our career' speech and 'not tell anyone', even though nothing happened.

I go home and don't snuggle up to Her. Something inside of me withers every time I don't tell. But I know how these things can't be explained, even to someone who used to understand everything you said or did and trusted your motives, bathing unashamedly in your integrity. As quickly as a jail door slamming I wish I'd had a filthy session in the office with the new girl on my desk next to the unstapled report in the orange jacket. I wish I had broken her in on her first day at the office when I smell the distinctly potent men's cologne on Her, the same one as last time.

My favourite day of the week is Thursday. On this day, which always seems to provide renewed hope as it means you are past the halfway mark and the weekend is within spitting distance, I chose to drink coffee. Not a particularly good coffee, but coffee nevertheless. Cheap coffee that perfectly rounded out my hour-and-a-half lunch break.

The steaming almost-done cup balances on the chipped table in front of me along with a half-eaten overly sweet cinnamon and raisin bagel which I refuse to finish in the interests of health and safety. The coffee shop is full of foreigners yet quiet so I decide to delve into my mail that now lies in a week-old bundle in my bag. Nothing new for the most part – bills, statements, direct mail offers (how they ever get my details baffles me) and one from a magazine company. The magazine logo is stamped onto the envelope with red circles depicting the curvaceous form of a woman on her side. The envelope is light pink and psychedelically mesmerises me as I move it to create alternate forms of the woman.

I start picking at the envelope, vaguely remembering having bought this men's 'lifestyle' magazine a couple of months ago because it had an article on boybands and their favourite West End nightclubs, when I stumbled onto an interview that intrigued me. So much so that I entered the accompanying competition having just emerged from a fresh round of arguments with Her. But then abruptly everything comes into focus as I distinctly remember the details of the prize. The guilt is now pumping through my body like thick chocolate, filling my veins so that they're ready to explode and I secretly hope it's a standard rejection letter.

The letter is now open and I'm reading it in the gloomy light, my eyes straining to focus on the profligate text. I read it three more times before slumping back into my chair, shoving the remaining bagel crescent into my mouth and almost chipping a tooth on a fossilised raisin. There's no going back now: I was going on a date.

CHAPTER 4
HOT DATE

Not telling Her is like lying on the couch in the middle of the night, tired beyond belief, but refusing to traipse through to bed – you do it because of the effort associated with not not doing it. Plus the story never needed to hold water; it just had to be vaguely plausible in a work-friends-interests sort of way. It did require some planning though. Getting a tuxedo to and from work without being noticed either by Her, Christie or other interested colleagues requires guile, finesse and above all dexterity (creased material not really an option for an evening such as this). I had to disguise the tux as a suit for the dry-cleaners and deter any sniffer dog colleagues snooping around my desk.

From five in the afternoon anxious glances at the

skew hanging wall clock became frantic stares. Once out, I ducked into a grimy public Tube toilet, changed sufficiently well to be drop dead presentable (somehow remembering how to knot a bowtie and satisfyingly now able to get the top button fastened without feeling like Hawley Harvey Crippen) and disposed of my work gear (the rectangle of meagre bushes outside the office the only available refuge). I was ready. The chase. The buzz. After all, I was about to go on a date with a woman who had walked into a surgeon's office and uttered, "Give me double G breasts".

The limo picked me up at the specified location later than expected. The chauffeur was not a man of words. A simple greeting followed by a description of the amenities within the car was about as much as I got. The nerves began to tingle slightly as we meandered off so I took advantage of the facilities and began downing my own version of a Bloody Mary. I tried to light a cigarette too but was promptly told off by the mute driver. Even though limos are now about as common as beggars on the street, everyone still stares. From within the lush and safe confines of this tank of an automobile I see their faces. Wondering. Which Arab oil sheik sits inside with his harem of local girls, topping up each other's champagne and licking lipstick off their teeth? Which bachelor party has splashed out for their groom-to-be while the bride-to-be licks oil from the inside of a fireman's crotch in Bournemouth? Which sorry young punk has just won a competition and why is he cheating on his cheating girlfriend?

All these thoughts are quickly dispelled as the restaurant comes suddenly into view, the array of expensive cars shuffling through like airline passengers. We are flagged through by a red-coated overweight man to what seems to be the special parking lot for long cars. When the engine is turned off I thank the driver, down another drink and exit, momentarily wondering whether to tip and maybe shutting the door a little too forcefully. Nerves. A man approaches as though he's about to mug me.

"Welcome welcome, Mr Stipps," he says brightly. "I'm Jacob David, editor of Triple A Magazine. Congratulations!"

"Thank you." Is it an honour? I'm not quite sure, but I am glad to be here.

"Kitten is running slightly late; she's really a wonderful person, you know. Don't let the appearance fool you," he says, gently glancing down towards his chest with a wry smile fighting to hide itself on his face.

"I'm sure she is."

"It was a tough decision; we had over ten thousand responses to the competition. I wasn't even sure that many people read Adam's Ample Apple."

"Did you pick?"

"Well we narrowed it down to about thirty based on Kitten's initial criteria and then she made the final selection. You know she's just broken up with her manfriend of six months. The footballer. You know the man who…"

"Yes, I read it in the article."

"You a big fan?"

"Of the footballer?"

"No. Kitten."

"Actually not really. Never even heard of her before I picked up a copy of your mag. But once I saw the picture…"

"I know, it happens to most men. Most, but not all."

"No, what I meant was…"

"I'd like you to meet Jim; he's sort of my right hand guy if you know what I mean."

Jim's a lanky, dark haired, pale skinned, blatantly homosexual man standing with his hand out in front of me. His head is cocked slightly down at an angle and one of his hips is thrust forward. I make a lunge for his drooping paw, catching it completely wrong, accidentally indenting my palm on one of his rings. He snarls at me I think, then winks.

Jim and Jacob, the happy couple, lead me into a private drinking booth which is showered with fake flowers and bottles of champagne. The magazine's hired photographer is waiting and starts measuring my facial dimensions in the air with his hands, his one eye shut, bending onto one knee and up again in paroxysmal jerks. His camera is the mother of all cameras and before I've even been introduced or settled down, it's going off like a shotgun in front of my face. With each snap I get what I imagine to be a brief glimpse of the inside of my brain, the passages of dry white tissue networking in spirals alongside one another.

Before I can blink Kitten's breasts arrive. I won't exaggerate but they were magnificent. They shine like inflated golden beach balls, the frozen glitter speckled along and down and up again like disorganised hikers assailing the heights of two forgotten mountains. Her pink outfit, which really was just a frilly bra, acts as the unneeded suspension sending the mammoth creatures forth to do damage to men's toilets and auto repair shops around the nation.

> All hail to thee, Kitten oh one of magnificent
> cleavage.
> You are my goddess and I worship thee with
> all my soul.
> A pinch doesn't work.
> This is real.
> They are not.
> I'm on a date with a double G.
> Halleluiah.

"Kitten this is Paton Stipps," and my brain is fighting my eyeballs which are straining to point southwards. Brain in the red corner, eyeballs in the blue; eyeballs coming out swinging, the heavier of the two and with a longer reach. I can feel the twinge as the Gs loom inches below my sightline, a quick glance more taboo than farting, my brain constantly murmuring 'you'll get plenty of opportunity'.

Be patient.

Sit still.

Remain focussed.

And look her in the eyes.

And her eyes are actually quite pretty and my mind is off her truly hemispherical mounds for a millisecond.

Round 2.

And I'm fighting.

Don't look.

Don't look.

Please don't look.

She's testing me.

And her eyelashes are also quite nice.

If they're real.

Given her track record I'm in the wrong arena on this one.

"You have lovely eyelashes, Paton and it's great to meet you in the flesh."

Where's the squeak?

Girls with double G breasts are meant to sound vacant and squeaky.

It's in the manual.

'Everything you ever wanted to know about girls with double G breasts'.

Flesh.

My flesh.

She mentioned it.

Oh and how I want hers.

Or just to look at it.
Them.
On my hot date.
O Lord deliver me from the double G cup.

CHAPTER 5
MOVIE CINEMAS

There is seldom a greater experience.

The lights dim.

But not all the way. That's reserved for the feature presentation.

The trailers set your visual appetite alight. I sometimes feel the pour of saliva down the sides of my tongue and feel as though I'm levitating effortlessly above my seat when a preview launches. Some movies are great and some are really crap, but let's be honest, the trailers are all good. Three full hours of back-to-back titbits of movie tantalisers would make this pirate shiploads more toothlessly happy than sitting through a high budget extravaganza starring a linguistically impeded Neanderthal and his two close friends: shot and gun.

And the obligatory accompaniments:

Peanut M&Ms; the new ones. The extra-large diet coke with straw unable to reach the bottom. The holder for the extra-large diet coke complete with straw unable to reach to bottom.

The big blaring boisterously brilliant big screen.

The digital sound – which must always be too loud (better to hear too much than too little).

But people always seem to fuck it up.

Or the people I sit next to anyway.

Maybe it's a curse and the cinema gods have never shown me pity or maybe I'm just incredibly unlucky but I always seem to end up sitting next to someone who I'm sure their friends describe as 'quirky' or 'a whole lot of fun in small doses'. I even have my pre-movie prayer which I make on my knees on the sometimes clean cinema floor (because I'm always early so as never to risk missing even a second of the first trailer unless I'm with some silly date who is monkeying around in the rude-staffed sweet shop; and then she's dumped as a movie buddy anyway because the first trailer is always the furthest from release which means it's the one with the most intrigue which means it's the one I know the least about which means it's the best) but it never seems to work.

Never lately.

The latest time I'm next to some kind of granola girl who has conspicuous underarm hairs which flay into the sides of her white vest like porcupine quills. I'm not one hundred percent positive but I would hazard a guess that the musky whiff dragged across my view emits from those unruly clumps. I sense she hasn't washed in a while.

Perhaps a month.

Shifting past me in the darkness, late for the movie, interrupting my trailer viewing pleasure, she kicks my shin, hard, fails to apologise and almost sits on my lap, as she inconspicuously drips a zigzagged line of mustard down my jacket sleeve.

I'm convinced she lets off a little exertion fart in the process as well. But I wouldn't swear to it.

She plonks herself aggressively down in the seat next to mine and shoves my settled arm off the armrest.

I let it go.

The movie starts and she starts sniffing.

Not delicate little feminine snorts accompanied by a raised lace handkerchief and an "Excuse Me" with a slight hint of scarlet in the cheeks.

This snort sends shivers pulsating down my soul and I wretch because I have a thing about snot. I hear her swallow the glob like it's an oyster and then she clears her throat to bring what must be a green amoeba shaped clump back into the real world and plays around with it on her tongue. Where it ends up I'm not completely sure but hopefully nowhere near me.

It's not once.

It's not consistent.

Ad hoc.

Catching you like a left hook just as you are being lured into the complacency of enjoying the dialogue.

Smack.

Hllllllwwooooppppppp.

I will not leave the cinema.

I refuse.

The first rule of cinema attendance is don't leave the cinema. Don't let someone make you leave. Don't let the granola girl win.

Another time there's the loudest couple in the universe, discussing every possible facet of the picture. "What did he say?" "What was that?" "She's so funny, isn't she?" "Oh, clever, clever." "Wow" "Phew" "Jeez" "He's so hot!" "I think she's just leading him on." "This is really good, isn't it?"

And so on.

Until I have to say, "Excuse me, would you mind keeping it down a bit?" and they both look towards each other, the tips of their noses almost touching in unison and scoff and mumble something derogatory behind me. Something, for once, I am unable to decipher. But they keep talking so I sit up as straight as I can and spread my shoulders as wide as they possibly can stretch to show them that I can and will block the bottom portion of the screen if the chatter continues.

They don't shut up.

They continue their useless commentary through the flick and it makes no difference to anybody in the cinema except me.

These people should be punished.

CHAPTER 6
NEXT DAY

There should be a pair of double Gs ominously resting beside me in an expensive hotel bed but there isn't. There's just that discrete smell of men's cologne which hovers in a haze above Her sleeping form until She stirs to get up and embrace the chasm that has become our life together.

Just before She arises my new clock radio tenderly nourishes me awake with a great tune that's just come out. I've been meaning to find out who sings it and the song is about to end and reveal who will benefit from my next CD purchase when She slams the snooze button down, leaning across me so that Her breasts slap my well-worn cheeks.

Real breasts.

Not double Gs.

I'm left to contemplate the blur of the dinner with Kitten, overanalysing each conversation and deciphering innocuous gestures. What did she make of it all really? It all seemed to go well enough without any hint of the discrepancy between her world and the monotony of mine. There was nothing drastic to suggest train wreck: chuckling at my anecdotal stories, competent wine selection, a dearth of tablecloth splatters, license to allow her free chatter – but all a bit formulaic, as though she was more interested in looking immaculate when she returned from the little girl's room than me. At least I managed to pay no homage to her two companions, although on the journey between acknowledging her coin pouch size dish and meeting her eyes to signal 'start your engines' for the course there was an indelibility which I am now trying to rejuvenate. And that discussion on the boybands. And her definitely mentioning something about meeting up again. Encouraging.

In the evening I'm surrounded by sweaty, hairless, short, orange, narcissistic panters all aiming to trim that inch or add that edge or drip a crap load of sweat all down the side of the stationary bike so that I heave in the fumes and gag, arching my calves to avoid absorbing the concentrated uric acid.

The way I figure it is that I should continue the regime I began; it would be a shame not to. All those weeks of running up stairwells, sweating and starving and drinking raw egg whites and midnight push-ups for nothing?

I don't think so.

After all, she mentioned meeting up again.

So the abs need oodles more 'sculpting' (or 'chiselling' according to Fabio, the on-hand green-spandexed very-personal trainer) and the chest, well, you know what they say about the chest – it can never be too solid.

But it must be tone not build apparently.

There's a cute couple in the steam room and they make it obvious that I should leave so they can resume their heavy petting. I don't, just to piss them off, and watch the overly oiled grease monster fight his urge for a hard on as his girlfriend teases him by exposing half her nipple.

A gay woman with a crew cut joins us, which upsets the entire sexual balance of the steam room, so I leave and head for the sauna.

This gym isn't so bad after all.

The sauna's crap but empty and the thought of knocking one off isn't the furthest thing from my mind.

(It was a reasonably impressive half a nipple)

Fifty laps of the cramped swimming pool serve as an ample substitute.

My locker key gets stuck in the keyhole which makes my head itch and makes me wonder who's been trying to break into my locker.

There've been rumours.

About thieves jamming the wrong keys into the

gaping generic holes that make up the locker room.

My anti-dandruff shampoo doesn't work even though I don't have dandruff.

A slight itch that won't go away.

Made worse by the crappy cold London air.

The shower's good; better than at home. The water manages to mix without scraping my skin from my body and exposing the tender nerves.

I use the soap from the dispenser that looks like cum as it squirts into my palm. Now there's a sight: all the gym instructors jacking off in the middle of the night into the brown tinted rectangular holders so that all the members can attain that warm glow after a workout.

My exit from the shower is greeted by something unpleasant.

Dangling in front of the basin.

Manfred Dill.

One of the most influential people in the firm complete with river facing office and big pay cheque.

It's not good because he looks up and recognises me.

We're both naked and it just seems wrong. I'm not sure why. Just wrong. I see this guy most days in a conservative suit with his hair neatly styled and black leather folder resolutely under his arm.

He's respectable.

Decent.

In charge.

Now he's a potbellied shaving cream encrusted locker room boy.

With a penis.

That stares at me and refuses to look away.

"Hi," he inauspiciously drones realising that his towel is too far away for him to grab and it would be silly doing so now, so he just stands, impotently proud and self-conscious.

Just like me.

I do not know this man.

I do not want to know this man.

I do not want to know this man naked.

Me: "Hi."

Keep it short. Keep it simple.

"Good workout?" he asks.

"I suppose. Bit of chest and abs. Yourself?"

"Yes, can't say I'm into the whole weights thing. Seems far too energetic. Also all those iron pumpers are really fags aren't they?"

This rings out and echoes in the changing room among the muscle bound heavies, deafening me. I'm so stunned the itching stops.

How do you reply to that? Agree and cancel your gym membership. Disagree and cancel your career membership.

He looks at me expectantly.

I shrug.

A weak shrug.

I like this gym.

Others look at me expectantly.

One with biceps the size of Manfred.

"Do you prefer to cycle?"

Comeback?

"When the cycle's not full of pumped out gay sweat."

Back to phase one.

The changing room is now restless. Onlookers await my response.

Again.

Like a bullfighter in a ring with a hundred bulls.

These socially repulsive situations usually intrigue me. I should be able to say what I feel.

This Manfred prick might not be so bad after all.

But I wimp out.

"There's a new machine. In the corner. Sort of a cross between a cycle and a rowing machine. Have you tried it? Oh, did you hear about Jack Domonivic from Actuarial Finance? He won the lottery."

"No! How much?"

Unscathed and back to full form.

Tangents rule OK.

"About £11.8 million. Should see him through the next couple of weeks."

"As if those fucking actuarial queers don't make enough as it is," says the actuarial homophobe who definitely makes enough as it is.

But in a strange way I like this guy. He's honest and he dispelled the horror of the naked situation in the most efficient way. He's a pioneer and I'm sure there is room for him somewhere.

Somewhere.

CHAPTER 7

MY BROLLY HANDLE

A less than attractive woman with more than attractive zigzag hair leaned out slightly too far whilst waiting for a bus. The bus driver did not even try to avoid her and clipped her shoulder spinning her like a wing nut before she collapsed on the cool tar. Her face failed to register the pain but her eyes captured the distress, the red lines darkening and the pupils weaving from side to side as the driver unceremoniously flagged down a taxi, more intent to get on with his route.

A great story for people to tell their loved ones after an otherwise uneventful day full of boring office gossip and nevereverending meetings.

But unconcerned remained the key word.

No one to hold her hand while she waited in the emergency room and begged the doctor for painkillers, her cheek grazed and bleeding, diamond shaped bits of tar tangled amongst glutinous blood.

No one to see her home safely after discovering that her family couldn't give more than a 'That's terrible' over the phone.

No one to check up on her as the adolescent doctor deemed her condition 'not serious' and the hospital refused to keep her.

No one except me.

On the way back from her flat I boarded the same number bus.

Number 43.

Another driver nonchalantly relieved me of my pound coin and issued me with a ticket to clutter up my wallet or briefcase or pocket.

This was the last bus I think.

Just after midnight.

Empty.

Until the next stop.

Four youths, their cumulative age not above sixty, enter like orangutans, pounding windows, spitting vociferously and getting physical with one another.

Do these kids' parents know where they are?

I can smell booze. Or is it petrol?

I'm a fly to them.

Not on the wall but on a bus.

I'm sure they have knives.

A toy. Me. Not the knives.

I mind my own business staring out the window trying not to imagine these kids as the future ambassadors of our great civilisation.

We would have never behaved like this, politely abstaining from adult interaction and working weekends for 85p an hour.

It is aggressive. Intimidating. Towards me. In the middle of the night. Now.

An exertion of their hormonal power.

Just like the young girls on the Tube.

"Oi mister, got a light?" says one.

"I don't think you're allowed to smoke on this bus," I say.

"Who the fuck are you? The bus conductor?" says the one with the worst acne.

"Actually I'm not too fussed…"

"Course you is not fussed," says the one with the grey cap just above his eyebrows, spitting a piece of chewing gum upwards which miraculously manages to stick to the roof. "Cause you has got some fags for us, hasn't ya, mister?"

"What's this on your collar?" says the skinniest one leaning over me from behind, his face stinking of glue and his finger Morse-coding the splats of Caroline's dried blood.

"Nothing. Why don't you boys just make yourselves comfortable in the corner over there and relax."

"Weez relaxed mister, we just want something to suck on," says Acne again followed by frenzied laughter.

Cap Boy now almost straddles me and sits on the opposite facing seat putting one foot on either side of me in a sort of pathetic teenage knobbly knee vice. I can see the reflection of the silent one as he approaches more quickly than I am comfortable with, pulling something from his jacket and plunging it towards my stomach.

The smell of stale seat foam welcomes us all and now I'm on the floor as the boy wrestles his blade free from the seat like an inexperienced fisherman.

I'm about to be mugged by four frigging teenagers!

These little twerps are fast little twerps and they're on top of me like midget warriors, suddenly brave now that their embattled hands all hold metallic weapons, probably stolen from overaffectionate Uncle Colin's tool shed.

I feel a tinge of pain but I'm not sure where.

The bus driver is wholly unaware of what's going on atop bus number 43 I'm sure.

Standing up, I feel like a Christmas tree with four abused ornaments dangling from me.

The pain comes again.

My brolly is within reach.

On the seat.

The one with the wooden handle.
My Excalibur.

The first swipe actually digs into one boy's skull (I cannot remember which), the sharp well-polished wooden edge comfortably finding a newfangled home. He crumples to the floor, then crab scuttles sideways to safety. The next combination is blurry because the pack of teenwolves now severely doubts their ability and strength minus a member, haphazardly aiming their metallic objects at my midriff and retreating behind the pack. Again Excalibur slashes down an enemy, this time tearing open the side of his cheek (unfortunately it was Acne Boy which meant the spray was 60:40 blood:pus).
Roughly.
With two down the pimply posse disembark from the bus at the next stop without thanking the driver for his troubles.
It was, after all, the last bus of the evening.
As the driver pulls into my stop I cordially thank him as I step through the open front door, feeling slightly guilty for wiping my brolly handle clean on one of the upstairs seats.

I lay awake for almost four hours after the experience, Her snoring blissfully missing my conscious like far away thunder. My heart pumped full blood for ages as I went over the scene again and again.

I so badly wanted to thank those teenagers. I felt as though I had done my community proud; I'd been unselfish, attempting to right the wrongs.

When eventually I fell asleep I could barely feel the two puncture wounds that decorated my side like a snakebite, carefully tended to with the blood stained cloths, now right at the bottom of the dustbin.

CHAPTER 8
PARTY

Knowing what to wear when is equally a problem for men as it is for women, the difference being that men do not actively verbalise the mental anguish and indecision with one another. Every day we all tread a precariously fine line in the fashion world between pathetically ridiculous and unmistakably cool.

My frame now fills the full length mirror and unmistakably cool is nowhere to be seen. Pathetically ridiculous sits on top of my shoulders laughing at me, daring me to step out into the world of self-proclaimed fashion gurus and pretend to look anything but pathetically ridiculous.

I want to burn the trousers I have just paid £120 for.

Watch them die and suffer for making false

promises.

Watch the leather flanks and beige corduroy curl up and crumble as the heat engulfs and spits them out.

What was I thinking?

Leather!

Flanks!

Almost like dark black sideburns rolling down the outer legs in between the rough straight lines of the corduroy.

It's back to the boring drawing board and time is ticking away like my life and I can't decide which look will ingratiate me to Kitten and her extended circle.

Kitten called me at work and the conversation was anything but pleasant. Not only was my tone the usual office *stop fucking listening in on my call* monotone but also the supposed follow up date was more like a fill the numbers obligation.

Her party.

Her 28th year of life.

(I wonder how old the double G's are?)

A plus to be invited I suppose but after the apparent success of the first date I had hoped for something a little more personal and intimate and quiet.

Where I can begin to turn listening into real progress.

The party's a heaving success and I can scarcely believe how many famous faces I don't recognise. They're famous because their expressions say so. The way they stand. The way they hold their cigarettes. With a cocked wrist and a false laugh and too much make-up.

Boys and girls.

The house is impressive in a sort of *I have no taste whatsoever but loads of money* sort of way.

A bit like the Double Gs.

But I still like them.

The bathroom is where I spend most of the early part of the evening as I conveniently have the runs. I'm convinced it's something She popped into my food; perhaps an attempted poisoning. And She wouldn't struggle to hide the taste of the poison either because the food always tastes so foul. The only reason I scoffed it down was because I was drunk the night before and all the gourmet fast food joints were closed.

Shut early even though the sign lied.

So the tuna and vegetable bake had to suffice and now I'm paying for it.

Bending right over in an attempt to fart quietly and praying to Christ that I don't send a little soft serve spiralling into the real world.

I can't sit comfortably on the toilet seat as it's one of those modern ones shaped like a guitar (minus the strings) and (for heaven's sake) a different tune is played (from where I do not know) every time it flushes. And I know there are only twelve tunes that revolve and play in the same order.

I know this because I'm about to embark upon squirt number fourteen.

Geronimo!

Lenny Kravitz's *Are You Gonna Go My Way* marks my exit from the uncomfortable instrument, my legs now stinging from the extended stay.

My conversation has been particularly poor tonight, probably because I don't know anyone. Jim and Jacob, the happy couple from the magazine date, provide little respite as I enter the hallway dominated on one side by black painted walls and on the other by sheets of soft leather. Their chuckles and twitches suggest they're about to embark on some kind of sordid activity in the bathroom. I castigate myself for wondering if the smell of shit will turn them on as they… who knows? Snort crack from each other's cracks?

They're due for Soft Cell's *Tainted Love*.

But they're sweet guys and they seem to really like me and they might be my only way to get to Kitten, who has not even welcomed me to the party yet.

I've barely laid eyes on her.

Jim: "Love the suit. Prada?"

Me: "Actually yes." A lie.

Jacob: "And the shirt? D&G?"

Me: "M&S"

They both erupt in raptures, swirling around me.

Jacob: "You look divine. Seen Kitten? I think she looks soooooo fantastic. She had a really wonderful time wining and dining you – oh and the follow up on the date will be in next month's…"

Jim: "Shhhhh, loudmouth! We don't want to ruin the big surprise for our soldier here."

Me: "Why, was there some sort of problem?"

Jacob: "Jim's just yanking your chain. She really thinks you have a nice, well – arse."

Me: "She liked my bottom?"

Jim: "Well part of her mandate was to pick her favourite body part. And she picked your bottom – we devote a whole paragraph towards her description of it."

If only she could see it now – swollen, numb, raw, clenched and all tuned out.

Are You Gonna Go My Way?

Me: "What else did she like?"

Jim: "You little minx! What else did she like…"

Jacob: "She liked it all!"

Jacob now stares at my crotch which is strange because Kitten unfortunately went nowhere near it.

Jim: "The pussy's out the bag now. Look out, Tiger. Grrrr."

There's a gay man growling in front of me and I'm excited.

There must be something wrong with me.

The two retire arm in arm to the loo giggling and tossing their shaven scalps back. Jim sneaks a final glance at me and blows a delicate kiss while Jacob mouths what I think looks like 'Good Luck' before they collapse through the brightly varnished door.

I blink.

Something round and solid is pressing into my latissimus dorsum. And it's cold.

I blink again.

A hand is followed by a bright green frill that surrounds a well-tanned forearm like the collar of a golden circus bear.

I blink once more and I'm moving.

With her.

The pressure on my lat is now close to painful.

It can only be.

The baby cat hath arrivedth.

With her companions.

"Where are we going?" I stutter, trying to look around and acknowledge her eyes.

"Away from the toilet. Where've you been? If I didn't know any better I'd think you were avoiding me."

"Jim and me and Jacob were just exchanging pleasantries, that's all."

"Those two love to fuck at parties. I hope they don't make a mess in my toilet again."

Again!

The thought makes me want to run back to the guitar and stick my head down there rather than my arse. But not directly after Jim and Jacob.

"How's the party progressing?"

"Terribly! Completely horribly! The caterers were late and most of the food had been eaten by one of the new staff who got a little too friendly with a couple bottles of Mezzopane in the back of the van. What he didn't manage to eat he threw up on."

"I was wondering why there were peas and carrots in the foie gras."

She laughs. A genuine laugh. And I see her teeth. Perfect. We pass a fountain with fake pink swans and white flamingos heading along the stretch of overly manicured lawn towards the pool house.

"I love what you are wearing," she mutters, looking away and greeting the oncoming traffic of guests all making their way towards the guitar.

"You look really good too," but she doesn't hear which is just as well because it's such a line anyway.

I'm suddenly on my own again as though I dreamt up the whole encounter in order to make the two toilet lovebirds go away. But I know that's not true because even the toilet lovebirds are better than standing around like Norman No Mates for an entire evening. My stomach seems to have settled down and it feels almost bottomed out. The alcohol has begun to flow quite nicely and I can feel my eyeballs start tingling and my inhibitions wearing away.

Defence is the best form of attack.

Bullshit.

Attack is the best form of defence.

There is a woman standing in the frame of the wooden pool house door sipping a Mai Tai and looking around expectantly and agitatedly. I approach with purpose and ask her for a cigarette. She doesn't smoke and informs me she has a boyfriend.

Shot down.

I try again, this time the woman is better looking and not alone. She's with a bunch of other females and our chatting reveals a mutual friend which is a Godsend given my circumstances. I'm listening with one ear and looking for Kitten with the other. Before long her (I think her name was Jade) hand is on top of mine and she's almost on my lap sucking her straw a little too deliberately. I try not to look but end up staring down her top and her breasts hang which means they are real which means she is real which means she is not Kitten. I strongly consider a cheeky one in the toilet or the bushes (it's warm enough) and then abandon the idea when her head flops into my lap. My initial reaction is that she's passed out and I'm planning how to make a run for it without letting her head down too brusquely when she resurfaces from an exaggerated laugh.

Apparently I said something funny and am very funny.

Kitten back to the rescue, this time after a whole host of blinks. Way too many for my liking — a full symphony of blinks.

One, two, three more blinks and I'm being introduced to a bunch of guys that I recognise. And I can feel my stomach juices tossing and splashing like a violent storm and my oesophagus is burning as my smile extinguishes the flame and I'm shaking hands greeting them with interest and fervour.

But they're whisked off once again, Kitten caught in the slipstream which might just as well be in everyone's best interests not only because number fifteen introduces him or herself with a loud knock but because no destiny can be complete without preparation, control and, most important of all, definite purpose.

A boyband.

CHAPTER 9

PROBABLY THE NICEST PERSON I'VE MET

Caroline bends over to gather something from the bottom of the oven and I try not to look at her large behind bulging from her navy blue stewardess-like skirt. I sit patiently, staring out the window of the modestly furnished flat complete with poo brown couches and overwhelming light shades. Somewhere in the south of London. Sidcup I think.

The tea is great. Her arm is still in a sling and I

completely forget to jump up and help her with the hot cross buns until it's too late and she's wiping sweat from her shining forehead with the free hand and the buns decorate the too clean floor. She steps on one sending a raisin shooting from the side of her flat shoe which makes her slightly embarrassed so I calm the whole situation down by whistling for her Labrador who cannot believe his luck. I'm sure she would normally disallow this feast but she lets it slide because I'm there and because I helped her and because she has a crush on me. But how she loves that dog. Which is admirable.

The dog slops up the buns and I pat him in a congratulatory salute because he polishes them (and the floor) off in under thirty seconds. He (or she, the name is Biscuit which is difficult to attach a gender to) even has space for more I'm sure, his tail slapping the open cupboard in regular inharmonious beats.

She smiles.

I smile.

The dog smiles.

Then runs off to lick his balls or piss on another dog's piss.

Caroline Maxwell Davies is a thirty-something-year-old divorcee who lives with her pet Labrador Biscuit and likes to cook. She's not very good but she likes to do it. To try new things like mixing fish and chicken in a sort of stir-fry casserole hybrid. She loves to eat which has contributed to her metamorphosis from plain thin country girl to plain plump city girl. She works as a part-time maid cleaning flats and houses for London's way too busy. Her husband traded her in for a newer model when he began noticing that strippers were far more attentive to his needs, falling in love with a young thing named Desire who he religiously visits every second night for a private dance and in order to part with one hundred pounds.

She is probably the nicest person I've met in twenty-seven years because, although she frequently misfires, her heart is in the right place.

Beating steadily beneath a rib cage thermally contained by her wobbling bosom.

That is why a situation such as this is dangerous. Caroline has already attached to me and although the physical side will never be reciprocated I am reasonably convinced that I am falling in love with her kindness.

Because it's rare that sort of thing.

Unconditional kindness.

The kindness she perceives I am showering on her as I sit on the poo brown couches, staring at her slightly squint eyes and unfairly generous smile.

One of her most endearing facets is that she talks too much.

It's the nerves but it's cute and I can't help hugging her inside my mind.

For her kindness.

I'm not a saviour.

This is not charity.

Charity is forgetting about the fifty pence you throw

to a street person or forgetting about the fifty-pound cheque you write for the blind.

I haven't forgotten.

I haven't forgotten how the back of her shoulder swelled to twice its normal size.

I haven't forgotten the terror and loneliness in her face as people fled, intent on running back to their own selfish existences.

I haven't forgotten how she cried when I sat beside her on the hospital bed.

Stroking her face.

I haven't forgotten how the injustice of the world boiled up inside me that night.

And I acted.

Decisively.

For Caroline.

For me.

Now there'll be more.

Much more.

The boybands must pay.

CHAPTER 10

COUNTDOWN

I'm so looking forward to settling into my routine at the gym one cool Sunday afternoon with comfortable headphones blaring down my throat on the stationary bike to get the juices pumping – perhaps some rock or even the latest hits; the MTV chart of something.

But what do I get?

What the frigging hell do I get?

I get the top 10 boyband songs of all time.

And they actually call it this which means they've acknowledged the evil.

A boyband.

Now a boyband is not merely a band with boys in it.

Iron Maiden is not a boyband. The Beatles were not a boyband. Radiohead is certainly not a boyband.

A boyband is a cluster of vain, short people who love themselves so much that they have little or no time to write their own music or learn how to play a musical instrument or (heaven forbid) learn how to sing. Boybands do not form bands – they all merely try to outsing and outharmonise one another with over pronounced dance routines and clothes that look as though they've puked all over themselves. They gaze longingly into the camera, undoubtedly sending teenage pulses racing, giving us, the viewer, a true insight into how in love they are with themselves.

So I'm cycling – 100 rpm; heart rate 130bpm when the countdown begins. I know I'm now gripping the heart rate handles of the stationary bike a little too firmly when I see the veins in my hand and biceps bulge a little too purposefully so I decide not to let it worry me.

I will not let the boybands win. They will not win. Like the cinema. I will not leave. I will stay on the bike until the chart is over. I will watch it even if my arse and head and thighs all hurt. After all, how else will I learn about theses maggots who are all going to be extinguished?

#10 *All My Love Is True* – All For Love

One brutha, one cholo, one white boy and one

something stand on a stage surrounded by reams of model-like fantasy woman. The women cheer and scream and clamour for their attention while the wannabe pop gods stand atop the podium (if they stood next to the girls they'd be up to their armpits) and wave just as Caesar would have to a gladiatorial crowd. The song is, at best, a take-off of a cheesy love ballad and the boys all wear Day-Glo suits that collectively look like a television test pattern.

Verdict: Death
Method of Execution: Mace decapitation (high skill required yet possible)

#9 *Love Is In My Fingertips* – Z9

(I'm sure there's a porn movie similarly titled). These golden armpits are dancing in the rain. Correction - pretending to dance in the rain. They're ripping bits of each other's wet white t-shirts off in what looks like a gay wrestling match. The camera succeeds in showing sculpted glimpses of their unsculpted bodies. A pec. An ab (someone else's probably). A shoulder. The fake tan cream they use stays on miraculously well given the pelting counterfeit rain. The wet hair in the face is a personal favourite for this lot who have made a couple of videos where they try distinctly to look manly by peering upwards through matted hair that will probably need to be replaced by transplants in another twenty years.

Verdict: Death
Method of Execution: Drowning

#8 *Love Is For Me* – TunedIn

The first of relentless cover versions where the boys prove their true inability to write original songs. What really worries me is the fact that the people who write the songs for boybands have run out of lyrics! I know I am not alone when I say that covers are never (NEVER!) as good as the original. So why do it in the first place? All it does is bastardise the music. These teen idols have been around for a while and the first glimmers of facial hair are beginning to appear at the ends of their chins (well three of the five anyway). I am convinced the follow up video will feature a full bearded member. The video exploits this puberty with close up camera shots and plenty of bright lights to bring out the seven-and-a-half hairs between them.

Verdict: Death
Method of Execution: Skinning with a cutthroat razor

I need a quick pee brake and dash off to the gents, which is a way off, determined not to miss anything as

MTV's overdone, overobscure advertisements flood the minds of the other cyclists. An old friend holds me up at the urinal and I'm immediately annoyed because he wants to talk about hedge funds and all I can think about is that he's taking time away from my boyband mutilation plans.

I'm back on the cycle (the same one because I purposely left my weights gloves at the base) but I've missed the beginning of number seven.

#7 *Didn't You Love Your First Time* – Colours

This is a new entry and a new band and there is clearly no sign in the industry of improvement. These clowns are all clad in blue denim jeans and white t-shirts. The pumped up look doesn't work on these lads because firstly they're too short and secondly they're too short. They're doing something with their chairs which I envision to be a substitute for a homosexual act. You see these idiots parade around as though they love women but all they really want to do is hunt for chocolate down their buddy's pants. No space in these jeans – sorry fellas.

Verdict: Death
Method of Execution: Suffocation

#6 *I'll Be Your Love* – Moonsnap

Last week's number one (these songs are never eternal; fads more than fashion). If I remember correctly these jokers were part of a television programme where the band was 'created' from hundreds of hopefuls. You'd think with such a large pool of untalented young men they could have found at least five with anything more than dreadlocks and an IQ of 80. But nooooooo. They pick the rejects. Always. Without fail. And these real life TV dramas are so in it makes me want to retch. Are all viewers so sad and bored in their own lives that this shit excites them? All these aspiring 'musicians' hugging each other and loving each other and forgiving each other every time they squabble like babies over who's getting more camera time or who's making 'the band' look bad or who's using whose toothbrush.

Verdict: Death
Method of Execution: Chainsaw limb severing (individually and slowly)

#5 *Love Can Fly* – Madfly

When tattoos (real ones) were in, they still wouldn't have looked cool on these prepubescent all toothed fairies. They're so gaunt that they all look as though they've got teenAIDS and the tattoos – unskilfully painted on by an about to be unemployed makeup artist – are a weak attempt to make them look hardcore. They are not. They are not even softcore. They're wimps. Short wimps. With no idea. Only crap voices and fabricated lyrics. This lot are even holding guitars in an even weaker attempt to display their lack of acoustic skill. They've got the chords all wrong – it's so blatantly obvious that my foot slips out of the pedal…

My revs momentarily drop from 120rpm to 50rpm before I'm back and focussed once again on these vermin.

Verdict: Death
Method of Execution: Shoving a tattoo needle through their eyeballs and leaving them to bleed to death in an African desert while hungry vultures 'clean the carrion up'.

#4 *The Road To Love* – Boyz

This quartet has been around a while and can probably be forgiven for starting their band before boybands were officially invented (or excreted). But they still have no idea how to sing or dress or be humble or dance or create good music. They suck and they're all black which makes them suck and try to bend a note while sucking. Amazing how the word 'baby' pitches up after most lines. One of two scenarios here – one, they couldn't find anything to rhyme with baby and two, there were two syllables missing from the end of the line. The real pain emerges when there are three or four or five or six syllables missing. This is when these wincing head-shakers try to bend the note and extend the word *baby* over too many syllables. They look as though they have a down syndrome twitch and they believe it makes them look as though they can really sing. But they can't. They just occupy space and must be exterminated.

Verdict: Death (or perhaps eternal pain based on the fact that they began before boybands were being churned out like Pokémon cards)
Method of Execution: Ripping their jaws apart using an electronic wrench.

#3 *A Special Place Called Love* – Front ND

An abundance of shirts there is not in this video: another cover version. Every full 360-degree rotation of my pedal equals a gratuitous abdominal shot. Now let's give these post-teen hopefuls their due – their liposuction has proved effective: all eight ab striations with little or no sign of the scaring. I picture the director yelling after each take, 'Right lads you can all breathe out now'. Their arms are permanently on their crotches for the primary reason of squeezing their pectorals together to create a false tanned line of unwrinkled hairless post-teen cleavage. They never expose their legs. Ever. But their top halves receive so much coverage that I notice most of the men in the cycle line averting their eyes either because they're straight or because they can't bear the thought of how many hours they will need to cycle to cut their beer bellies down to that. I have a quick feel under my now drenched white vest and can feel some real progress. Fantastic.

Verdict: Death
Method of Execution: Disembowelment

My water bottle is as dry as my throat and there's an ad break so I hop off to suck on the germ infested stainless steel water fountain (don't you hate it when those sweating panting grimy gym patrons slobber all over the outlet? Have gyms never considered signs like *Don't Slobber on the Tap* or *Fuck off if you are Diseased* above the fountain?)

My glove rests delicately on top of the seat and, as I return with a mouthful of unfiltered water, it falls off as a sweaty flat stomached woman takes the opportunity to rest her sweaty behind exactly where my arse was, just seconds before.

There are no free cycles left.

Everyone is loving the top 10 boybands of all time.

I'm panicking.

She's not allowed to just steal my bike.

This isn't junior school.

Number two is about to start.

I can't miss it.

Not now.

No matter how flat her tummy is.

"Excuse me," I spit. "Those are my gloves; I was just on this bike and popped off for a sip of water," motioning politely for her to get off the bike.

She totally ignores me.

I cannot believe it.

I say it again.

This time louder and with more purpose.

I hate myself because I believe in chivalry and women should always get first say.

Except now.

I wipe my brow with the bottom of my vest because now I'm really sweating at the prospect of missing the final two. She glances sideways at my exposed midriff and slips out a tickle of a nod of approval. I get hopeful that I'll retrieve my bike for a nanosecond. Her cycling slows down as if she's teasing me and then quickens up again. I want to cry. I want to tell her how I plan to murder these narcissistic fakers on the screen and that this research is crucial to my quest but realise that she's gone over to the dark side when she starts gyrating from side to side and clicking her fingers, her earphones now embedded in her sexy earlobes, as number two jumps onto the screen like the h bomb.

I'm frantic now.

Looking backwards and forwards.

Everything's busy.

Even the air walkers.

And I'm not so desperate to cycle but more desperate to plug my headphones in.

Like I'm horny and need a hole.

Thank God a big gaping one opens up in the far corner and, like a polecat, I'm off towards it, determined to beat the steroid freak lumbering from a shorter distance.

I'm almost there.

I jump.

And make it.

Sort of.

The apology is complemented by the fumbling of the cord and getting the headphones comfortable on my head. He mutters something and marches off to shoot up in the toilet.

Suddenly everything is clear.

I have purpose.

He hath spoken.

To me.

#2 *Lovechild* – Boy Meets Girl

All I can see are scantily clad pulchritudinous females and for a split second I forget that there's anything wrong with the pathetic self-proclaimed genre that has become boybands. But then the boys arrive. And man! are they adored. And there's not a hope in hell that any of these back-slappers would ever even warrant a glance from one of these beauties in the real world. But they're being adored. Even though they're all standing on boxes to be eye level with the full chested waifs. Then the director's creativity momentarily overshadows the band's camera hogging and there are glimmers of hope. I think I might have seen them on some talk show or music awards ceremony and I remember hearing the crowd booing because some synthesiser broke and the singing sounded wretched. It was so blatantly embarrassing that I wished I could shove it down all the die-hard fans' throats because they were, are and will always be hopeless. And they are all happy clappers or something; thanking the Lord at every turn; the squeaky clean image the mandate from their PR manager. When the press finds one of them passed out with puke down their string vest in a public toilet with a needle still attached, where will God be then? He, like me, will be planning how to extract these ersatz stars from the planet.

Verdict: Death
Method of Execution: Crucifixion

I can barely contain my excitement as again the 'trying hard to be funny' presenter cuts to another ad break. I stop cycling and reset the timer just in case mine ends during the song which would force the tension to reduce and me to stop and avert my eyes from the champions of the known boyband world. The bestest everest boyband song; the number one; *the* song.

#1 *She's From City Love* – Coastal Love

Can this be another cover version! When I see who it is I bite down so hard on my lip that I feel the warm blood seep down into my throat. It's them. They've got the hairstyles. Way too late. The unruly ruly look. Spiked in all directions. The style adopted before these locals began kneeling down to examine each other's first pubic hair, nestling above an undropped testicle sack. They're in a barbershop or something as my headset malfunctions before the music has even started and I can't hear anything. But this makes it oh so much clearer. Watch a boyband video without the sound; I dare you; I urge you. You will see how truly ridiculous and fabricated they look singing what normally is someone else's song. Shame on the greedy artist so desperate for cash that their once immortalised song is now bastardised forever. Only three of the five ever sing. I'm not sure what the other two do (the good looking ones); perhaps they're like porn fluffers – keeping the others in the band ready for optimal performances. Their raised eyebrows and longing, pained expressions deep into the camera's soul makes me choke. It's them. And they're trying so hard to dispel the boyband image even though all their fame and cash and cars and houses and teenage boys and teenage girls are all based on the premise that they perform songs created by others and mixed by further others. It's them. I recognise them. And they're shorter in real life. And more arrogant. And more stupid. And they love themselves even more than they do in the video. The greatest boyband song of all time. They will die. And suffer. For their portrayal misleads the youth of today and taints the youth of tomorrow. Like those degenerates on the bus. I must teach. The song ends with a famous cameo appearance and the boys exit the barbershop hugging and congratulating each other like victorious footballers. Until the final picture which is etched in my mind forever. Of the band in tattoo form. On the celebrity's arse. How she had degraded herself. I will never see another of her movies again. Even though the tattoo is fake. Like them. An image on an arse.

Verdict: Guess?
Method of Execution: Wait and see
Urgency: Critical

My thighs are now cramping and I've snapped my headphone cord (or bitten through it, I'm not sure). It's time to go home.

CHAPTER 11

MEETING

Ever experience that feeling when your mind is awake but your eyelids are as heavy as lead, as though each eyelash is tied by a tiny invisible string to the Titanic? I can feel this phenomenon as my head becomes excessively comfortable in the palm of my hand and my notebook looks more like a Picasso than a doodle pad.

Overcrowded.

Manfred drones.

Which is unlike him because everything he usually mutters makes sense as though each tiny bit of information is gracefully bestowed upon us after an immense period of consternation, debate and thought. But uncharacteristically he's droning.

Like a boring bee.

I think because he has to: his boss is present, literally the CEO of the division which should make all us mortals sit upright, straighten our ties and pay attention. I tried this for the first ten minutes, getting that attentive contemplative look upon my brow like a customs official. I even wore my favourite tie: the silver one with the dabbles of bright blue; Versace. But it's back to normal after ten minutes, the tiredness and boredom setting in like a virus.

She's looking attentive though.

The one with pen fragments in her eye. Sitting bolt upright like the teacher's pet, eager to add her two pence worth until all management applaud and beg her to run the company. I see her squirt a sideways glance at me because the crack of my pen reverberates around the room as a piece lodges into my tongue and scratches the roof of my mouth. She's wary now. I can tell. It makes me happy. This. My pen hath become my sword. Felling the weak and incompetent and ensuring the strong and true arise again to rule the world; to take back what is rightly theirs and what has been unjustly ripped from their grasp in past times.

Christie's smug comment goes down well and I'm in the process of planning how to remove her spleen with my jagged chewed pen when my name rings out from a galaxy far far away. I disregard it as imagination when it happens again and I trace the source to be Manfred Dill's lips accompanied by all the eyes in the room.

"Could you repeat the question please?" I say, the

pen now safely clenched between my fist.

"Ah yes, we were just wondering if you shared Christie's unfaltering support for the prediction?"

Christie's support for the prediction.

Christie's support for the prediction!

Absolutely not!

If I ever support Christie's anything I would have to make sure that my nuts spend an eternity dancing inches above the soothing whirr of a blender.

"Christie's support. Mmmmm. Not quite sure I do."

"Why is that?" this time Jonathan, my boss, who at the second he mutters this, realises he has made a horrible mistake, as my eyes bear down on his and he averts them in an attempt to divert the potential power I have now that I have been privy to witness his manhood bestowed upon the mailroom boy.

"Because I don't think Christie has truly assessed the holistic ramifications of the prediction."

I need a slight hint on what exactly the prediction was as the eye weights have now reluctantly been slung over my shoulder.

Christie, in her infinite pen slugging wisdom, inadvertently comes to my rescue, blissfully unaware that a more effective method of kicking me whilst I was down would have been to keep quiet.

"What I failed to add was that the prediction includes potential revenue streams from retrocession fund manager kickbacks. Sometimes as high as sixty basis points," she says.

"But are you taking account of the ever increasing trend of fund supermarkets who demand a retrocession payment of as much as one hundred percent on the annual management charge, coupled with a cutting edge J2EE technological platform and a non-existent initial charge?" I retort.

The stunned silence even stuns me.

Manfred Dill's nodding smirk is secretly in admiration.

I can tell.

Christie looks like a puppy that's just been smacked for crapping on the lounge carpet.

Later the same day I'm enjoying a rare moment of sun splashing my face through dark clouds and a dusty tinted window, when Homer yells 'D'oh!' on my computer to let me know that new mail has arrived. It's pretty late in the day and the thought of addressing some menial concern and potentially biting into my leisure time annoys me. So much so that I'm about to shut down without opening it when I notice it's from Manfred Dill. Curiosity more than obligation seeks a quick double click to open the window.

Half an hour later my tie is back to where it was just prior to the meeting and I'm sipping expensive filtered coffee watching the deceivingly clean Thames water saunter along far down below. I hate the word *swell* but there is no other word to describe this office. There's more leather in here than a sex shop and the paintings are in frames that probably cost more than my apartment. The only nauseating element is the screensaver, which, in Manfred's absence, keeps grabbing my attention similar to how one is unable to look away when someone is eating badly: chewing with their mouth open so that the mushed up food is inexplicably visible, mangled with saliva strings that connect to the molars. It's of a girl group.

"Lovely little honeys those, aren't they? Anyway you're probably wondering why I asked you up here. Well the truth is I want to know why you do so little. At work I mean?"

My initial reaction clicks me straight into *corporate answer* mode.

"Well sir, I just don't feel there are enough challenges for me in my current role."

"Bullshit! You know it. What's the real reason?"

He now has a look in his eye that makes me want to fess up.

"I have a higher purpose in life than working for a wet blanket like Collins. I've been sent for a specific purpose, you see. I've been sent to educate the youth and rid society of meaningless unfulfilling corrupt shit that dictates our everyday lives."

"Interesting marketing concept!" he coaxes almost expecting what I just gave him. "I have a little proposition for you. You see I quite like you. I don't know why. Maybe it's the way you disdainfully look at Miss Franken's annoying little pug nose or the way you never stop chewing your pen or maybe it's because you're one of the laziest pricks in the department. Which astounds me because you are one of the brightest too. You churn work quicker and better than anyone yet you only do the bare minimum. Just enough to get by; enough to pay the bills. What's that all about? Why are you messing with your talent and potential?"

"I have a purpose. Now, anyway."

"Well how about the purpose takes on another sphere. We have two choices here – one, leave the company. Or two, take Collins's job, come work for me, triple your current salary and kick-start your very promising career."

I'd like door number two please.

"Why the drastic change? What's in it for you?"

"To be honest I'd like a number two. Someone who doesn't roll over and take it in the arse like Collins. Someone who wants to make a difference. Someone who's willing to stand up for what they believe in, even if it means getting into a bit of trouble. Someone exactly like the person sitting in front of me right now. Someone who just needs the right guidance and a little kick-start."

"Can I think about it?"

"No. Here's the proposed contract. Don't take time to read it. If you don't sign it now, collect your stuff and don't ever come back. No pressure, but you can move into your new office tomorrow morning. The one on the top floor. We're all moving up there; the Executive

Board and their nominated representatives. You'll see there's a relocation package (even though you don't need relocating), a company car of your choice, share options, medical, dental benefits and a partridge in a pear tree."

CHAPTER 12

NEPHEWS

Her nephews are in town and I can tell things are different when firstly She talks to me and secondly She's nice to me. She still reeks of men's cologne, which is inexcusable, but I'm quickly thinking about how many of my breakables are exposed when my current favourite song wafts from the radio like onions frying. My little jig on the lounge floor is a poor attempt to get rid of Her even though She's offered to make a lovely cup of tea. I'm just about to jump online and order the tune when She springs the nephew timeline thing on me.

Tomorrow.

My one free weekend.

They're jetting in.

Like unwelcome flies.

Ready to make everything dirty.

Again and again.

Now these kids are the worst behaved children in the known universe but, to Her credit, She loves them to bits and seems to extract the nice bits of their evil. They're on their own this time which is a crumb of a Godsend because the mother (Her sister) is one of those trying to be progressive 'I'll never spank a child' ethno-bongo 'I've lost my youth and blame my children for it' leeches. The last time the entire family graced our doorstep (complete with husband who managed to mutter something about a steam train and a plastic windshield the entire stay), mayhem: the level of discipline between the households (London and Devon) like the gaping hole of Calcutta.

Snapping priceless inimitable African art was obviously acceptable in the country, so when that wanton destruction of other people's things moved cityward there was clearly going to be conflict. I mean, call me an old fuddy-duddy, but if some little twerp is wiping their crap all over the walls, I say: 'Fine, do it in your own home; but in mine either follow my behavioural doctrine or ship out, bucko!' This idea of your home being your home gets trampled to death when kids are involved.

Stampeded.

But I'm open minded about this visit.

What choice do I have?

None.

"It's only the kids. We can control them. I promise." Her words ring in my ears until my head feels like it has swelled to an enormous size, ready to explode all over the lounge to join the imminent mess created by the children.

I haven't done the dishes in weeks which means I have very little bargaining power (I did do the toilet last Thursday though!) which ultimately results in me in a park with a child on my shoulders and ice-cream splashed down the side of my new shirt, the material now firmly stuck to my flank.

And there was no apology.

Just "Get me another!"

Like I said, badly badly badly badly badly behaved.

And ungrateful.

And impolite.

But secretly I love these kids to bits.

I think it's the parents who messed things up for them.

I love them the most when I'm away from Her and a summer jogger or Frisbee girl bounces over to tell me that they have my eyes.

Mine are green.

Theirs are blue.

But they love it.

A single father has the sex appeal of a God.

A single mother has the sex appeal of a Dog.

Unfair societal values really.

But these girls can't believe their luck when I hand

them the sticky, screaming, whining, crying, demanding, dirty youth. They cannot believe their luck.

(Also because these kids are relatively good looking which makes them start to assess how viable and potentially attractive the gene pool is.)

They're holding the kid and the ball is now in their court. I'm saying, "You look as though you'd make a really good mum", and the pressure's on. Them. They're on show. As a mother.

Then I start assessing the gene pool.

Just in case I missed any of it when it bounced over.

Of course I'd never hand one of my girlfriend's nephews over to an ugly girl.

Apart from sending the wrong signals no child wants to be manhandled by an ugly person.

One of my mum's friends, when I was a wee kicker, used to pinch my bottom and always comment on my eyelashes which made me run away and eat tinned spaghetti in a dark cupboard with a plastic spoon. I don't like being around ugly people. Just like I don't like the sight of puke. I'd rather look at an old building or a nice cuff link.

She's off with the little buggers, granting me feeble respite which is spent sunning my stomach and smoking a cigarette. I'm loath to watch them but do and realise how fantastic She is with kids. Every movement reeks of patience and Her smile that I once loved returns in its entirety to greet the charging tykes as She substitutes for a jungle gym.

Maybe I should talk to Her more often.
Like we used to.
But first She must stop fucking men with such cheap cologne.

CHAPTER 13
DOG

There's a whimpering dog and I've got blood all over my hands and hoping no one saw me. It's late so it's dark. This is a good thing. There was no sound when I made my move; none whatsoever. Just something inside. Bubbling.

The first swipe was somewhat useless, me swinging full circle and almost slapping myself in the forehead. The second speckled the wall behind with a collage of black blood, the effect adding to rather than detracting from the graffiti. The little sucker then decided to fight back and bit my hand like a dog. So the blood on my hands is also mine. But mainly his. And I can smell his saliva mixed in with the blood and fear.

Cowards!

Not because they run but because they strike.

Helpless.

Strike.

Again.

Again.

Again.

Until the thud of the jaw smacking against the pavement made my teeth rattle and made me cough a tiny splat of vomit into my mouth and spit the acidic mess out as my stride quickened and I approached to calm the situation.

And save the animal.

But it was too late.

With one harsh boot accentuating gravity's direction he stomped the dog's spine, snapping it into a V shape, and then ground the creature into the wet textured tar.

That's what being a bully is all about.

And I hate bullies.

So I smacked him around until he was in the same position as the hound: flat on the ground and begging for mercy, his back exposed like a mother's breast.

His spine wouldn't snap the first time I stomped on it, his arm firmly twisted and bent behind him.

It didn't break the second either.

Or the third.

But eventually his silence silenced the crack of the small dog's spine that now no longer rings in my head and my throat and my heart like a pistol shot.

Loud and eternal.

I had to kill the dog to put it out of its misery.

The man who hit the dog I tried to kill to put him out of his misery.

EXPERIMENT

Everyone has a price. Ask yourself this: for two hundred billion dollars? Would you cup your father's balls? Now this would be no routine cup. Although you would walk away with the money, the man who unselfishly raised you and put all his faith in you will go to the grave knowing that you cupped his balls. How you do it is up to you but he will never know that you did it for money. All he will know is that, whilst innocently drying himself on the soft pale pink bathroom mat, his beloved daughter or son, purposefully approached him, stuck out their right hand, inserted it under his scrotum, and cupped his balls. Delicately. Would you do that for two hundred billion dollars?

Now that's obviously a suspension of disbelief because he would certainly notice things were different when you pitched up for the local rugby game in a Learjet or bought your little brother a racehorse. But if you can just imagine the proposition and the potential scenario: riches beyond your dreams versus humiliation and eternal dignity loss.

We go through these little tests every day of our lives. Do we take the crap job which pays more or do what we really like doing for a pittance? What's better: putting together business process flow charts or helping an autistic child to swim? The smile on the boss's face when he realises the flow chart is implementable or the smile on the child's face when a width is completed?

What about if these unconscious decisions were consciously turned into conscious ones? I gave a homeless man ten pounds yesterday morning. I promised him another twenty a day if he gave up drinking. He agreed, his commitment to beating the bottle both passionate and unfaltering. A fleeting encounter? No. The steam rising from the pavement clears revealing the same man in the same place at the same time. He's my regular. Have passed him every day for the last couple of years just near the office. He's a certainty. The perfect lab rat. Summer or winter. The heat bellows through the grids from the surrounding offices: his respite from the cold. His skin and hands are crumpled like brown paper packets and his outfit gleefully denies the changes in fashion. Would he have cupped his dad's balls?

"Remember me?" I say.

He can barely muster the energy to raise his eyelids and does so with such an effort that I feel like a drill sergeant in the army ordering a young recruit out of bed.

He grunts something which I can't make out and follows this with a hay fever salute, a straight clear snail trail of mucus now decorating his palm. I crouch down nearer to him.

"You've been drinking."

It's eight thirty am.

"No I fucking haven't," he says, his eyes now slowly recollecting my face. "I haven't, mister… sir. The twenty. I haven't eaten. I'm hungry and cold. Help me."

"What did you do with the ten I gave you yesterday?"

"It was stolen. Right out of my hands. Those little street buggers."

"I'll tell you what. I'll give you twenty pounds right now if you tell me the truth, the whole truth and nothing but the truth. What'd you really do with the money?"

He's now crying and his upper lip has joined his palm in the mucus decoration genre.

"I'm sorry, sir. I spent it on the booze. I tried, but it's so tough."

I take out two twenty pound notes from my wallet and place them in front of the dribbling man, taking severe caution to not get into the mucus firing line.

"This one is the one I promised you yesterday," I say,

lighting the note with my cheap red plastic lighter in the shape of a chilli. The man lunges forward and only succeeds in burning his hand and receiving a shoe in the chest.

"This is the one I promised you today," I say, sliding the note over towards him. Like a dog with a bone he snaps it up and clutches it on his heart, anxiously tick-tocking his head from side to side.

"Our original deal is off because you broke your promise. Had you stopped drinking, you could've had one a day."

"Oh please, I'll try again! Please sir! Please! One more chance!"

"Sorry mate. You had it."

My new office is nice but sufficiently boring which means I'm not going to describe it. I need another guinea pig. Fast. I haven't spoken to my old boss, who is now one of my senior managers, since I leapfrogged him on the corporate ladder. I've done most of my work and Manfred is in Zurich so I decide to continue experimenting. How does one convince the pig that spinning the wheel in the opposite direction is for the good of all mankind, womankind and futurekind? How far will a human being go?

I compose an email. It reads, *Jonathan, it is about time you and I got to know each other a little better. Cancel all your afternoon meetings and meet me at my car in half an hour.* Twenty-eight minutes elapse and he hasn't replied so I call his secretary who informs me that he's ill. Gastric flu or something.

"What's his home address?"

After I'd figured out how to get to Surrey it took me even longer to find Jonathan Collins's residence: a cute three bed cottage tucked down a cul-de-sac behind a small brewery. I was just settling into listening to that new fantastic song I keep hearing when the large golf ball post box accosted me like a visual rapist. I ring the doorbell three times before banging forcefully on the rattling door. Still nothing. Not even a murmur from the inside; just the disjointed hum of distant traffic. The garden looks well-kept with young trees and too many daffodils, which dissect the trees like paint ball splats. At the rear of the house is a small fence which I quickly hop over and into another smaller garden strewn with children's toys and metal chairs. There's a window ajar.

It's a bedroom window and I peer in waiting for my eyes to adjust to the darkness. My ears adjust first as I hear moderate regular breathing. Then a mound in the middle of the room comes into focus. A duvet covering what is hopefully a sick man. Sleeping. Resting. Recovering.

"Jonathan," I whisper considerately. "Jon, is that you?"

A sudden pang sears through my body as it dawns on me that this might not be the correct address. The highlighted map and scribbled address match.

Thank God.

"Jonathan," I whisper again, this time a bit louder

and he quickly sits up like a snapping mousetrap.

"Who's there? Who's that?"

"It's Paton."

"What are you doing here?"

We're both whispering for some reason; no one's sleeping anymore!

"Let me in and I'll explain."

In an hour I've convinced Jonathan that he's feeling better and the fresh air would do him good and we're on the road heading for north London. The conversation is polite and work orientated. He keeps inquiring why we are doing this and I sweep it under the guise carpet of getting to know one another a little better.

Squeeze.

Tighter.

Camden.

Late afternoon.

Getting chilly.

"Where are we going?" he says.

"There." I point to the neon lights flashing in the window.

He looks at me; not a look of wonder but pure confusion. My return look is not one of mischievousness but one of forcefulness. I think he's about to contest when I lean closer and whisper into his ear, "You'll ensure my silence for a month."

Eight foreign women sit on white plastic chairs with their breasts bubbling over their tops and their legs crossed, the thick high heels of their shoes dangling in unison with their earrings. Jonathan is pale and makes a break for it, probably believing I'm trying to snap him out of his homosexuality by getting him laid by a gorgeous hooker. That's not the case at all. It relates to the boyband thing, I suppose. If men are sexually attracted to other men they should embrace it and be proud, not live a lie and pretend. I like gay men. Not in that way. But I like the fact that they openly embrace what they like. It's not their fault. It's not A fault. I know not why I like women but I do. This man has two kids and a wife and might be far happier without them. But does this man have limits? I still struggle to see the mailroom boy with his suitcase on the doorstep in Surrey but this is a start.

I catch his arm back upstairs at the entrance and, coupled with a quizzical stare from the large Nigerian bouncer, I drag him back downstairs. We have a quick sauna together and top it off by joining the selection process. The establishment is quiet and I haven't spotted any other patrons, which worries me. The intercom rings and one of the girls prepares for takeoff. Jonathan is nervously smoking, sometimes missing his lips and stubbing the filter of the cigarette into his lip or cheek. I lean over and tell him to relax. We're both clad only in white towels and the conversation begins to flow as the girls start their sales pitches. The best looking girl departs just before a tall reasonably good-looking man enters.

He looks around and the dynamic is unusual but potentially hilarious. Encircling him on the cheap white plastic chairs, a crappy soap opera flickering unnoticed in the background, is a load of available beauties and two men, smoking cigarettes and topless, only covered by white towels. Jonathan looks up and registers at the exact second I register, the supplementary man's face widening like a child's in a candy store. Jonathan is a small man and his frail shoulders and smooth face give him the appearance of a young man. His lack of chest hair further accentuates this illusion. My plan takes on serious new dimensions when the man bites upon his finger in a quizzical expression and turns towards Jonathan.

I take the man aside while Jonathan looks around in terror.

"You want a three-way?"

"Was it that obvious?"

"Yes, but we could have a slight problem with the management here. I'll go upstairs and sort it out while you have a chat to my friend over there."

The big Nigerian stands over me and I can feel his shadow trap me in a half nelson. The woman manager, who I pray to God was never involved in the industry because she's so ugly and it would be cruel to impose her warts on anyone, lays down four conditions: one girl in particular, a shitload of money, no anal sex and not to make it a habit.

Sorted.

When I get back downstairs the two men are coyly staring into each another's eyes and chucking the usual signals: hand through the hair, chewing the fingernail and unintentional one-two eyelid flutters. My experiment is taking on complicated proportions and this annoys me slightly so I call Jonathan aside and test his limits. I tell him that I will tell his wife everything about the mailboy unless he does exactly as I say. He's to undertake a threesome with his new boyfriend and 'Magna' (the one in taut orange) and only focus on the girl. He cannot under any circumstances even touch the other man and has to have full sex with the whore. But not up her arse.

His protest takes the form of a raised eyebrow and a little shake of the head to which I restate that his failure to comply will mean full disclosure. I light up a cigarette and settle into the sauna as the three make their way to one of the angular wooden enclosures for sex. Two hookers join me and offer me a group discount. The one isn't bad but the other I wouldn't touch with a ten foot barge pole: her arse hangs only slightly lower than her breasts and the gaps in her teeth make her look like she's swallowed a piano. So I decline, the thought of paying for it too harsh for my fragile ego and the thought of my pubes mingling with their crab infested bushes too frightening for my fragile immune system.

Jonathan emerges before the other two, smiling yet obviously anxious to escape the cringe of having just slept with a hooker and a brothel patron. I fix his collar which I hope he doesn't take as a kind gesture. Or a friendly gesture. It's neither. And my expression tells it that way. He's still confused, so I decide to provide the clarity.

"How was it?" I say.

"I don't know what to say really," he says. "Pleasurable, I suppose."

"What did you do?"

"Just as you told me."

"Which is?"

"I made love to the hooker."

"Which end?"

"The correct end."

"Which end did your buddy go?"

"A bit in the mouth. Then he took over, once I'd um, finished."

"Bend over."

"Pardon?"

"Bend over."

"Why?"

"Because I want to see your rectum."

"You want to see my rectum." His interest in the subject suddenly amplifies.

"Yes, I want to see your rectum so that I can see how swollen it is after you lied to me."

"I swear he didn't."

"Wait here, I'm going back to ask him." I'm jogging back downstairs when his louder tone stops me.

"Wait."

"So you couldn't resist. Even at the prospect of losing your wife and kids and everything. I have to tell her now of course."

"Oh please, dear God, I beg of you."

"I can't go back on my word. That's just the way I am. And besides, this is what you really want isn't it. Why live a lie? I'd be doing you a favour."

He's now forgotten to disguise that his arse is aching and he wobbles like a cowboy as we approach the car. He drops to his knees, clutching my coat and sobbing hysterically.

"Did you use protection? Wait! Did he use protection? You know you're putting your wife in danger."

"There's no danger," he sobs. "We never … and I did use a condom. And he did," he sobs on, touching the side of his mouth.

"Did you involve the woman at all?"

"Yes, in the beginning, and then she concentrated her efforts on herself and Giles."

"Giles!"

"That's his name."

"No shit. Are you going to see him again or was this just a once off?"

"Just this time I think."

"You're lying again! Why don't you just tell me the truth? I'm one of the few people in your world who might understand, but you continue to lie. And renege on deals. Which means I have to tell."

"Don't, don't, don't. I'll do anything. Anything."
"Anything?"
"Anything!"
"Anything."

CHAPTER 15
PHONE CALL

I decide to phone Kitten and my nerves are uncharacteristically on a knife-edge. I call her four times and hang up before the phone begins to ring. If it rings once you are caught. Even before the days of caller recognition, if you called and it rang you would find yourself explaining a mere ten minutes later how the phone cut off or you dropped it. Girls have heard all this crap. Kitten has heard all this crap. That's why it cannot ring: my hang-up skills are luckily in check even though my hand is shaking like a vibrator and my lips are sweating.

Eventually the ring tone slips out and I'm stuck to face the music.

One ring.

Two rings.

Three rings.

Click.

Oh my God.

"Hello," says a male voice.

Hang-up?

No.

Caller ID!

Remember the caller ID!

"Hello," he says again.

My mouth is now twitching like a bad actor's.

The receiver is millimetres away from being slammed down.

I'm leaning towards it.

Slowly.

Painstakingly.

"I don't think anyone's there dear," he says, muffling the receiver.

"Hi, can you hear me?" I say.

"Yes, yes. Can I help you?"

"It's Paton Stipps speaking. Sorry, could you not hear me? I could hear you perfectly. Those mobile phones are sometimes a bit dodgy, aren't they."

Downright. Blatantly. Obvious. Liar.

"Can I help you?" he says again.

"Yes, thank you. I'm after, I mean I'm … is Kitten around?"

The pause is longer than feels normal and I can hear his dissenting tone when he mutters, "Someone called Paton Shits or something" and a longer gap as Kitten tries to remember who I am. "Oh Paton Stipps," she eventually registers. There's no sign or groan which is encouraging but there's also no "Halleluiah, it's him!" either.

"Paton, hi! How are you? It's so wonderful to hear from you. I'm at the gym working up a bit of a sweat."

And I imagine the purposefully formed glistening trails of sweat casually resting on the slopes… stop it!

"Great. Super. Forcing a few extra reps out are we?"

Lame comment.

She giggles. Expectantly.

Waiting for me to confess why I called.

Time to cut to the chase.

"The reason I called is just to see what you were up to on Saturday?"

"Oh sorry honey, I've got a fundraiser for the restoration of steam engines."

Nobel.

"No not this Saturday; the Saturday after next?"

Longshot.

"Next Saturday?"

"Yes."

"Why what are you up to."

"Well it's just a friend of mine. He's having a bit of a get together. Nothing big, well, it probably will be quite big. And festive. Anyway I was hoping I could return the favour for such an excellent birthday party…"

Are you Gonna Go My Way?

"…and invite you to another."

All my good and hard work undone in one phone call.

"Who's your friend? Is there, um, I mean will the normal crowd be attending?"

The normal crowd?

The normal crowd!

"Yes the usual abnormal celebs will be buzzing around. He's one of those high flying social butterflies, if you know what I mean."

She's distracted by the male voice, which I'm hoping is her personal trainer's.

"Um sure, next Saturday. Looking forward to it. We must catch up anyway. Is eight alright? Pick me up, okay."

"Sure. See you then."

We hang up and two small tasks lie portentously before me. In less than two weeks I have to find a famous friend and persuade him to throw London's bash of the year.

That night ends up being one of those rare occasions when me and Her are together. Sitting on the cream couch, slumped in separate corners staring at Robert Redford undress a woman at gunpoint. She's a stunner and there's something strangely erotic about watching a good looking man make a woman take her clothes off while casually nestling against a hand-made wooden chair holding a revolver. Sundance. Then she mounts him like a sex starved Amazonian woman.

Then She speaks. During the film. I can scarcely believe my ears because I'm consistently scolded for talking during movies and TV programmes. I'm not sure whether to give Her some of Her own medicine and shoosh Her or ignore the comment altogether. Something about 'Us' so I coyly ignore it. She has another go and again I play the ignore card. She smells of men's cologne. Again.

Then we're in bed. Both sitting bolt upright like wide awake planks. Reading. Ignoring. Not even absorbed in the story but pretending to be so. Like a game. Where the magic went maybe only a clairvoyant knows. There were days of slow blinks and soft words down the receiver of a long distance telephone. Where considerate was not a four letter word and communication was something that existed without imposing itself like overspread peanut butter. And it's gradual: the decay. It sets in before you can smell the flesh decomposing, or perhaps you forget to notice when every day is more of a chore than a pleasure.

More of a chore than a pleasure.

When splitting the last stick of chewing gum became scoffing the packet and stinking of men's cologne.

CHAPTER 16

HOT DATE, ROUND TWO

Kitten is pissed off with me despite having just toyed with her meal at the Ivy and seen the best, most impossible to get into show in the history of London theatre. Her lip is hanging about an inch from the floor which is half an inch higher after she discovered there was no party and certainly no celebs. These things happen. Contracting Hepatitis A is common and most young actors can be expected to fall prey to this ruthless virus every once in a while. Not that plausible but believable when coupled with puppy dog eyes and an alternative that should have seen to it that not only does the smile reappear but perhaps the knees are grazed by the end of evening.

I suspect I'm just not good enough for her. That's the only explanation because my charm levels could never again attain the heights they set for themselves that evening. I am the man with all the interesting and fruitful chat, but she doesn't think so. She continues to slurp her Dom Pedro and gaze wishfully in any direction but mine.

I've run out of this bounty of conversation so severely that I'm about to kiss her forcefully on the cheek, get up, go to the bathroom and never return when the shiny wooden door of the quiet after dinner pub swings curiously open. A man with a moustache and a ribbon-like ponytail walks in, bathed in gold jewellery and a light mink coat. He's followed by two boys and two girls, all young and painfully thin with dark rings beneath their eyes and plastic smiles.

Kitten's neck almost snaps out of joint as she twists around and pulls her top slightly lower to reveal more of the arse-like breasts beckoning to be released. She smiles at the man who smiles at me, stopping and squinting in my direction, his head cocked to one side.

This goes on.

For an uncomfortable amount of time.

Until his stare burns a hole in the side of my neck and I turn to help him.

Something's familiar here and Kitten waits, poised like a skydiver.

"Paton. Paton. Paton? Paton Stops! Paton Stipps!" Jackie the Jackhammer.

"Jackie the Jackhammer?"

"Yes," he says grinning, Kitten's hand now conveniently on my leg, her smile almost matching his.

"How long, you elusive little person?"

"Not sure. A while I think…"

"Ever since the shoot," he says.

Kitten is now more excited than a raccoon on heat and is squeezing my thigh high up and clearing her throat trying to get her breasts closer to the visitor.

"Oh, how rude. Jackie this is Kitten; Kitten – Jackie."

"Kitten. What's your mum's name? Pussy? Paton, I'd introduce these idiots behind me but I'm not quite sure who they are. Or what the fuck they are doing hanging around me. Go away!" he says flicking his wrist. "Go to the bar or the toilet or something. Go on. Shoo."

The herd trot off like robots towards the toilet fishing around their pockets and trying to stay upright. Instead of being disconcerted Kitten jumps right back in.

"What do you do, Jackie?" she says, shifting just short of sitting on my lap, after Jackie has sat down across from me.

"Two Kir Royales," Jackie yells towards the waiter.

"What was that um, what's your name again? Mitten?"

"Kitten, and I just wanted to know what you do."

"As little as possible! Listen Mitten do you mind if

me and Paton have a little chat. You can run along and join the others in the toilet if you want."

"I beg your pardon?"

"Listen, here's some fun money. Go and have some fun," he says handing her a wad of notes.

Kitten's face turns to something in a severe dilemma. She doesn't want to offend the ostensibly powerful man but also doesn't want to blow her big chance by leaving.

"I'm out tonight with my boyfriend Paton!"

Boyfriend!

That's a step up from *Scum Of The Earth* five minutes earlier.

"I tell you what," Jackie says, losing patience. "Whatever he's paying you, add a zero on the end and come back when he needs you again."

"I'm not a hooker! I'm a model and an actress."

"Aren't we all?" he says, levelling his moustache with his baby finger. "An actress, eh? What's your latest picture? Captain Phallus's Mandolin? Shitty Shitty Bang Bang? Or perhaps Good Will Humping!"

I'm an innocent bystander in all of this.

"You want acting? You should chat to your boyfriend here. He could've been something, you know."

All attention on me, despite the embroidered statement of the year. Kitten turns to face me only missing her stake entitled *Struck Gold!*

"That was a long time ago Jackie and, as I told you then, it wasn't for me."

"In all my years of directing, I've never seen a face eat up the lens like this kid."

I think I hear Kitten come at this exact second.

The Kir Royales arrive and Jackie deliberately hands one to me and toasts us, giving me a nudge on the chin with his fist after which he downs the drink and orders two more. This becomes three when he realises that there is no chance Kitten will unglue herself from my side.

She's stuck.

Like a Garfield car ornament stuck on the inside of a windshield.

A Garfield with double G breasts.

After about nine dozen Kir Royales I can feel the room begin to levitate. Jackie's spent the entire evening singing my praises and trying to get me to join a play he's directing and cast for a movie he'll be directing in the new year. I've spent the entire evening trying to keep up with his drinking and protest my innocence.

It was, after all, only a handful of commercials I did whilst studying at university. Extra pocket money. Jackie had since gone onto bigger and better things, leaving the world of commercials for the world of commercial people. Like Kitten, who has spent the evening trying more-than-desperately to spark her 'big break' into flames. She takes an enormous amount of heart from one of Jackie's comments which went something like, "With those accessories I'd only be able to cast you as a dancer. But that would mean writing a scene where there actually are dancers!"

The four join and leave as regularly as Kitten's forceful chuckles at Jackie's jokes. There is a maximum of five syllables between the lot of them. Just as suddenly I blink and they're all gone and the bar is closing, the upturned chairs casting shadows across the room like stilts and Kitten is sucking on my neck, her hand groping my chest as I try to focus on the ceiling without passing out.

A taxi takes us somewhere. I'm arguing with the driver, I think, as Kitten paws all over me, clearly aiming for the lost city of Nether, her blinkers now firmly attached and eyes facing straight down the racetrack.

This is what I wanted.

But I can't do it.

The driver is driving with his eyes firmly on the rear-view mirror while Kitten undoes my belt buckle, the clank of the metal snapping me awake. I manage to shift over to the other side of the cab and lean forward, struggling to mutter my address and shove a twenty pound note in the driver's pocket. Kitten luckily does not hear this, after insisting on her address only moments earlier, and sits upright fetching each breast slowly and deliberately out of her top until they both stare at me like two solar systems.

And I'll be honest, I cannot avert my gaze.

They are magnificent. False and magnificent.

Everything I've ever dreamed about.

No scars.

But she's not magnificent.

No longer.

The driver has a full view of her bare shoulders and adjusts his mirror, but to no avail, because she moves onto trying to shove one of her enormous nipples into my mouth like a hungry baby.

Except I'm not crying.

And I certainly don't need milk.

Not now.

Not from her.

A block from my apartment I tell the driver to stop and somehow squeeze myself from her grasp and stumble onto a low dirty brick wall, knocking over a dying pot plant. Kitten follows, putting herself back into her clothes and I try to escape yelling to the driver not to go. She's following me so I run around the cab puking slightly against my teeth from the exertion.

Three in a bed is a glorious thought but not one I wish to spring on Her now. Because there's a new Her in town. One far more persistent and even armed to the teeth (well, to the collarbone anyway). I need a clear head for this situation so I stop to face her approaching ding-donging figure.

"Kitten. I'll call you tomorrow. Please go home."

She mutters something and fumbles with the belt I've just refastened, dropping to her knees.

The grazed knee ideal never seemed so unappealing.

"My mum is visiting and she's ill. I need to go home

and look after her," I say ripping free again lifting her up.

"You'll call?"

"Yes."

"You promise?"

"Yes."

"You swear?"

"Yes!"

The tail of the taxi is a beautiful sight as I hear two lovers slamming a headboard in an overhanging apartment and a dog snoring. The air is muggy and misty and I can feel that my watchstrap has been ripped off in the scuffle. My neck has scratch marks, which will be difficult to explain, and I know my boxer shorts will smell of expensive perfume.

All in a night's work.

CHAPTER 17

LONELY WOMAN IN A PARK

My eyelids are stuck down; no, cemented down. I can somehow feel the world around me but am unwilling to embrace it. I'm so tired that I feel queasy and even a few forceful gulps of water fail to eradicate the sickness. From the cute plastic cup with the shiny yellow pyramid-like indentation at the bottom.

I summon the energy to sit up in bed and stare past Her at the outdated, bright red numbered, never clear, digital alarm clock. Wish I could smash it. Especially now.

3:30

One-and-a-half more hours of rest.

Panic suddenly. But surely the driver would have buzzed?

4:55

Bonus, a full five minutes of anguish and torture as I try to rip the duvet from my warmed flesh like the skin off a chicken.

The radio alarm.

Must've dozed off because it slaps me awake again like a boxing trainer.

It's that song again. The one that I haven't yet sourced.

Even at five am it sounds brilliant.

Snooze button gets abused twice and each lasts four minutes which means I have twenty-two minutes until the driver arrives.

Five thirsty.

Off to Zurich. Flight at seven am.

I'm up. My eyes are red, shoes dirty and the driver's annoyingly on time.

At the airport my shoes get cleaned, my body caffeinated, and the plane is annoying late.

For the first time ever my drool patch wakes me up because it's so large that it soaks into my shirt and is cooled by the air conditioning which send sensors from my clavicle to my brain yelling: 'Wake up!'

I'm in the front seat of business class so the embarrassment is selective: the airhostess pretending not to see me slurp the bungee jump of saliva back into my mouth as I wake up.

The meeting, or should I say workshop, is so boring that my 'concentration' face deteriorates into my 'interested' face which eventually becomes my 'oh please dear God not another slide' face. Lunch isn't that bad because no one understands my accent and I can lure them into laughing at my comments that are neither funny nor make any sense.

Just by laughing at the end of a sentence.

In the afternoon the Italian representative makes an early dash for the door armed with the excuse of an early flight. I try desperately to join him but am vetoed by France and Germany who insist on taking boredom to a brand new spanking level. The day winds to a close more excruciatingly slowly than finding the cure for cancer and I eventually hear the real final lap bell and the horizon appearing as a mirage in the distance.

The taxicab driver is Italian and old and I try to make polite conversation after spending ages trying to enquire about whether he accepts credit card payments. Plus the Italian representative wasn't half bad so, I suppose, I owe his countryman a little respect. And it would be rude not to share some of my basic Italian.

He's quite big for an Italian and mumbles a lot in my direction, waving his arms in the air as though he's composing a symphony. He's not smiling so I smile and nod, absorbing the setting sun reflecting off the pale brown buildings while he hoots and whistles at the dark-haired women.

When we arrive at the airport there appears to be a slight problem. His voice level has been raised a few octaves and the hand signals have matured from composer to rave dancer. This time in my direction. My credit card flapping impotently in front of him is clearly *not* the correct method of payment which leaves me in a predicament, as I have no Swiss Francs on me.

"Credit card? Do you not accept credit cards? Visa?"

"Mumble, mumble, mumble, che cazzo stai dicendo, vaffanculo! vai in culo!" he yells, the greying curls on the side of his square head lifting up.

He then grabs my collar, leaning all the way from the front seat into the back and rips my top button open, snatching the credit card. In the split second before he's about to snap my card and when a cartwheeling chunk of saliva embeds itself on my glasses, I slam the heel of my hand into his nose. So shocked, he flicks the mirror down in order to examine the damage and then turns to charge. The next smack is way more satisfying partly because it's with a full fist and partly because it draws blood. His face is then more definitely engulfed in his hairy hands and very little happens before I slam his head three times onto the steering wheel.

Fast.

And it's awkward because it's on the left-hand side.

No one notices despite the placid hoot emitted from slam number two. The card lies at his feet and I pick it up wiping the three-and-a-half specks of blood off on the back of his sweat stained white shirt before exiting without paying.

The flight back is incredible. I feel like I'm glowing and the airhostesses pay me extra attention keeping the red wine flowing like their practised wrinkled smiles. The food even tastes good. No, better than good, each mouthful a mini sensation of chicken and olive oil (with chillies). The Camembert slab rounds off a thoroughly enjoyable flight and end to an exhaustively entertaining day. After a slight absence, my cape and tights are both firmly back in place, ready to resume the quest.

I leave the podium with a slight wink and a nice pen, back in London.

Back.

The chocolate stain on my shirt even fails to dent my virtuous elation.

Cradled and nurtured to suffer another obscure and non-existent life.

At work later that week I avoid the barrage of phone calls, one time counting seven between one and two in the afternoon. Every time the display is the same and the red light of the mailbox seems to grow brighter with every phone call. And the phone is not the only victim. My email inbox is filled like a garbage disposal truck, my Homer Simpson 'D'oh' alert going off in regular intervals, rattling my chair and my spine.

I'm feeling like an animal trapped in a snare with the rusted metal teeth embedded in the flesh of my ankle. And I feel like I'm being watched; as though my every move is under scrutiny from a woman who has named herself after something usually followed by *pet food* or *declawing available here.*

Her claws are way too sharp. Hunting for my flesh. Hungry.

I've got to get out of the building or I'll suffocate. I can feel her running out of communication channels and popping down to the building with her…

Does she know where I work?

…double G breasts and asking for Paton Stipps.

The name rings out in my ears like a hot air balloon bursting (if that's possible) and I try not to imagine the aftermath.

I see her standing in the foyer, probably dressed in pink, saying my name, her collagen boosted lips painfully mouthing the three syllables –

"Paton Stipps. Paton Stipps please."

Then her smiling. That dumb smile. And the men in the office falling over each other as they are transfixed by her hemispherical mammaries. Oh God. She doesn't know where I work. She wouldn't remember. She's too stupid and she can't digest that many syllables. But what if she looks up the number or tracks down the venue somehow or is transferred to reception or figures out the email acronym domain name!

She'll be here before I can tighten the noose or get the child proof pill lid off.

I dial. It reverts to voicemail, probably because she's calling me. So I wait. Patiently. About as patient as a child. I dial again after a forty-six second wait. Still voicemail. Then my phone rings and I freeze because again her number pops onto the mini-screen like a fast food order.

"Paton Stipps."

"Paton Stipps!"

"Hello."

"Paton it's me, Kitten. I've been trying to get hold of you all week. Where've you been? Why haven't you returned any of my calls? I was about to come looking for you, you naughty little rascal."

"I've been busy, um, away. In Zurich. On business. Very busy at the moment. Everyone's coming and going and coming and going. Not quite sure if I'm coming or going, you know?"

"Well you're coming. Friday night. To Mash Mayfair. At eight-thirty."

"Friday … damn! Any other day. I've got a business dinner on Friday. Any other night…"

"Oh great because I was thinking I should probably be more involved in your professional life now that we are practically going out. What should I wear Friday?"

"You know I've just opened an email and it seems that the Friday dinner has been cancelled. That's a pity."

"Maybe we should meet for lunch sometime? I'll come to your office. What's the address?"

"Hun, got to rush now. Meeting's just about to start. Did you say eight-thirty?"

"Yes, make sure you're there," and then she hangs up as though she's completely aware that she's playing me like a toy xylophone. Her breasts are weapons now, at first the unattainable fantasy and now balls of doom.

I'm at a depressive loss so I call Caroline to see if she's able to hook up for a late lunch. Voicemail. So I do something I haven't done in a very long time. I call the Bitch.

We meet in the park equipped with expensive sandwiches bursting at the exposed edge and thin at the apex corner, not dissimilar to a burger billboard that leads one into believing they're about to munch into a six inch high char-grilled delicacy. She's there already, on a bench swinging Her legs, waiting in the sun. And there among the exuberant dogs and cut grass and picnic blankets and cement slabs She even still smells of men's cologne.

"Nice day," She says.

"Mmmm."

"Are you having a good day so far?"

"Not really. Too much crap to sort out I suppose. What about you?"

"Why don't we talk anymore? You and me?"

I feel a bug settle on the side of my temple and deftly flick it off. Dismissively.

"Because whenever we do we fight. Argue. All the time."

"Let's go talk to someone. Or something."

"Why? So we can spend a fortune to discover we're not meant to be together."

She averts Her eyes and blinks a puddle down Her cheek. Her sniff is well disguised yet not effective, a tissue from my pocket handed over between forefinger and middle finger.

"In a strange way I'm glad you said that. I'm glad you said something. It's better than the silence; the nothing. Your dumb face staring at the television screen. All the time. Say something horrible again."

"Why bother. I've got to go anyway. I have a meeting."

"Talk to me. Please."

"You know why I can't talk to you."

"I don't."

"It's so fucking obvious. And even if it wasn't, we ran out of steam a long time ago. It was you who stopped loving me first."

I relocate the crumbs on my lap to the floor as I stand up to leave. She says nothing, staring straight at me then away. And towards a child running after a dog, the leash lapping behind like a tapeworm and the child screaming for the hopping mutt to return. My throat feels dry so I sip from an overused fountain as I make my way towards the Tube. From above the rim of my glasses I see the blur of Her distant form, Her hand cupping Her face and the slow regular jerks of Her convulsions depicting another lonely woman in a park.

CHAPTER 18

ENTER MR BRYAN K

There are a hundred million little annoying orange plastic worm-like stalks hanging from the ceiling giving the impression that we're under water. I'm always ducking as the ceiling feels like it's about to collapse on top of me, as all the others lean across and sip from the beer rack, smiling as though they're interested in what anyone has to say.

I find myself hiding in the toilet for prolonged periods, unable to cope with the plethora of stupidity and shallowness that exists at the restaurant table. After all, the toilet's quite nice without any noticeable filth or blatant disregard for proper toilet behaviour.

Back at the table and Kitten is slobbering all over me as she fiddles with her duck pizza, the others at the table so obviously wrapped up in their own lives that they're almost drowning in it. I think most of them are wannabe actors and popstars and models and even lawyers. There's a space next to me which is vacant, a bit like the people surrounding me. I have to end this non-affair with Kitten before it becomes messy. Perhaps I'll set her up with Jackie somehow and then reluctantly return to my sombre existence. At least then I can go back to the fantasies that are no longer tainted.

When I get back from toilet excursion number seventy-five there's a young man sitting in my seat, kissing Kitten on each of her cheeks and then smiling. A winning smile. Confident. He's wearing something very similar to the outfit I almost wore to Kitten's birthday party and he annoyingly pulls it off ten times better than I ever could. Maybe it's because his shoulders are narrower than mine. Or because he's shorter.

"I'm in your seat, aren't I? You don't mind swapping."

"No not at all, carry on," I say reluctantly sliding in next to a girl that looks like a stainless steel manufacturer.

Kitten swaps the slobbering to this guy, who I swear is wearing mascara, his eyelashes curving up towards the orange stalks like a skateboard ramp. And I'm strangely jealous now; excluded like this. Me who rules my own world and who listens and who always does the right thing. Maybe this is her ploy, but he looks too young even for her. As though she could be his mum. My God, imagine the poor sucker who has to feed from those milk tanks.

Some fat baby!

"Paton, this is Bryan," she yelps at me. "He's in a band." The tone so deathdefyingly boastful that I consider dropping to my knees in unworthiness.

We greet each other, him unable to look me in the eye, more concerned with the surrounding fauna and flora.

"What do you do?" he says without even looking in my direction. I'm not even sure he's addressing me and the gap gives Kitten just enough time to step in and flex her social muscles.

"Paton's an actor. Well was an actor. Used to work with Jackie the Jackhammer."

The slight tinge in Bryan's eyes cannot be disguised as he flinches slightly.

"Jackie. Interesting choice."

"Which band are you in?" I ask.

"Coastal Love." The words march forth in slow motion. He blinks and it seems like forever as I recognise that he's one of the anti-people; the façadites; the corruptors.

"You're in a boyband," I say without knowing it and suddenly the whole table falls silent as though I've muttered a four-letter word.

"You could call it that. We're starting to write our own songs now though," he says turning his back towards me and focussing his attention on Kitten again as though, from this point on, I fail to exist. He orders something from the waitress, winking and running a hand down her slender flank.

She enjoys it.

Like a stupid cat in the sunshine.

I sit alone for the rest of the evening watching Bryan. Totally transfixed. He runs his own reality, innocuously tracing the line of Kitten's cleavage with his baby fingernail while the rest of the table whisper between themselves at the supposed humiliation of the man she's introduced as her boyfriend. Sitting just inches from them all. His back is so squarely facing me I can see his spine protruding from his tight shirt and the Giorgio Armani label of his underpants peeping above his trousers. His next move is to pass an ecstasy pill from his mouth to Kitten's and then cut a line of cocaine right there on the table and snort it, his false decadence impressing everyone.

"What a rebel! How dangerous! Oh that Bryan!" are some of the giggle-accompanied comments that fly around the table like Pac Man. I want to leave but can't, the humiliation now settling on top of my nose like a militant bee. Or perhaps I'm paranoid because everyone's eyes are dancing around Bryan as though he's a one-man stand-up comic. They're laughing, trying to get nearer to him as though some of his fame and gall and confidence will rub off on them, and they'll behave differently suddenly in their demure boring little lives.

"You see that little girl over there," he says, turning towards me eventually and directing the comment I think at me, but I can't be certain. "I fucked her downstairs in the toilet last week."

Congratulations!

"She said I was hurting her," he laughs, still refusing to look into my eyes and scanning the room in a regular radar-like arc.

The pictures on the wall are staring at me now. Each black and white print beckons me to get involved but I cannot. They scream and yell and chastise me for being a silent observer.

"Get up you lazy coward and make a stand! Make a difference…"

"What do you think of her?" mutters Bryan, interrupting the pictures and placing a cigarette in his mouth.

This girl does not look legal. Her eyes are too big for her face which makes her look young and her waist is so narrow that I reckon I could get the tips of my fingers to touch if I put my hands around her. She's smiling; a girly smile as though she was peering out of a tree house. Until she spots Him. And her eyes take on a new dimension; a simulated sultry dimension, her hips acquiring a pronounced wiggle as she approaches.

"Drink, sir?"

"What about a blowjob in the toilet?"

Just like that. A verbal agreement. Legally binding.

She disregards her apron on the way to the downward spiral staircase that dissects the room like a colon. Bryan winks at me without looking at me and gets up to go for his blowjob. Just like that. And the patrons subconsciously applaud him; admire him; wish they were the little girl on her knees in the better than normal toilet.

Until he hurts her. Again. But she'll still want more.

This is the injustice that needs to be rectified.

He's back in no time at all, the smug grin on his face darkening the room like a plague. Kitten slaps his shoulder playfully and mutters something like, "What were you doing with that innocent little thing?" and everyone laughs in unison.

I'm sick to my stomach and matters don't improve when he shows me his finger which is coated in drying blood.

"Little bitch was up on blocks; you know, the painters were in." He wipes the small remaining moist patches on the tablecloth leaving an almost symmetrical bloody impression. The girl returns looking older and continues with her duties as though she hasn't just been abused.

Suddenly the world makes sense. For me anyway. The blame has to lie somewhere or with someone; have a source. A core. The eye of the storm.

Mr Bryan K. Co-singer in the boyband Coastal Love. Entertainer and soon to be deceased drain on society. End pollution. For good.

CHAPTER 19

BEWARE OF THE COFFEE MACHINE

I never believed I liked violence. As a child I was always the one standing up for the unfortunate kid getting the crap kicked out of him behind the woodwork room. Violence was always a final resort; when absolutely everything else has failed and composure and reason became merely descriptors in a self-help book.

Lately though the world is begging for violence. There seems to be no other solution. People no longer listen or learn if your tone remains uniform and polite. People need to be *shown*; fear works.

The death penalty. A great deterrent.

Fear works.

And when something's bubbling: take the lid off; let the steam out; uncover the motion.

This image has been doodled on my A4 light blue lined page which is supposed to be capturing the 'essence' of the meeting when I hear my name in the distance: an all too familiar occurrence lately. And I don't even notice it, cocking my head slightly to admire the picture of a pot atop a stove, the liquid inside dripping down the edges and the lid hovering elusively above.

Like a UFO.

"Perhaps Mr Stipps would like to share what is so enthralling in front of him with the rest of the group," says Manfred, sipping water from a plastic cup.

"I'd rather not," I reply. "Do I really need to be here?"

There's a cautious buzz around the room now, the attendees shaking their heads in patronising disbelief.

"Unfortunately for you Mr Stipps, you do. So get comfortable, stay awake and try to concentrate."

I don't have the energy for a retort so I slump into my chair and prepare for the imminent torture held by the remainder of the afternoon's meeting.

It finishes at seven fifty-one pm. I shit you not. And to aggravate matters Manfred says he would like a word with me and heads for the kitchen for a top-up of machine cappuccino. I follow, dutiful yet annoyed that this waste of time has encroached upon my television time and I was also meant to meet with Jonathan to discuss something.

Now Manfred's yapping and he's ranting and raving telling me what a fucking loser I am and how my days here are numbered and I can feel I'm about to go deaf or die of boredom. I make a suggestion, one which, in hindsight, probably wasn't the best. I say, "Can't we discuss this tomorrow," and this sends him spiralling further towards hysterical nirvana. I even think he's about to burst into tears and he's slamming his fists on the kitchen counter. I feel sorry for the man because I'm not listening to a word he's saying and he's putting so much effort into his rendition of Mr T.

I make another suggestion: "Do you want to talk about something? You having problems at home?" which results in him lumbering forward at me like an off balance drunk. He gets me in an embrace and I'm not sure whether he's trying to strangle me or kiss me. Either way I deem it to be unacceptable behaviour and I push him away. Like a spinning top he does one and a half rotations and ends up slammed up against the coffee machine, his head somehow jammed in the space where the cup usually goes.

I'm not sure what he pushed or bumped or whether it was me, but the gyration of the black dispenser lets him know that he is about to receive a black coffee with one sugar. His scream echoes through the pipes and I think I try to pull him free but it's all happening so fast.

This human coffee episode.

Then the machine unloads just as it has been instructed to. Who says machines rule the world? His pink, fleshy, large lobed ear is the first to get it, the boiling hot black liquid filling and flooding the cavity like a dirty river. The liquid then goes pouring down the front of his face burning his one eye, his hand too late to shield the molten lava.

The screaming momentarily continues until I've pushed a few more buttons and I'm convinced that he's deaf and unconscious.

Black tea.

Black tea with two sugars.

White coffee with no sugar.

Cappuccino with one sugar.

Hot chocolate.

Chococcino with extra sugar.

Boiling water.

Boiling water.

Boiling water.

To end the drone.

Surprisingly, the coffee curdling screams don't draw any attention; no one comes running with the cavalry. No one gives a shit that a man might die at the hands of a brutal coffee machine. Safety should be a far more regimented doctrine in the office nowadays. You never know where the next accident might happen.

The silence is gorgeous. Manfred is slumped on the counter, his head penetrating the coffee machine like an interracial sexual encounter. White in black. Black coming. Repeatedly. White tired and limp and unconscious. There is brown liquid everywhere, the kitchen floor a tanned skating rink.

Maybe he drowned because it doesn't look as though he's breathing. My two fingers on his neck reveal that he is alive but not breathing easily. It's time to get him out of the jaws of coffee doom, so I smash the surrounding plastic clasps after turning the machine off at the plug. It's not an easy job because the machine is well crafted and sturdy in the extreme. But eventually I triumph after smashing the cup floor to bits with a heavy stapler that almost embeds itself in Manfred's coffee coloured hair.

Pulling him free reveals that there is something severely wrong with his neck, the pronounced droop slapping the wet counter before being pulled to safety and lain on the dry carpet in the coat room. He's sleeping like a baby and a few playful slaps are certainly not enough to wake him. I'm not quite sure why I do this but I squeeze his nuts in order to rouse him from the dead. It works and he blinks up at me looking confused and wiping a dried coffee concoction from his eye sockets. His eyes try to go back into his brain as he tries to pass out again before another slap wakes him and he proceeds to puke in a pair of shoes that have recently been re-soled and rest below a dry cleaned suit next to us.

"What happened?" he gurgles.

"Are you feeling alright?" I say, concerned.

"What? I cannot hear you. Ow, my neck! It hurts like shit. What's going on?"

"You had an accident," I say pronouncing the world slowly and clearly.

"I can't hear you. Where am I? What's this all over me?"

"Wait here," I say, motioning for him to stay where he is. "I'll call an ambulance."

I'm back in seconds after dialling 999 and endeavouring to make the story not seem like a practical joke.

"Ah yes, hi, a man just had a near fatal run in with a coffee machine," is substituted for: "There's been an accident in the office. A man has damaged his neck."

Far more plausible.

The ambulance arrives relatively fast and I can see them sniggering and cackling as I explain my version of the story while they put a neck brace on Manfred and place him tenderly onto a stretcher. As they're taking him away Manfred yells in my direction, "That's the one. The man who saved my life. Had it not been for him I would have been stuck there all night. Thank you Paton, thank you!"

Always a pleasure, Manfred. See you in a while.

Parks, for me, provide the small amount of tranquillity

and delicacy that exists in London. There are a number of factors that conspire to ruin this idiom, the first and foremost being the weather. Summer is a fleeting experience reserved for those wide awake enough to notice that the cold weather is gone but will soon be returning.

Central London is manic all year round, and this manic state intensifies when the sun comes out. Londoners seem to take on a new hysterical dimension when there's warmth, exposing their pasty white flesh and eradicating the three-line frown customarily reserved for shielding the pissy drizzle that fills up the rest of the year.

Another conspirator is the chore: always needing to be done. Weekends mean that park excursions are limited to a two in seven chance and that leaves little time for the all-important, life consuming chores that are required in order to fulfil an orderly and clean existence.

Washing dishes.

Drying dishes.

Vacuuming uncleanable grimy carpets.

Cleaning bathrooms.

Toilets.

Washing windows.

Washing clothes.

Colours and whites separately.

Hanging them up.

Folding.

Sometimes ironing.

So let's assume that all of these are either done or blissfully disregarded, and the sun is shining and there's no wind. Islington Green: the park slapbang in the centre. A perfect spot to let the skin absorb some of that elusive much needed sun and bask like a seal while sipping on a Frappuccino from Starbucks (the wait is well worth the shit service and exorbitant price). Enjoying the day. Enjoy my existence with Her leaning on my shoulder quietly reading Her study book. Everyone around us loves it too, the smiles jumping between faces as their stories multiply and a few nice cold ones are consumed.

There is very little that can ruin a setting such as this. But there is something. A loud noise. Static. Then a greeting.

"Hello everybody," says a tramp with a microphone disturbing the serenity like a mirror shattering and sending my jaw pressure back to clenched.

"I am not a tramp, you know," he yells through the microphone, and now my jaw is not the only thing that's clenched. "I am a human being and deserve to be heard." Everyone sits idly by, pretending the protrusive noise doesn't exist. "Do you all know what the government is doing? They're fucking us all," he says struggling to stand upright as the booze pulls him onto on knee.

I wonder where he is able to get a microphone and speaker. Does he hire it and if so who lets him hire it? Does he buy it and if so how does he afford it? All those bloody idiots who feel compassion and drop a nugget into the open guitar case truly believing they are helping when all they're doing is making sure that these bums buy some more alcohol and cigarettes and glue. And a microphone with a very loud, very annoying speaker that's spoiling the majestic concord already established. Buy the man some bread instead. Or give him twenty squids to stop drinking.

"Fucking cunts, the lot a ya. Staring at me like I'm a fucking animal. Well I'm not. I'm a man. A proud man. Who has come to speak to you today."

A few parents leave with their hands cupped over their children's ears.

Someone yells out, "Go home!" to which he replies, "This is my fucking home!"

His tone is unadulterated aggression and I'm not quite sure where the fear lies because he's old and filthy and drunk, but everyone becomes submissive and shuts up. Then he starts preaching, the noise so loud that I can feel my brain rattling in my skull until I cannot take it anymore.

I crave peace.

And quiet.

"I'm going to hurt that man," I say, looking at Her above the rim of my dark glasses.

"Just leave it alone. He's not worth your trouble. Let's go elsewhere?"

"I can't leave him to ruin someone else's day," I say, standing up and dropping my shades to the floor.

"Paton, please don't. You can't solve the world's problems all the time. Leave it alone. Please. Please."

"I can't."

He sees me approaching from afar and begins chastising me, "Oooh here comes a big fella without a shirt on to try and shut me up. Well come try you little piece of rabbit shit. Try! Maybe you've got something to say," he says thrusting the microphone in my face.

"Would everyone who would like this man to shut up please raise their hands," I say into the microphone, keeping my distance as the alcohol fumes are enough to get me high.

Like a symphony of medieval arrows the hands fly skywards, supporting their champion in the quest for silence.

"Is that enough for you? Would you mind keeping it down from now on," I say in a surprisingly composed and calm tone.

"Fuck off!" he yells swinging the microphone in my direction, clipping me on the side of my temple. "I have a right to be here, you know. I have a right to speak my mind," now throwing his beer can at me which wets but misses me.

"You – are – dis – tur – bing – the – peace," I say looping the microphone cord around his neck and watching the life drain from his eyes. Just before he's about to pass out I let go and kick him towards the speaker which goes crashing in a fireworks of plastic and sparks. The audience applauds as I return to my seat and the man rolls over to puke in the gutter and lap up the remainder of his liquid diet.

"Was that really worth it," I get from Her on my triumphant return.

"It shut him up didn't it?"

"Yes but you could have hurt him."

"He's fine. Look at him now, trying to throttle one of those poor pigeons."

"He's harmless."

"He's annoying."

"He's got nothing better to do with his sad life."

"He attacked me."

"Where's the anger coming from?"

"What do you mean?"

"Why'd you hurt him like that?"

"It was self-defence! And besides, he isn't hurting."

"You went looking for a fight."

"I never go looking for a fight. They just seem to levitate towards me, like flies to that piece of shit down there. Let's just try to enjoy the rest of the day. Look, everyone around here is back to doing that after he shut up."

"Okay," She says, uncharacteristically backing down from a mini-argument and snuggling up to the warmth radiating from my body.

"Studying going well?" I ask.

"Not really, but it's going," She says starting a new chapter called *The Manager as a Communicator*.

CHAPTER 20

Take one

And action: a skinny pale man wearing an overcoat and a cap slinking among the shadows down an alleyway in London's West End. He's nervous, biting at his nails and pacing backwards and forwards, waiting for his cue. I've shown him a picture so he knows what to aim for. The first time he saw the man he was clearly taken by his good looks or it could have been the air brushed effect of the print. Either way it annoyed me.

Kitten's incessant onslaught died down considerably after the dinner at Mash Mayfair, probably because she went home with Bryan to screw his socks off and because she is away on a shoot. She did manage, however, to call from Spain to see how I was doing which gave me the opportunity to discover more about

Bryan K. Where he likes to hang out in particular, disguised in a surfeit of false concern and witty comments.

We're waiting. Me in the club. At the bar. Just metres away from the man himself, surrounded by adoring young girls and boys, all kissing up to him and laughing at his jokes and buying him ridiculously over-iced drinks. Some of them don't even look drinking age. Whatever the case he's there and he's being watched as he mingles, most of the time blatantly disinterested and trying too hard to be cool. As though he could drop his trousers and piss ice cubes right there, from one of his drinks. Recycled and processed to display just how cool this guy thinks he is.

It's a very long evening. I try to stay as sober as possible but end up getting slightly tipsy as I watch and wait. As the evening progresses he flits in and out of the VIP lounge, coming back each time with a redder nose. It's three in the morning and I've made sure Jonathan is ready at least a dozen times via mobile telephone. Each time he tries to convince me that he's not up to it and that I should do it alone, and each time I have to remind him of our agreement.

Bryan K has his coat and finishes sucking on some young girl's tongue, pinching her little nipple and making his way towards the exit, nodding at the bouncer. I set off in pursuit but am headed off at the pass by a gaunt redhead wanting to buy me one final drink before the club closes. I thank her but refuse which gives Bryan the split second needed to escape my vision and potentially ruin my entire plan.

Without being too obvious I step the pace up and trot outside also nodding at the bouncer who fails to nod back. In the cold early hours of the morning there is nothing; the street is quiet bar the club's patrons streaming out like soft serve ice cream.

I phone Jonathan. "Did you spot him?"

"No, but I can see you know," he says. I see him loitering across the street.

"Well done! But where the hell is Bryan? You didn't see him coming out of the club? He must have been out literally seconds before me!"

"I think he's behind you," which is enough for me to terminate the call and casually glance behind me as Bryan appears from an alley directly adjacent to the club. I'm under the impression he's gone for a slash because he zips his fly up, but, true to form, the real reason is revealed when directly behind him, following like a stalker, is a young girl. I manage to twirl around doing a quick semi-circle and end up walking a couple of metres behind him.

It's perfect: he's so drunk he can hardly stand up straight and his attempts to hail a cab are as futile as they are fitting. He spits at one of the cabs as they drive past, the 'available' light shining bright yellow in the hazy evening. I stretch my arms straight into the air, giving the signal which I know Jonathan sees because he jumps slightly and makes a feeble attempt to approach, wasting valuable time with his hesitation. He's now about ten metres from Bryan and the adrenalin thumps through my body causing my knees to crouch slightly in anticipation. Of all things to happen now, Jonathan trips and falls flat on his face at about the same time as Bryan stops. Jonathan gets up quickly and runs in the opposite direction, a taxi beckoning Bryan to enter.

I blink and they both disappear along with my plan. It's cold and it's almost time for sunrise and everything has gone painfully wrong. The smoke discharging from the club forms a shroud around me and I cough violently as the redhead exits blowing me a kiss. My clothes stink of smoke and the thought of getting up for work the next day makes me feel even more depressed than I already do. It was so simple.

BaR

Jonathan and I sip beer in a horrible pub where the walls are redolent of wet vermin hair and the wooden banister down to the toilet is begging to give way to a tipsy patron and introduce them to the lavender coloured cement floor feet below. Jonathan's crying into his beer and I'm amazingly patient given the circumstances. He keeps adjusting his crotch, between sobs and grunts.

"Is there something happening down there?" I ask.

"No," he whines. "Just itchy."

"Itchy. Don't tell me, I don't want to know."

"I've been shaving to prevent the crabs."

"Aaaahhhhh," I yell, blocking my ears. "I didn't need to know that."

"Sorry."

"It's okay."

"Okay," he says, calming down slightly at the sight of a rectangular black man with a shaved head, glasses and a tattoo on his neck. Of a moon crescent.

"Now Jon, what happened? We had an agreement; a simple agreement. What happened?"

His choking returns and he lengthens each syllable like a siren when he says, "I-I-I-I d-d-d-o-o-o-on't know. I was shaking and I tripped and I thought, I thought I heard running. Towards me, the cops or something. So I ran as fast as I could to get away. I don't like this sort of thing. Oh ple-e-e-e-ease."

He's now slumped at the bar, the angle of his spine resembling the letter C.

"It's for a good cause, I promise. You'll see. In the long run you'll be doing a massive service to your community, your country, your children and the world."

"The world?" he says, sniffing potently and wiping his nose with his forearm.

"Yes. Now listen, we've got to go through the new plan. It's going to be broad daylight so it is imperative that you get it right this time."

I see him get that nervous shudder as his mouth turns into an upside down quarter moon.

"Now don't worry, it's not that difficult. All you have to do is stick to the basics. Approach, attack, attain, abandon. Come on, say it with me – A…"

"Approach," he reluctantly begins with me, "attack, attain, abandon."

"One more time. The four As."

"Approach, attack, attain, abandon."

"Excellent. Two more beers," I say, pointing to the extra cold Guinness tap.

"Why are you doing this?" he asks.

"For humanity. And for you, I mean, people like you. You see, people like him are the reason human beings suppress their natural desires. They dictate a false culture where little pathetic men are champions among little pathetic girls. This narcissistic fetish is why homosexuals such as yourself have to pretend to be happy in a heterosexual relationship. It's a sick illusion. We've just entered the third millennium for Christ's sake. And besides, he annoys the crap out of me."

"Who is he?"

"He's nobody. That's the point. That's the statement. That's what the world needs to witness. I've been sent to snap the illusion; shatter it and then watch how the world fails to remember their insignificant contributions. If there is something to aim for in your life, let it be 'making a contribution to the world'. That way when you're rotting away in a box or scattered all over someone's shoes, you'll be remembered for righting the wrongs; for making a difference; for setting standards. Not prancing around in the false belief that you are a champion because your make-up guy is talented or your songwriter is gifted or your hair stylist is an award winner or even maybe because you were lucky enough to be born with good cheekbones. No way. Praise those who deserve it; those who work hard for it and possess the talent."

The sermon nature of my speech suddenly slaps me back to reality at about the same time as the bar lady slaps the two beers, complete with indented foam clover, on the bar counter. Jonathan's expression is somewhere in the void between utter confusion and sceptical awe.

On the fence balancing like a snooker ball on a needle.

"You see Jonathan, things have slowly begun to get clearer lately, as though I've been looking through a telescope for years without ever seeing a ship. And now the ship is tentatively coming into focus but is still a blurry blob in the middle of my circled vision. And the clearer it has got, the more I've realised that my true destiny is not to turn the light on, but instead steer the ship towards the rocks, until it's flogged and in a million pieces, back to dwell with nature."

"I'm not clear. I'm sorry, it's just that we were on something about the world and now it's something about the Navy?"

"Never mind. It will all become glaringly obvious soon. So soon I can taste it. Cheers."

CHAPTER 22
MANFRED'S COMEBACK

The foosball table in the office is abused while Manfred sits in a hospital bed performing various acts of hearing therapy.

For coffee radiation. Or the medical term *Inhalus Caffeinus*.

The true joy that is foosball cannot be easily described. When the table arrived those of us who had never played before were circumspect; wary; even against this red and yellow intrusion occupying space in an empty office at the end of the corridor. A few of the diehard fans, most of whom weaned on spanking the white ball into the back of the tin, would selfishly gang together and have a game. But it would all change once the new breed 'took over' as it were.

Now the addiction eats my conscious and unconscious mind like a corn on the cob munching cartoon. If I lose I go home depressed and unnerved, mentally replaying the silly mistakes my partner made during the course of the game. It's an annoying addiction because those who are not addicted can't get near understanding the trauma of not getting a fix before lunchtime.

Because it's bad office policy.

It creates a bad perception.

As if we did any work anyway.

The band of merry foos enthusiasts are the good people. The ones who are true to themselves and their sport without pretending and without holding back. We all play to win whether it's a flick-slam from the back or a gentle touch from the front. The objective remains the same – to score goals and reach ten before the other team thus immortalising your name in the foosball archive and potentially climbing the weekly ladder.

Manfred hates foosball. He hates it so much that there was speculation in the office that he was bending the bars in the middle of the night because he knew his popularity would wane if he blatantly got rid of it. He knows the joy it brings to the unchosen few yet he persists in branding the activity 'unproductive'.

A waste of time.

A children's game.

We got him on the table one time after a work function and a couple of bottles of Italian wine and did he suck. I think he connected the ball once and that time was to snap it back into his own goal. We were all drunk and all amateurs, foosball virgins, but he somehow christened himself as the Virgin Mary. That was the last time he played. For certain.

This is how it goes – you have three men in the front who are your strikers. Now with the exponential improvement in defence these men seldom score unless they sneak one through the dead zone or a lucky angle. The midfield is five able-bodied plastic men who serve as the powerhouse from kick-off. The slam-dunk. Good for a couple in a game if the put-in rolls in your favour. The two defenders are your control men, able to shoot but just as able to feed the goalie who often has the best shot from the back.

Four (real) men play – one defending, one attacking. And it's aggressive. But men are like that. Always able to tell each other what frigging morons they are in the heat of battle and then able to laugh about it afterwards over a few drinks. A few beers perhaps. Or even red wine. It can be masculine.

London in midsummer is a place where it is not advisable to sweat during the day in your work clothes. When the foosball was in the infant stages of the mania it was winter – a double positive if the inclusion of a shower between work and pub was nowhere to be seen.

But the intensity has increased as the temperature did, as if the two secretly conspired like the soaring red line of an old-fashioned thermometer. We all pong like discarded shoe soles after a potent game, the obvious incriminating stench following us to our desks as we all pretend that there are no beads of sweat decorating our temples like unsqueezed pimples.

The building pulsates and the heat clambers to get in and attack the flimsy air conditioning. And still we continue to flick and block and shoot and score and slam and touch and spin and sweat. Until Manfred's imminent return, spreading through the office like the Jaws theme tune. Everyone refuses to play and there's a cacophony of deodorant sharing and dabs of water on the forehead and a mad scramble for desks and offices as everyone tries to find something that will make them look busy. As though they haven't been sitting around getting in at ten, leaving at three with six hours of foosball and a thumb delicately inserted into the arsehole while the boss has been away.

The boss is back, the very thought as frightening as the aftermath. But maybe the caffeine insertion into his auditory apparatus did him some good. Maybe he's unclenched and widened his smile. Maybe the clear sky and muggy heat has brought with it the delicate ray of sunshine that is Manfred, his forehead lines gone and his pointing finger safely accompanying the other fingers as his outstretched hand shakes all of ours rather than wagging at us. Although I know he has taken a special interest in me, I choose to join the masses and rebel against this power after I've witnessed his single-minded quest for greater power and obnoxious cruelty towards the little people.

Personal assistants never get thank-yous for coffee (perhaps now, they'll get a shudder instead).

Junior team members get laughed out the room.

Senior team members get humiliated in meetings and chastised behind their backs.

Although it could all just be his pious efforts to fit in with the rest of our venerated leaders where self-service is a cult and the decomposing bodies the suicide bombers who've been stepped on. And we don't cure cancer for heaven's sake; we just move money from those who think it's better placed elsewhere to those who know it's better placed with them, until at the end of the chain the rich are richer and the poor poorer.

Most of this is speculation of course, and speculation can often be more dangerous than naivety.

I haven't shaved in about a week, which scars me like a ruffian, my neck a swirl of dark hairs to match my eyebrows. It's really the five o'clock shadow look, except midnight would be a more accurate description. I've got an emergency tie in one of my drawers, I'm convinced, as I feel my scrabbling become more frenetic as those oh so distinct uniform rapid footsteps become louder from the outer edge of the corridor. The footsteps become even louder, a mere long jump away and thank bejezus the tie is knotted and it's around my neck and hopefully under the collar as the shadow appears through the tinted glass and I can't get my final top button done as the door opens and swish it's up just under my Adam's apple.

"Anyone home?" he says, his voice marginally louder than normal.

"Hi Manfred. Welcome back. Are you feeling any better?"

"Absolutely," he yells this time and I squint slightly giving away my discomfort. "Sorry, still struggling to hear out of this ear," pointing towards the pink pulsating flesh that not so long ago exposed itself to the coffee machine funnel as though it were a soon-to-not-be-recycled white plastic cup.

"I suppose you enjoyed yourself," he says, this time in a normal tone.

I feel colour explode into my face like ink in water. I've been found out; smoked out of my hiding hole; the protégé held to account for his betrayal.

"It was an accident. Don't you remember?"

"I meant while I've been away. In the office. Keeping everyone working hard – heads down – focussed. Maintaining the good name of this great company."

"Oh yes. Of course. It has been quite amazing the different angles we've taken, strategies selected and goals scored. Quite a performance really. I've not seen improvement on this scale for quite some time."

"The cops were, you know, enquiring whether there

was any foul play involved."

I have to bite the sides of my cheek now. I'm imagining the sketch artists depicting various brands of coffee machines and scribbling captions like: 'Have you seen this coffee machine?' and 'Beware, coffee machine on the loose! Call your local authority if you spot one loitering around your nearest corner shop.' It's as though he's teasing me, manoeuvring me to fess up that I slammed his brain into a coffee machine.

"But I said no of course. That would be tantamount to what? Attempted murder? Assault…" he laughs, gingerly fingering the lonely lobe.

… with a deadly coffee machine with intent to harm.

"How do you put someone in a coffee machine?"

"Oh God no, I wasn't implying you did it on purpose or anything. Just funny how these things get misconstrued sometimes. Or can get misconstrued."

Manfred takes a moment to wander around the office, looking at my desk, deliberately surveying the terrain. My paper inbox is higher than the top of the computer screen and leans to one side then spiral-staircases upwards. Manfred seems to like the chaos; like the way my effort to output ratio is disproportionate, approving of his handiwork somehow. He nods continuously running a mesmerising finger though the dust on my desk snow-ploughing to a squeaky stop in front of my gleaming silver letter opener.

"I'm sure you'll keep doing a good job though," he

says.   "Keep me informed of all dealings in the company; what everyone is doing. And not doing."

"Of course."

"And Collins?"

"He's fine," I answer a bit too rapidly.

"You two adjusting to the role reversal?"

"It's taken a while to really get him on the same page, but I think we're making real progress. In fact I think we're about to go through something quite special."

"Good. I'll make sure not to stand in your way."

He returns to his origination point and I see his swollen ear waft past my nose. The hole is almost completely shut, frothy shiny purple balloons of swollen flesh rising above each other like coagulated lava. There should be guilt but there isn't; there should be an apology but it is not forthcoming. Manfred lives, breathes, eats and shits this job. It is his everything. I cannot necessarily blame a man for living through his career but to Manfred this goes beyond normal utilitarian corporate mountainclimbing. He's sending a message now; a message as to why he dragged me up the cliff face behind him. No fuck-ups. Keep it all flowing nicely. Onwards and upwards, telling him of underperforming climbers. Or else. Or else the free-trade white tea without sugar comes out of hiding. But I don't think he's satisfied with that. It's just a small reminder that the boss is back.

"And thanks for pulling me out of that thing," he says and I can't accept that I'm the hero; can't accept that I saved his life. But can accept that he must be sorely pissed, except Manfred would take corporate performance over pain and humiliation any day of the week it seems. "It made a real difference. What else have you been up to?"

"The usual. You know. Reports. Clients and their events. Client events. Helping clients. Figure stuff out. And making money." I'm babbling; my mind searching for one constructive thing I've done in the last few weeks, darting into dark corners (nothing), peeking into small holes (still nothing). Almost as though I've forgotten the art.

"Last week there was a transaction I put through for two million. And another of the same amount the week before. The ones you asked me to focus on."

"Did you use the updated account details I provided?"

"Yes."

"And you kept the signatories blank like I asked you to?"

"Yes."

"Good. It all sounds very encouraging. I always had a strong feeling about you, Paton, so keep up the good work. Keep pushing it all through. Keep doing exactly what we talked about. Let's not deviate from the process at this stage, when it all seems to be going so well. We wouldn't want anything to get in the way of that progress, now would we?"

Would we? Well there is one thing that could, no

wait … should.

He continues, "There are always people in this world who want to dent progress; impede real gains. Bureaucrats and internal fuckwits so intent on following the same boring formula that all the true innovators leapfrog right over them. You and me Paton, we'll set this place alight. As long as we all sing from the same hymn sheet, if you know what I mean.

"I know what you mean," I lie, winking.

His knowing smile leaves the room at least half a minute after he exits. I'm still standing and unnervingly I can feel my heart pounding against my breastbone like a prisoner slamming a fist against a cell door protesting his innocence.

I am innocent.

Guilty maybe of pushing him off me and into a kitchen accessory.

Guilty maybe of adding milk and sugar where I should have stuck to decaffeinated black earl grey tea.

CHAPTER 23
OH CAROLINA

The tourist's hooked worm; the lights and vigour of the West End can be as intoxicating as they are piquant. The attack on the senses is relentless. There is never any interval, the neon kaleidoscope creating unnatural shadows across the millions of movers transgressing between shows and clubs and restaurants.

I sit on the steps below the statue of Eros, waiting patiently for Her. I've invited Her to the restaurant Criterion, billed as the most scenic place to eat in London. A bold statement given the superfluity of eating haunts speckled all over this city.

A punk with wonderfully manicured pink and green, statue of liberty spikes sleeps next to me, the chains and studs tinkling precariously as he breathes, stretching the chain that connects his nose to his belt almost straight. On my other side a woman with psychedelic tights and a runny nose pleads for change and then runs off screaming before I fail to pluck a pound coin from my wallet.

She's late.

So late that I start to doze off which is a potentially dangerous activity in London town. I haven't been sleeping well for a while now. At least a couple of weeks. I lie awake staring at the ceiling, occasionally glancing over to the curtains when a welcomed breeze forces its way into the bedroom. An incessant humming sound had begun in my head. I'm not even sure when it began or if it regularly decreases or increases in volume. But it's there.

I feel my mind blur and my eyelids are heavy, quivering in a pathetic attempt to stay open. Like a clam. Wanting to slam shut with a clap sound. I'm singing *We Are the World* with a big white guy with an even bigger afro, my bellbottoms luminous blue when a cold hand touches my cheek and drags me from neverneverland back to suck in the green TDK endorsing rays.

"Sorry, did I startle you?" says an out of context yet familiar voice.

"Caroline!"

"What are you doing here?"

"I'm waiting for, um, for someone."

"I see," she says, turning her eyelashes towards the

floor and lifting her leg to reveal an amoeba shaped grey-purple blob of chewing gum beneath her shoe. She awkwardly tries to scrape it off catching most of it under her badly painted nail that chips, I think, because she quickly pops it in her mouth, which makes me feel slightly ill. Depending on who was chewing it, and standing on it of course.

"How've you been, lately?" I ask.

"Not bad actually. The shoulder feels much better although it's still making that grinding noise when I twist it too far. It's not sore though, listen." She does an almost sexy circle with her shoulder followed by a grinding that makes me want to go back to thinking about the origins of the chewing gum.

"I got the birthday card you sent. Thanks. I really liked the little caterpillar and how he squiggled around on the screen."

"I tried calling but you weren't home."

"I've met someone."

"That's fantastic. Who is he?"

"I met him at the fundraiser. For the new kids' playground at the local nursery school. He's nothing very special in the–" she pauses. "He's no y–" she pauses again. "He's no Brad Pitt, but he seems good. At this stage."

A small cough echoes out to the right of Caroline's injured shoulder and there She is, standing with hands on hips, tapping Her foot. I'm not imagining that – She's actually waiting for an explanation.

Then countenance sets into Her face when I think She notices Caroline's appearance. A soft smile settles on Her as though put there by the tap-tap of a butterfly's wing. She looks into my being, almost knowing the unselfish nature of why I have been doing this. Like the old days. Her smile ping-pongs onto me and I smile back, then Caroline smiles and we're all smiling like idiotic ventriloquist puppets, until the pink and green punk awakes suddenly, vomits on my shoes and then rushes off back to slumberland.

In the comfort of the light brown cement steps.

CHAPTER 24
Take Two

Following another human being in broad daylight in London is more difficult than one would imagine. There are the obvious obstacles: remaining inconspicuous, not losing the person, and of course, watching where you are going. Then there are the less obvious obstacles; the ones that only become truly apparent when this exercise takes place, for real, with a very clear, very definite objective in mind.

I'm slumped down behind the wheel of my vehicle chewing overly sweet chewing gum and finishing off the remnants of a McDonalds medium sized diet coke. The slurping effect coupled with the shake of the ice sounds out coincidentally like a ringside bell, and the boxer emerges from his corner wearing tan leather trousers and a bright blue buttoned down shirt to reveal his hairless rib-filled chest.

The Chelsea townhouse is about three stories and the door is Georgian: large and square with a shiny gold doorknob. When he reaches the street he reverse sniffs, blowing a separate chunk of snot from each nostril onto the pavement, as he swaps index fingers. His car, a Bentley, is squatting with one wheel on the pavement, the taillight of the car in front sprinkled all over the sidewalk like a mosaic. There's a note flapping under one of the Bentley's windscreen wipers which suffers the cruel fate of more snot (this time expelled from the mouth) which acts as glue, as the note is slammed onto the taillightless car, the adhesive strong enough to hold it and set it up for a day of baking in the sun.

The Bentley thumps off the pavement and nicks the car directly behind as the music is turned on and the windows rolled down. Following someone who doesn't know how to drive is a bit like trying to hit a moving dartboard blindfolded. But somehow I manage it and before long, after a terrifying parallel parking into a space the size of a thimble and a red traffic light violation, I'm walking behind him along Kings Road, Sloane Square. My passenger walks on the opposite side of the road, shifting nervously between the abundance of shoppers. I beckon for him to hurry up and get ahead, pointing and stabbing the air.

My victim walks without compunction with the attitude of a swollen rap star, although his rhythm lets him down, the exaggerated strut and single shoulder wiggle making him look as though something is lodged inside him from the back. His head is cocked slightly back and he purposefully takes no notice of anyone walking past him. A few recognise him and whisper among themselves, in particular a group of young girls. One runs back to retrieve an autograph and returns wiping her mouth and rubbing one of her arse cheeks.

The human traffic intensifies and his height deficiency makes the following more tedious and even more obvious. He's about twenty feet in front of me one second and the next, like a rabbit, he's gone. I feel myself getting frantic because I'm sure he hasn't slipped into one of the stores as I reach the spot where I last saw him. The mass of people sears through me and I have to move on, swept along by determined brand addicts.

"What happened to him?" I say into my mobile after submerging into a small café.

"You eat?" an impolite foreign voice asks.

"No, I'll just be a sec."

"If you are not eat, you can't stay. We very busy today."

"Okay, okay," I say re-entering the human bloodstream. "You still there? Jonathan? Jonathan!"

"Yes, here. What's going on?"

"Can you see him?"

"No. Can you?"

"No. Where are you?"

"Where you told me to wait; to wait for your signal."

I feel the solid knock of a tight perm against my ear

as an overweight woman impatiently shuffles past me, muttering under her strong breath and sending my mobile clattering onto the sidewalk to dwell among the stampede of boots. I'm scrabbling around on the floor as though I've dropped a contact lens when, in the same moment, I find the phone and catch another knock on the side of my head from a pair of tan leather trousers.

The phone looks in check and I pray it works as I resume pursuit, a bit groggy.

"Be ready, he's coming your way. Don't fuck it up!" I hang up fearing having to go through another reassurance talk. My vision locks onto a package dangling in his left hand. Something small. And easily accessible. In a panic I redial and get Jonathan's answer message. He must have turned his phone off! I try again and, to my relief, Jonathan's very shaky voice answers.

"Listen, change of plan. This will make it much easier for you I promise. He's carrying a black bag in his left hand. All you have to do is grab *that*. Clear?"

"Yes," he replies, fighting back the fear tears.

"Good. I know you can do this. I believe in you. Good luck."

So much for avoiding the pep talk.

I spot Jonathan in the distance, fully loaded with cap, shades and overcoat. The whole street seems suddenly to shift down a gear, everyone's steps more pronounced and in slow motion. Jonathan sets off, an unsteady walk, in my direction, the fox sandwiched between us as we close in like two hands clasping over a ball.

It happens so fast that I don't even see it but Jonathan shoots off in the opposite direction and I see our boy throw his arms up in the air like a spoilt schoolyard brat. That's my cue and I can feel the blood in my thighs begin to pump as I step out onto the street and begin rapid pursuit, dodging stationary cars and avoiding people. The commotion in that area is luckily pretty subdued as Jonathan (who, to his credit, is amazingly fast) escapes the scene. I reach the scene of the crime.

"Anyone hurt?" I say, looking directly at the victim, his hand on his chest and rolling his eyes, people in the crowd consoling him. "Which way did he go?" I say not waiting for an answer, just following an old lady's wobbly triceps. To my surprise, the accostee jumps to his feet and begins running after me, yelling and cussing.

My head start on him is not much but his little legs don't seem to pose a threat, his bowlegged shuffle barely enough to keep me in his sights. I reach the meeting point to find Jonathan crouching behind a dustbin, his disguise shoved into the adjacent bin.

"Jon." I'm out of breath. "Quick, put your clothes back on, it's back to plan A."

"What?" he says, now more nervous and bemused.

"Just do what I say! Now! He's right behind us."

"What about others?"

"No one else followed. Now hide where you were. I'm going to the other side of the alley. Remember what we practised."

He fights his tears, reclothes himself and reluctantly crouches again, fishing the instrument I gave him from his overall pocket which now arbitrarily dangles at his side. Once I'm on the other side of the alley I see the out-of-breath pursuer appear. I make it seem as though I've lost him and shrug my shoulders, walking towards him, his head nodding and then slumping down as he rests with hands on knees. I see Jonathan pounce, taking one of the dustbins with him, but inexplicably managing to stay on his feet. His surprise attack sends the victim into bomb blast position, crouching on the floor, his head contained under his crossed forearms, screams echoing from beneath. Jonathan flails a large blade in his direction. He actually seems to enjoy it slightly, going right up to the man and putting the blade against his throat to make him shut up. I begin running towards the scene and can only hear the mumble of Jonathan's rehearsed demands and the wailing. Jonathan takes off, clutching what I hope is a wallet directly towards me, and I wait delicately until the wailing subsides and he looks up.

"Sorry Jonathan," I say as I kick him gingerly in the ribs. I then flat hand slap him once and dummy a few punches into his stomach. He swings the knife at me a few times, opting for the sideswipe for maximum aesthetic appeal. I bend his wrist back and retrieve the wallet before a woman yells from above and a few more people appear where the heap watches with anticipation and intrigue. I grab the packet and my eyes widen.

"What are you waiting for?"

"I can't!"

"Do it! If I have to…" the warm sensation of blood streaming down my arm and the even warmer sensation of Jonathan running for safety, the knife burrowing back into the overcoat after slicing open the side of my arm. It hurts more than I had planned, the deepness of the swipe ironically pleasant and symptomatic of the adrenaline and exigency of the situation. I can feel the flap of skin being pulled down by the material of my shirt, Jonathan having exited down instead of along, the only flaw in an otherwise perfect performance.

"Are you alright? Do you need an ambulance?" says a voice among the crowd, who make way as the words "Let me through! Let me through!" cyclically ring out while I clutch my arm a little harder.

"I'm fine. It's just a nick," I say as he appears. "Here's your wallet and your package."

"Oh my God, how do I thank you?" he says. "I had over a thousand pound in there!"

"Don't worry about it. Just upset the guy got away."

"I know you."

I look up for the first time.

"Yes, hi. It's Bryan isn't it? We met at Mash Mayfair…"

"Did we? That's right. You're a friend of Kitten's. What was it again? Daniel?"

"Paton. Paton Stipps."

"Well whatever, you've done so fucking well. I will

make this so up to you mate."

"Really, it's not necessary."

"Of course it's fucking necessary. A thousand quid! Even for me that's a bundle. And the mission of cancelling credit cards and renewing gym membership and all that shit. You're a life saver."

"What about the packet?"

"Just a book. A novel."

"Which one?" I say the pain now starting to spread into my joints and bones.

"Don't know," he says, shaking the packet free and holding up Luke Rhinehart's *The Dice Man*. "Something about gambling, I think."

I start to feel the air around me as most of the onlookers depart and a car hooter bellows amongst the surrounding noise. Bryan K is smiling, looking directly at me, nodding and chewing gum so that the strands of saliva make him look like something from Hellraiser. He flicks a thumb through the notes in his wallet and seems to smile even more, his better than average teeth glistening as he spreads the gum across them like bread dough. He slaps me on the good shoulder and says, "Amazing coincidence this. This sort of shit always seems to happen to me. I'm lucky. That's it, I'm lucky. Some fucker is watching over me right now. And he sent you. Made you take the blade rather than me, sending me a message. Amazing coincidence this. Amazing."

"And some people say miracles don't happen," I say,

shielding my face before I sneeze, a loud and reverberating one that makes me wish I'd given Jonathan a blunter knife.

CHAPTER 25

THIEF IN THE NIGHT

She sits up in the middle of the night, clutching the duvet and ripping it free from my bare chest, scaring the crap out of me as my rapid eye movements turn into rapid ear movements.

"What is it?" I whisper.

"What was that?"

"What was what?"

"That noise? Like a door opening?"

We both stay silent for a couple of seconds, the only noise the toddler-like pitter-patter of our hearts thumping against our ribs, completely out of sync.

"It's nothing," I say flopping back down onto the bed and ripping the duvet back over myself. "We're not living in fear."

"Go check."

"No. Jesus! It's what? Two in the morning? Go to sleep."

"Paton, there's somebody out there." The pitch in Her voice is softer yet more assertive.

"Where's your mobile?"

"In the lounge."

"Shit. Wh..." I stop, now also paranoid in the uncertainty that some crazed drugged-up person with a weapon is lying on my sofa eating potato chips and laughing at unfunny television moments.

But there definitely was a sound.

A creak.

It could have been nothing.

But it was a sound.

There's a full size baseball bat behind my bed. My rationale was always to have a good-reaching weapon in the bedroom, but make sure it's hidden and accessible to avoid dying at its hands and not being able to draw it in time. I've never actually had to use it, even to hit an inanimate object. It feels solid and smooth as I run my hand up and down the shaft getting slowly out of bed.

"No matter what, stay in the room. If you have to, push the bookcase in front of the door."

"What about you?"

"If there is someone there, either I'll persuade them

to leave or make enough noise to make sure they leave. This lot can often be talked to; just ask them to get out. Put some clothes on and don't come out."

It feels as though my heartbeat is speed-fucking the end of my chin as I slowly turn the bedroom door handle and peer out of the crack directly down the narrow hallway. I'm not sure whether I can't move or if I stay motionless to wait and see if anything is out there. I can see the lounge curtains in the distance rollercoastering as a receptive breeze shuffles into the room. The breeze isn't coming from the window though, the curtain's moving to one side in the opposite direction to the balcony door.

That's the entry point and I want to scold myself right there and then for not getting the lock fixed.

I could see it coming.

I asked for it.

I begged for it.

For a stranger in my home.

Just then a shadow appears from the balcony door entrance and I see him point. Then someone else appears holding what looks like the VCR. I'm tempted to let them leave without doing anything, the VCR's absence not that much of a tragedy. They must have a host of stuff and a quick mental inventory reveals that, at most, the lounge's stash will reward them with about two dozen spoonfuls of heroine. Then as I think they're leaving I feel as though I've been raped; abused as though some external force has interrupted my harmony and taken something sacred from me.

Hurt my privacy.

Dented my confidence.

Put their filthy, shit encrusted nails on my stuff.

My shit.

The humming noise disappears in my skull as I burst through the door, gliding stealthily over carpet, baseball bat dangling behind, making certain it doesn't knock on the corridor. I don't know who's more surprised when I reach the balcony door, but the dark orange glow of the streetlights clearly depicts the connection. One man has straddled the black balcony rail while the other lowers a black rubbish bag down with a rope.

The shock sees the sickening crash of all my stuff becoming acquainted with the pavement as one lets go of the rope and also gets into straddle position, the other man now clambering along the windowsill. It's too good to be true as I bring the bat across the closest one and smash him on the side of the temple, the hollow echo of the blow sending him flying towards me in unison with my follow-through, which almost spins me completely around. The second man, seeing his friend assume the foetal position on my moss dominated balcony floor, starts crying and begging because he realises that the windowsill deceptively ends and the jump across to the adjoining flat is just that iota too far away.

"It's not a very nice fall is it?" I say, returning inside and lowering the bottom half of the lounge sash window onto his fingers so that he is trapped, like a rat without the cheese. I lower the top half, standing on the windowsill from the inside and peering over the top to admire my masterpiece.

"Oh please, don't let me fall," he sobs. "You can call the cops, but please don't let me fall."

"I reckon if you fall you'll land on those bricks if you're lucky and maybe buckle your knees back at right angles. If you're unlucky, one of two things will happen. One, you'll land on your head, split it open like a cumquat and die of severe internal cranial injuries. Two, and probably the worst of all, you'll land on the iron fence below you, which will split you in two; directly in half. It'll cut you up through your scrotum and you'll probably be in that position until the ambulance arrives, one of your nuts on either side of the fence and your penis a severed, never-to-be-used-again bit of flesh in the neighbour's garden, waiting for Sigmund the poodle to munch on it as a midnight feast."

This banter sends the burglar into what looks like a full epileptic fit, and he starts trying to swing his body in order to wrestle free and perhaps make it to the next-door balcony. But there's no way he'll achieve this, his fingers squashed onto the chipped white paint of the sill as I press down on the window. I take one second, as the universe stops moving, to examine this man. He's not badly dressed and he doesn't look dirty. He is very thin with bulbous eyes that jut out like breasts and a scarred chin that makes his complexion look like

Japanese literature. His hands are covered in needle wounds, some septic, all self-induced.

"I've never tried heroine, but is it really worth it? Is each hit worth hanging for your life just before the guy whose house you've broken into sends you to your death or eternal pain?"

He stops sobbing and points his eyes up towards mine, the glazed fear now turning to harsh reality. "Fucking kill me! I dare you. You'd better, because if you let me live, I'll be back with some other junkies to make sure you and your bitch wish you'd both died at birth!"

The crack of a finger snapping through the skin as you smash a baseball bat down on top of it can be a truly invigorating exercise.

I've been given no choice now.

Which, even if it is a relief, is a cop-out.

I break each of the man's fingers with the base of the bat. They now jut out towards me, held steady by the window, like wriggling silkworms. Each one breaks in a different way, some allowing the bone to pierce the skin, others not changing for a couple of seconds and then swelling. One looked as though it snapped completely off, but it was only the nail being ripped completely off as the bat came down at a deceptive angle. Lifting the window after the ten stage procession seemed the most logical ending to a truly beautiful ballet as Swan Lake took on a morbid new dimension as the happy burglar buckled like a doll on the fence, cracking his head on the bricks and bending his one knee forwards.

So I was half right on two accounts.

The other man begins to move his eyes below his eyelids creating a drowsy cat in a sack effect. I see his one eye open slowly and then retract into his skull. He raises a hand to the side of his brain, his eyes still shut, and touches the slab of skin now purple with swelling where he ran into the bat. The bat is smiling as it takes on a speckled effect and now properly realises the purpose it was purchased for.

Protection.

Retribution.

Just good old-fashioned fun.

Finding its destiny.

"Where am I?" the man whispers. "Linc, you still there?"

"No mate, I'm afraid he's looking for his teeth and a section of his kneecap down below. Take a look," I say, grabbing his shirtfront and dragging him to the window. Linc has certainly seen better days and the sight of his deformed angle and violent convulsions and screams sends pangs of terror through the other member of the audience. In a fit of adrenaline he turns and lifts me off the ground, his arms locked around my thighs, and barges me into my picture-laden lounge wall. While I'm trying to figure out if there's any glass lodged in my arse the door opens and there She is like a lamb to the slaughter, standing in the doorway in Her dressing gown.

"Get back in the room!" I yell as the man changes direction on his recoil and heads for the new hostage. She freezes like a deer in headlights, failing to scream or even divert Her eyes. The man's trajectory does not adequately take account of the low coffee table which sees him, a few candles, magazines and remote controls become a badly made casserole on the floor. This allows me time to pick the bat up and bring it down hard at the base of his spine, yet my aim in the dark is slightly off and all I really achieve is a forceful spank on his arse. The next swipe does generate a response from Her, in the form of a chalky yell because She is sprayed with the man's blood, as the bat drags through his face taking chewing gum-like fragments of his teeth and a chunk of his lower lip with it.

"Go wash your face," I yell as I wind up for what hopefully will be the decisive blow. "He could have AIDS! Keep your eyes shut! And mouth!"

He looks as though he runs on the spot for a couple of seconds as he inches towards Her, his face now making a terrible mess on the carpet. The bat bouncing off the top of his scalp actually hurts my hands, which means I drop the bat and shake them as though I've burnt them on the stove. He's no longer moving and She's sobbing hysterically. I go to hold Her.

"It's okay, it's alright," I say holding Her with one hand and shepherding Her towards the kitchen sink to wash Her face. "It's over."

CHAPTER 26

WAITING FOR CHAPTER

Some say that everything happens for a reason. I think the key word in that somewhat disastrous premonition is the word 'happens'. To think of oneself as a passive object upon which evil elements happen is as naive as it is ignorant. Shit does happen, but it's how you happen to react that makes for a remarkable existence.

To exist is boring.

To be passive is boring.

To let things happen to you is boring.

Sometimes when things are happening, what occurs after or during is almost completely out of your control.

As though through your change in mindset; your acquisition of blinkers; your glazed-over look, you become somewhat passive, behaving as you would if all were just in an unjust world.

To moan about the world is passive.

To moan about the world is cowardly.

Yet if you are one of the lucky few who obliviously breeze through society without a nick or scratch, choosing to ignore the injustice, then I say, "Good for you, well done", pat you on the back and wait for someone you know and love to be unfairly tampered with.

To snap you out of your complacent impotence.

There's a threshold somewhere in this too. Acceptance is accepted as part of higher evolution with tolerance behaving as the weak protégé. Taking a stand against whatever is always constrained by the excuse that is a person's values.

It's fear.

Real fear.

But anger can overcome fear.

Built up anger.

Like the drip-drip of a tap into an odd-shaped beaker until it overflows.

It's not always necessary to see that overflow as an explosion; a cracking up; a nervous breakdown.

Overflow can manifest itself in many forms – humour, escape, silence or even just overflow (bursting a blood vessel or something else physiological).

The important lesson is to manage the overflow. I didn't say control. Never control. Allow the water to flow over, but manage it, carefully cupping it and shovelling it in the correct direction.

Like towards those who have no water.

Or even more efficiently into another odd-shaped beaker for future consumption.

Then breathe in and love the world that lies before us like an expensive lady of the night. Get your money's worth, embrace the experience and then get out. And once out, start seeing the world from a new angle, this time perhaps as a slippery rock: ready to be mounted but with caution and without shoes.

But watch the tide.

Always face the waves.

Never turn your back.

And let the challenge evolve and run with it, until you're satisfied that you've done more than an adequate job.

More than an adequate job.

There will be guilt.

Sometimes insurmountable guilt.

Like that feeling when you put your foot into a shoe and think there's a large, hairy spider with personality lurking within.

The shock followed by brief relief then back to the droning fear that the guilt will control your every move turning you into a cautious obsessive freak, checking your shoes every time you put them on with a chop stick and a can of bug spray, poised and ready to squirt. Somewhere between dropping the shoe and fleeing to the kitchen.

Gather the courage, my friends, for you only get one shot at this thing called life. Let things happen. Let yourself happen. React. As you see fit. Manage the overflow. Don't try to stop it or control it. Make a difference. If not for everyone then for yourself. Make the humming go away. Then chase the guilt and wait for the next chapter.

CHAPTER 27

'ON YER WAY' WITHOUT THE SLAP ON THE ARSE

Kitten returns from what she calls a photo shoot but what I am convinced was a porno shoot as she's walking tenderly, each step a masquerading labour of movement. Her lack of presence in my life has been welcomed and hardly taken notice of, what with my diary full up with alternative activities.

Somehow she manages to squeeze back into my world like the roadrunner (with big breasts) and, as I watch her walk, I feel this intense sorrow for her. Not a patronising sorrow, believing that I am so much better placed in life than she is, but a real sorrow, one which tickles every pore of my body, rendering me unable to scratch it and deal with it, like chicken pox.

"Kitten, you will never make it," I say as she turns to wait for me at the entrance of the studio.

"What was that, hun-bun?"

"I said you will never make it."

Her face now looks as though it's about to crack up, the worn-out foundation creeping into her facial crevices as she scrunches up her face to fight the tears.

"You don't mean what I think you do, do you?"

"I do," I say, taking her hand.

She starts delicately sobbing, so adroitly the tears run the risk of turning into crocodile tears, while she mutters about the harrowing time she's had lately.

"Can I try to explain?" I say.

"No," she says, wriggling free, beckoning for me to grip her and beg her to hear my explanation.

"There's this guy at work who used to be my boss who is a gay man. He lives for men. Every waking second I see him dreaming of his knight in shining armour or perving over some guy's walk. He loves men. He loves sexual encounters with men. Yet every night he goes home to his wife and kids and plays the good husband while his wife cries herself to sleep and the kids wonder why no noises ever come from Mummy and Daddy's room."

"What are you getting at?"

"He's living a lie. A big lie. A lie that makes him so unhappy that he chews his nails until each finger bleeds. He allows convention to dictate his unhappiness."

"I still don't understand."

"He believes everything will sort itself out. If he just continues to fuck other men behind his wife's back he will be able to co-exist in his far from perfect world. It won't go away. He has to embrace reality. He's starting to realise that a divorced couple are potentially happier than one where both parties fancy the same sex."

"What has all this got to do with me?"

"You're not attractive enough to be a model or an actress."

"I am an actress and I am a model."

"I'm the last person in the world to impede someone who is chasing a dream, but Kitten, in all honesty, it's time to chase another dream."

"My career is just taking off."

"You've done exceptionally well thus far, but for your own good, you need to focus on something more. You know this doesn't make you happy. You're so keen to get in with the right people that you have lost your soul. You're a nice person. Why waste that on false breasts, too much make-up and a career that involves taking it up the arse?"

No tears follow.

"I let three men stick their cocks up my arse so that I could get a quarter of a breast and my elbow in an advertisement."

"You've had enough now; I can see it in your eyes."

I'm now hugging her and for the first time since I met her I'm thinking exclusively about parts of her that don't include her breasts.

"What did you want to be when you were a little girl?"

"An actress and a model."

"Then go to acting school. Become an actress. But let the casting directors cast you for your talent. Don't do things that make you unhappy. It's not worth it. When you are seventy it will be far more important that you enjoyed the journey, not fantasised about the end goal."

"I'm going to go home," she says looking up and blinking deliberately, resting between my locked arms for that moment in time. I lean down and kiss her gladly on the forehead, not at all concerned that my lips are now coated in beige powder. She gives me one more tight squeeze before turning from the studio to walk away.

"Look after Bryan, Paton," she says.

"You don't need someone like that around. He's an illusion."

"Just look after him, okay?"

"I'll take really good care of him. Really good care."

CHAPTER 28

TIRESOME FIVESOME

Of all the rewards for my heroic theft-foiling con, Bryan K invites me to the set of his band's new music video shoot. The elation building up inside me is equivalent to the anticipation that used to fill me prior to a three-hour church service at boarding school including an hour rendition from Father 'Drone' Carbone. The building is somewhat non-descript: a square monotonous orange brick structure nestling between a Japanese restaurant and a rundown pub, and jutting out of the pavement like a bunion.

Kitten's exit sees me fashion my entrance late and

hence able to sneak in and sit at the back. Before entering I take a second to watch a mother slap her child harder than I think the law allows and call her 'Stupid'. It reminds me of a similar situation I watched unfold a few days ago before work.

A couple of black kids dressed haphazardly in school uniforms, their ties too short and socks down, passed an old, unshaven, overweight security guard perched on a bright orange plastic chair like a discarded fried egg. I'm not sure what the earlier dialogue was about but the result was the guard yelling something to the effect of 'You stupid black kid' to the shortest of the bunch. The tallest of the bunch then unassumingly approached the man and informed him that Leroy was in fact third in his class and first in Maths which meant, if anything, he was a 'Smart Black Kid'.

The guard had no reply, stunned into stupidity by the intrepid child; standing firm and even asking the man if he thought smart-black was a paradox or actually an oxymoron, making sure to pronounce the oxy so as not to confuse the term with a more blatant insult. The guard then looked like a child. A ridiculed child. Standing humiliated in a playground. Because he had no reply. So he swiped at the kid, the back of his hand clipping the child who failed to understand why, his eyes unable to prevent the runny waylay.

Inside what turns out to be a cross between a theatre and an indoor set there's a lot of noise with little visible action. One of the stagehands is crying with his eyes buried in his palms and someone who is behaving like the director is trying passionately to resume shooting. There are over two dozen women wearing bright pink bikinis and slap bang in the middle of them like a dirty flamingo is our man Bryan K, sporting a black suit, the collar raised. All are shrouded in bright artificial lights which sparkle among the coats of make-up as they wait for resolve atop the set made up to look like a diner.

I sneak forward to make out the dialogue when Bryan spots me and waves. I half-heartedly wave back and pick a seat that looks as though it's hidden by a corner of a shadow provided by the gallery overhang. I am one of three people blessed to be part of the audience: a man and a woman to my right, sitting together and on the other side of the seating area. I coyly wave to them too and make myself comfortable.

"Okay, people – let's try to keep it together now. We've got a good many shots to get through. Come on, come on," the director yells but in an amiable tone.

The crying stagehand then reveals himself to be one of the band members and he hysterically storms off backstage moments before the director and one of the cameramen collapse in adjacent chairs. The director's assistant, a nimble brunette, rushes after the weeping willow followed by the man sitting with me in the audience.

"Let's all take five then," the director concedes, throwing his arms aloft.

Two of the remaining four boyband members exit the

stage from the front and trot up the raised angle of the aisle leading towards the exit. The woman left sitting in my row stands up, putting a cigarette in between her lips so as not to smear her brownish lipstick. She's wearing light large rectangular sunglasses even though the audience seats are dark and they almost bobble off her face when one of the security guards yells: "You can't smoke in here, love," from the back. His tone is not purposefully abrasive and fails to deter the skeletal woman from flicking the flame to light. The smell of smoke and the loud exaggerated drag on the cigarette like a gasp sees the guard approach quickly yet unassumingly to restate the rules.

"I'm sorry ma'am, but you ain't allowed to smoke cigarettes in these premises. It's prohibited for safety reasons. A lot a flammable props and gas tanks lying around."

The woman turns her head away from the annoyance and stares at the tallest member of the boyband, making an expectant face followed by a sigh and a hand on her ridged hip.

"Do you know who the fuck you are talking to?" says the tall one who is still short by comparison to his crane-like girlfriend.

"I'm sorry sir, these are the rules. You can smoke outside the building."

"Outside the fucking building! Listen Captain Security, I don't think you quite appreciate who you are dealing with here. I'm Jamie James, part of Coastal

Love. You might have heard of us."

"Sorry sir I haven't."

"And this is Amber Thai, my girlfriend and the new face of Klein. Calvin Klein. Have you heard of him?"

"No sir."

Violent laughter erupts around the burly guard like fireworks.

"Well I suggest you turn around and go the way you fucking came and make sure we're all safe in here."

"It is against the rules of these premises to smoke on site."

"You can quote all the rules you like dummy, she's not going to put it out, are you babe?"

She says nothing still refusing to look at the guard as though he fails to exist.

As though his presence on this earth and in this theatre is nothing more than the smoke that now wafts upwards, soon to disperse.

The guard then does something that makes me want to drape a medal around his neck. Without the slightest hint of aggression or impatience he plucks the cigarette from the girl's lips and squashes it in his palm. The group are gobsmacked and Jamie makes a weak attempt to rush at the guard, his gesture towards his fellow band member to stop him as obvious as an unsightly forehead pimple. So the scene is comical: Jamie's kicking and screaming while his mate feebly holds him back, the security guard standing proud and resolute and twice the size of any of them.

"You fucking common blue-collar piece of shit," yells Jamie. "You won't be working here again, ever! Ever!"

It's time to make an entrance.

Before Jamie cries himself to death or the guard actually does lose it and snaps a few boyband bones like twigs.

They'll get their snappage.

But not like this.

"Let's all calm down. This can be resolved," I say, taking the guard aside.

"Who the fuck are you?" I hear as I walk with the guard down towards his previous post. I tell him that I'll make sure no one smokes inside and that I secretly think what he did was fantastic. When I return the emotional levels are still erect. Jamie is being comforted by his all-elbows girlfriend while he mutters things like "I could've busted him open man, I was close." The man from the audience has returned and is embracing the short, soft-looking boyband member whilst also trying to calm Jamie down.

Jamie the livewire.

Bryan and another band member join the congregation just before I return which means introductions needn't be backed up.

The introductions are quick.

I'm the hero who saved Bryan's wallet and his book.

Jamie James is the livewire with the anorexic girlfriend who is about as interested in him (or anything) as a cat after it has been fed.

PJ Glow is the short, cute, openly gay band member with too much mascara, long hair and a good-looking boyfriend who hangs off him like a tail.

Floyd is the crying member receiving 'treatment' in the back and the sole reason for the five minute recess. Apparently the director was favouring his bad side or something.

The last member of the tiresome fivesome is Brady, who sports a Mohican and enough jewellery to challenge a satellite.

Coastal Love.

Can you feel it?

CHAPTER 29

DINNER WITH GIRLFRIEND

London in summer can be as welcoming as foreboding. We sit, almost seven million of us, for too many months of the year craving warmth and willing the delicate drizzle away. Willing wrinkled brows away, shielding our eyes from the rain. Willing unhappy Tube faces away, going to and from work in the dark.

And then the sun comes out and everyone goes slightly grand mal. The heat hath sprung making every public outdoor spot an area to drink and smoke and smile and laugh. Shirts come off. Tits come out. Everything changes. Hibernation ends.

But it's short-lived and the heat is a muggy rancid heat. Sometimes it's overcast and the heat still clings, determined to occupy every fold of skin or pocket of pores like sticky toffee. On one of these particular evenings, She invites me out to dinner.

I go.

We eat.

We talk.

A bit.

About nothing.

We're full.

Sickly full.

So full that it feels as though the food is about to force itself from our stomachs and ooze from the cracks appearing around our bellybuttons. Blowing the lid off: a manhole cover forced sideways rather than upwards; masticated shapes of food rather than hot air.

And we find space for pudding.

Somewhere.

And stagger home, half-pissed, the sun setting late and the heat now comforting and gregarious.

Sombre becomes tolerant becomes attentive becomes jovial.

Until we arrive home and there's a large, wrapped present on the coffee table, the pink and purple ribbons bubbling down all sides of the box like the overflowing foam of a pint of beer. At first I'm confused until She flings Her arms around me saying, "Happy Anniversary. I know we can do better than last year." Something inside me melts because She smells different; She smells not of men's cologne.

"I didn't get you anything," I say, guilt now infesting down to the tips of my curled toes.

"It's okay, we can both use the gift," She says. "Open it, open it!"

She's now jumping up and down and I can see the kindness in Her eyes that I fell in love with. A strand of hair falls past Her cheek and I smooth it away, drawing Her nearer and kissing Her on the forehead. I leave a slight mark, not in the shape of my mouth but rather in the shape of Australia. She starts to cry and then shifts focus, wiping away the tears which have become tangled with the resurgent strand of hair.

"Open your present."

I awkwardly unwrap the gift, hopelessly uncertain how to react. The smile I put on I can feel is forced and doesn't know where to go, as though my face is a canvass and the painter has drawn an arc that hovers in no-man's-land. It's quite difficult to get to but I eventually do and, to my surprise, it's a goldfish bowl.

"Lucky I didn't shake it or turn it upside down I suppose," I say. I watch the orange fish look expressionlessly out the glass and then dart back among the spiralling blue-green colours of the pebbles at the bottom.

"Does he have a name?" I ask.

"How do you know he's a he?"

We giggle together for a while as the moon intrudes

through the window lighting the opposite sides of our faces as we stare quietly at one another. The next few seconds verge on romantic as She takes my hand and I thank her while She begins kissing the side of my neck.

It's the first physical contact we've had for months.

Her tongue moves south and circles my nipples as She undoes my trousers, struggling slightly with the belt. She begins nibbling at my nipple, pinching one with Her fingers, the sensation visibly intriguing. When She sits up and takes Her top off it rekindles something of the attraction we used to share in my mind. Her body is as firm as when we met and Her breasts heavy and rounded. They're propped up by a black bra, a generous portion of cleavage waiting for my touch. At this stage we can think of nothing but ravaging one another, so we do.

She rips off my boxer shorts and takes my penis in Her mouth, forcing herself right down onto it until my helmet is well inside Her throat. My entrance into Her throat provides an all round sensation that Her mouth cannot provide and I start pawing at Her breasts, squeezing one hard after exposing it from the cup. She's now licking up and down the shaft and moves to suck on my balls as I feel Her slipping away, no longer able to reach Her with my arms. She kisses under my surely sudorific sack and begins popping a few fingers in my arse, Her nails hurting me slightly.

I cogently lift Her up and fling Her over the raised edge of the couch and rip down Her low cut skirt. Her symmetrical arse cheeks greet me and I spank Her once and then twice on the same cheek leaving a criss-cross of fingerprints, bright pink in the moonlight. She groans and begs for more as I rip Her black G-string aside and begin tonguing Her soaked vagina and anus. I'm plunging a couple of fingers inside Her and She's flopped over the couch in ecstasy. I shove my fingers in Her mouth and then plunge them into Her arse, Her saliva the tongue in cheek lubricant.

She tries to turn around and suck on me but I make sure She remains facing the repaired picture of the old Chinese woman on the opposite wall. I climb onto my knees on the couch and tease Her, putting the head of my penis at the entrance of Her opening. On Her request I spank Her a few more times and then ease myself all the way inside Her, afflicting a seemingly large orgasm which sees Her shaking and yelling at me to fuck Her harder.

The agglomeration at first is fast and forceful until She's come a couple more times. We swap positions and I even fuck Her in the arse a few times, which proves less effectual on the orgasm front and more effectual on the expression front. Nearing the end I find myself facing Her kneeling on the floor with Her legs straddling the coffee table. I'm about to ejaculate all over Her breasts and face when She locks Her legs around me holding me firmly inside Her ensuring I come at the same time as Her. Our bodies now go limp and glisten in the light, our stomachs rising and falling in perfect unison while the post-coital cigarette provides welcome relief.

"You okay?" I ask.

"That was so amazing," She says, rolling over and nibbling my belly button.

"You still on the pill right?"

"I've just finished my cycle. It'll be fine."

The phone rings and we leave it, blowing weak attempts at smoke rings and thinking no further than the moment.

CHAPTER 30

BIG BROTHER IS WATCHING

All a bit cloak and dagger really, but there's an email from Jonathan where a series of sporadic letters are capitals. At first I ignore it and then begin to wonder why he has sent me an email regarding a project that was handed on to another department weeks before. On closer observation the capital letters spell out a meeting place and time: a greasy spoon called Jenny's near Tottenham Court Road at noon.

As usual he's late and I'm early. The restaurant is lucky to be called a restaurant and the cup of coffee I order looks as though it will keep me awake for months.

The foreign waitress fills the coffee machine to the brim with coarsely ground cheap coffee and proceeds to pour the thick black soup-like liquid into a chipped and stained hostel cup with a light blue line around the saucer. The two don't match. But after all, it is coffee and I like coffee, so I drink it, feeling my eyes pulsate after each sip.

Jonathan arrives about twenty minutes late and orders food, an action I warn him against to which he replies that he eats here all the time.

"Okay, enough with the e-coli discussion, what's all this secrecy?"

"I feel as though I'm being watched."

"Big Brother again?"

"No," he chuckles coyly, playing his homosexuality trait like a weak suit. "At work. Manfred's been asking questions. Strange questions. About us."

"What did you tell him?"

"Nothing, although I'm not the best liar."

"Does he know that you're gay?"

"No! God! He's so homophobic he'd have me selling the Big Issue in seconds."

"Well what are you worrying about then?"

"He wants a daily progress report sent directly to him. Does he know anything?"

"No, of course not. He's so intent on this initiative we're running he has little time for anything else. All he does, all day, is insist on how this should all be run – what I do, what he does, why it must happen this way.

Boring corporate rhetoric as far as I'm concerned. He did mention you the other day though, wanting to know what we were up to."

"What *are* we up to?"

"Nothing."

"You won't tell me what that whole business with the faked robbery was, will you? And my ribs still hurt."

"Don't lie. You're lying. That was too long ago."

"Tell me what's going on."

"I will when the time is right."

"It's right now. Manfred's breathing down my neck."

"I wouldn't worry about Manfred – he's harmless. Just stay away from the two areas of discussion – your sexual orientation (for your sake) and the robbery (for my sake). He'll get nothing from me."

"What if he finds out?"

"You've done nothing wrong. You'll see. Say you can't remember."

"I'm not good in situations like this."

Then it dawns on me: I'm all talk. My bullshit speech to Kitten was rubbish. I'm not making a difference – I'm doing it for selfish gain. How have I helped Jonathan? I haven't! Things are worse for the poor man now. It's time to make a difference.

"Actually Jonathan, scrap everything I've just said." His face again obtains the all-too-familiar confused look, his mouth squelching into a ball on one side.

"The next time Manfred says anything to you, look

him straight in the eye, and tell him to fuck off. Tell him you're a gay man who loves men and if he has a problem with it then he should get with the times. Tell him you work hard even though you hate your job and your life bores you which means you have to resort to false robberies in order trick the wankers of the world into trusting you so that you can teach them and the world a severe lesson. Tell him someone has to be blamed; someone has to pay a price for the world's problems and if he's not careful that someone will be him. Sooner than he can imagine."

"I should tell him all that?" he replies, pinching the tip of his index finger.

"Yes. And don't forget to ask him how he likes his coffee."

CHAPTER 31

FUND RAISER

The song I've fallen in love with plays on the radio as the highest climber of the week. Caroline switches from radio to CD before the end of the song, her choice of music somewhere between Christian rock and a Country love ballad. On her way to the music system she stands on the remote control which she has been searching for for over ten minutes. It's partly hidden under the cream carpet which muffles the mangle of plastic and circuit boards.

Her embarrassment is beyond sweet, her cheeks bellowing redness like two dull apples. She's nervous, I can tell. It's almost as though she seeks my approval; as though I'm her father and she's about to introduce me. To her new boyfriend. The fundraiser guy. Who she's been seeing for a couple of months now. Her nervous anticipation again overflows as she kicks over her umbrella basket in her haste to get out the door, ending up flat on her face among a cacophony of brightly coloured umbrellas and wooden walking sticks.

I help her up and again she blushes, this time with a sprinkle of aberrant aggression as we're slightly late and Dave always embraces punctuality. I was meant to meet her at the fundraiser but ended up taking a slight detour after Bryan called on my mobile, asking to meet for morning pomegranate caipirinhas. We've become friendly lately. Well sort of. He's latched onto me in a way. Most of his decisions can now only take place once he's consulted me. Maybe it's the father figure in me. Or maybe it's because I'm in the 'business world; dealing with money and markets and cash and shit'. Or maybe because I use words with more than three syllables which makes him think I'm knowledgeable.

Intelligent.

Four syllables.

Eloquent.

Three syllables.

Cruel.

Two syllables (par to contrary belief and according to my English teacher when I was fourteen).

So this is where I am in my quest for self-fulfilment in the treacherous journey called life: mates with a boyband member who knows more about teenage anatomy than he should and with more money than he knows what to do with.

Reach for the dream.

Or live the dream handed to you on a silver plate.

Silver plate.

Handed to me.

For a reason.

To fulfil my destiny.

While I was getting ready for the fundraiser he phoned in a panic saying he had to speak to me right away. We met in a secluded restaurant in Covent Garden where the waiter recognised Bryan and asked for a signature whereupon Bryan made sure the manager fired him for the intrusion. Had it been a teenage girl the scenario might have been different. He probably would have signed something for her. He's always got time for that. Anyway, he gets me there and stares straight at me, his brow wrought with concern, the wrinkles decorating his forehead like shiny earthworms.

"I think the band is trying to get rid of me," he said, sitting back and waiting for my monumental shock to transcend down to him.

"No," I said, my brow mirroring his.

"They fucking want me out. I just know it. The signs are there. They're there, man. Those lousy fuckers. They're nothing without me. I make the fucking band. I make it! I always knew they wanted me out. I'm too fucking good for them."

The word 'I' appeared so often that I decided to get more information, saying, "Now tell me what happened?" and getting settled for the monologue.

"Well we're rehearsing dance moves yesterday, for our new video. It's a really good routine with a bit of a country flavour. You know like a cross between techno and a square dance. So Brady's getting some of the turns wrong and I make a comment about his jewellery weighing him down. Well! You'd think I fucking screwed his sister because all hell breaks loose: he starts insulting my dance style saying how my steps are heavy and arm movements too exaggerated and also how, when I look at the camera, I'm trying too hard to create the dreamy look. So I strike back and tell him how shit he is and how the girls fucking love my dreamy look and then we're comparing how many girls we've fucked in the last week and I know he's bullshitting because all the fans prefer me. All the polls say so. I'm the good-looking one. The one with the charm. The one with the body. The one with the smile. I'm the fucking glue of the band, man! Anyway so while we're listing and proving who we've fucked, the rest of the band just stand there and watch, refusing to confirm anything I say and not standing up for me when clearly I was in the right."

This continued for a while and I listened patiently, similar to how I did on my first date with Kitten. As though I'm more of a wall than a mirror: something to piss against or spray paint rather than reflect in. I spent the last five minutes before I had to dash assuring him that the world (and the band) were not out to get him and that it was just a squabble that would soon be forgotten. Had I more time I might have begun to plant seeds of dissent among the crew, but my creative juices seemed to be running on empty and his paranoia extracted some sympathy in an exhaustive sort of way. It did give me an idea though.

Bryan's dilemma or *national crisis* as he liked to put it meant that I passed Caroline's flat and decided to pick her up. She didn't want to say but I could tell she felt uncomfortable. For the first time since the bus snapped open her shoulder blade my presence was unwelcome. She had explained before that Dave preferred no other men in her life, in particular on the friendship level. So arriving at the fundraiser with her was clearly antagonising the relationship. What effect this antagonism would cause was what I wanted to find out. After all, he didn't know I was coming. It was a surprise.

We arrive amidst kids chasing each other, abandoned by their parents in their noble efforts to fund raise. The venue chosen is an outdoor amphitheatre with uncut grass that spills over the vertical cement slabs like the head of a latte. People mill like sheep, all decorated with badges and clipboards and hats and fretful faces.

"Where is he? Is he here yet?" I ask.

"He should already be here by now," she says nervously looking around.

"I'm looking forward to meeting him. What's his name again?"

"Dave. Dave Reddill."

"What's troubling you?"

"Well Dave's not really a social person. I mean he doesn't like anything new or surprises or anything like that."

"He won't mind. Surely?"

"Well he has sort of emphasised that he doesn't want any sort of external contact. 'Just the two of us, all the time' he says to me. He's not really interested in 'other people', if you know what I mean?"

"I'm not sure I do, Caroline, but if it makes you feel uncomfortable I'll leave. The last thing I want to do is jeopardise your relationship."

"No don't be silly. I'm just being silly! He'll be fine when he gets to know you. Maybe it's just shyness. I think that's him over there." She points at a man fleeing rapidly down the steps towards the car park. I'm not completely sure but from behind he looks vaguely familiar. Caroline calls to him, realising that his pace is too quick for her to catch up to him. He fails to glance back and disappears into a white BMW, speeding through the cars and into the distance, the trail of dust masking the rear of the car.

Caroline begins to cry faintly into her hands. "He must have seen us. Together. And thought the worst."

"He wouldn't think that you and me would be … would he?"

"I don't know," she says, sobbing more heavily into the handkerchief I hand her.

"I'm sorry, this is all my fault. Let me explain it to him. Have you got his mobile number?"

"I don't, but also I don't think that'll be such a good idea. Just leave it, I'll sort it out. It'll be okay. Everything will be alright."

"I hope so. Just be careful. Protect yourself, I mean, just take care okay?"

"Do you want this back?" she says, handing back my light blue handkerchief complete with damp blobs and a fresh splatter of mucus.

"No thanks, you keep it," I reply and cup her head to my chest as another bout of crying ensues. The fund raising folk continue to raise funds, a crying woman no hurdle in their quest to relocate funds from those who wish to give to those who wish to receive. And still the kids play, the pitter-patter of their little legs running barely audible above the fund raising.

CHAPTER 32

THE BEGINNING

There's enough cocaine to fuel a jumbo jet strewn across the glass table, scantily clad women rolling their faces in it like dough in flour. One of the girls accidentally dips her false breast into the white powder, coating her entire nipple over the bright red bikini in the opposite of a cherry on top effect. Her vacant laughter quickly attracts Bryan who proceeds to snort the drug from her nipple and then lick it clean.

"Having a good time, Paton?" he yells from the table.

"Yes. Great. Thanks."

"You just make yourself at home, you hear? Plenty

of delicacies to feast on," he says giggling and flicking the girl's wet nipple before running off somewhere else.

It's a fantasyland this party. Everywhere I look are women who make Playmates look like Cabbage Patch Kids. There are Jacuzzis dotted around the mansion not dissimilar to lilies on a pond and the indoor and outdoor pools complete the excessive water effect. The drugs and drink flow like water too. Everywhere I look I see young people shooting up and laughing, thrusting their heads back in surreal pleasure. I would be a liar if I say I'm not taken by this world. But taken in a strange sort of way. If this bevy of flesh had been anywhere near me as an adolescent I might have jumped at it, then burnt my fingers and dropped it to the floor beneath. But something's missing here. Now. Everything's vacant. There's no substance. Just abuse.

I'm sitting alone watching the world copulate with itself when I'm approached by a girl in a silver bikini and devil horns fastened to the top of her head. This is about the thirtieth approach of the evening and this girl can barely stand, her horns slipping to the side as she stumbles towards me.

"You anyone famous?" she asks, the brutality of the question somehow refreshing. Most of the others usually go the *round-about-what-do-you-do* route.

"Well, between mowing lawns and clearing rubbish, I warm toilet seats for top government officials."

There's a silence as she tries to focus on my face.

"You're funny. And you're cute. How cute are

you?" the 'you' going an octave higher as she pinches my cheek.

"I don't know, how cute am I?"

"You're the cutest guy here I think. What's your name and how big is your cock?" She lunges forward, slamming her open palm onto my crotch.

"Whoa, careful there, Buffy. I think you should go drink some water and lie down. How about it?"

"Will you fuck me after?"

"Let's just get you comfortable first," I say, lifting her up as I would a bride.

As I'm carrying her up the stairs I pass Bryan and Jamie who both whistle and motion thrusting movements with their hips before high fiveing one another and running down the steps. Most of the rooms are taken but not locked. I get the enviable pleasure of viewing PJ Glow inside his boyfriend with his mouth on another man while a third enigmatically plunges from behind. The logistics scare me and the fact that I'm thinking about it makes me even more scared. The second room I intrude upon after no reply from the knock has screams emanating from the bathroom so I leave. Buffy's getting heavy and I'm sure she's about to puke so my search for a bathroom becomes more frantic.

Rooms three and four are occupied by Brady and Floyd respectively. Brady's with a girl who doesn't look older than thirteen and Floyd's with a boy who doesn't look older than twelve. Each is oblivious to my cause and continue despite the onlookers surrounding the beds in heaps of drug stupors waiting for their turns.

I finally find a room that's deserted and manage to lay Buffy assiduously down on the bed. When I get back from the basin with a glass of water, Buffy is completely naked with two of her fingers deep inside her.

"Here drink this," I say lifting her head onto my lap and tilting the glass towards her. She slaps it from my hand dismissively and tries to shove her fingers in my mouth.

"Listen Buffy, can we just hold on for one second."

"My name's not Buffy. It's Bambi. Will you call me Bambi?"

"Sure. I'll call you whatever you want if you hold on and stop what you're doing."

She's amazingly strong for such a fragile looking waif and I have to physically hold her arms down at her sides pinning her to the bed. She starts sticking her tongue out trying to suck my neck and thrusting her pelvis up to me, the smell now distinct. The light from the door opening pierces my eyes as the crack widens to reveal another female form.

"Oh, I'm sorry," the woman says, beginning to shut the door behind her.

"No wait!" I yell. "Please give me a hand in here!"

The woman re-enters circumspectly trying to make out what's going on.

"Can you hold down her legs?" I say.

"Sorry fella, I'm not into that kinky shit."

"No! No! It's not like that. I'm trying to restrain her and get her to calm down. But she's an animal on heat. She won't settle down. I just want her to drink some water and sit still before she has a heart attack!"

The woman then dives on Bambi's knees, spotting a small tattoo of a white horse on her inner thigh.

"Is that you Bambi?" she says.

"Yes! Kim! Kim let's fuck this guy. He's a looker."

"Okay we'll do that," she says leaning over me to pick up the remaining water. "But first drink these pills," she says, plunging two pills into Bambi's mouth and washing them down.

"Mmmm, more drugs," says Bambi as my frown towards Kim leads to a small wink and a shake of her head.

"Yes Bama, some nice drugs first and then we'll fuck him."

In five minutes Bambi is snoring louder than either of my grandparents and I'm smoking a cigarette with Kim on the balcony overlooking the back of the house where there is only darkness and tranquillity. No yelling. Or mayhem. Or fucking.

"What did you give her? I say.

"Sleeping pills," she replies, putting the smoke in her mouth and shaking a bottle of pills.

"You just happened to have a bottle of sleeping pills on you?"

"It's a long story."

"Are you in a rush to get somewhere?" I say as a scream echoes out from down the corridor.

"It's a family thing. A private matter."

"So what are you doing here?"

"That's the family matter."

"This doesn't seem to be your sort of party."

"Nor yours."

"I'm a friend of Bryan's."

"Bryan doesn't have any friends. Well any real ones."

"I help him out."

"Are you his doctor? His psychologist?"

"His unqualified one maybe."

"So what do you come here for? To restrain little girls and make sure they keep their liquids up?"

"I tell you what, you tell me what you're doing here and I'll tell you. Fair compromise?"

I watch her debate the offer as she tucks her hair behind her ears and flicks her cigarette over the balcony lighting another just as quickly. She swallows and looks up directly into my eyes.

"I've got no loyalty to these idiots, I swear," I say, my tone resonating in a humble and genuine comportment.

She pauses for one more moment.

"That's my baby sister in there. Her real name is Jacqueline and she's fifteen years old. She's a model and a dancer and somewhere along the line got involved with this bunch. When all this started I tried everything

I could to get her away from it. But nothing worked. Eventually after getting my parents and the police involved we found her living in a council flat with four black junkies after her third attempt to run away. So I made her a deal: she could continue to go to these parties as long as she came home and allowed me to go with her. So I suppose it's the lesser of evils – Mum and Dad still don't sleep at night but at least they know I'm here. I can't prevent everything but it's got to be better than fucking junkies for drugs. Least at the end of each episode I know she's safe in her bed at home. It's the getting her there that's the difficult bit. So I can't play it too strong and police her. I have to pretend to be *into it* having a good time and flitting around between these people. Or I won't get invited. And I'll not know that she's all right. What's your story?"

"I'm not quite sure really. Something about this lifestyle intrigues me. Another side disgusts me. Either way there's a purpose in it. So if I can get a young girl to gulp some water and avoid her drowning in her own vomit then perhaps I've achieved something. Or perhaps not. Only time will tell."

"And you know Bryan. Bryan K the Cock with a capital C."

"The Cock."

"Yes, they're all good at something you see."

"What do you mean?"

"Well if Bryan's the Cock then PJ's the Face. The good-looking one. Jamie's the only one who can sort of sing, so he's the Mouth. Brady's the Body and Floyd's the Feet. All the gratuitous abdominal shots on camera are Brady's and all the dance shots are of Floyd. They're the perfect boyband you see, perfect. Lacking in no department."

"The Cock. The Face. The Mouth. The Body. The Feet. It couldn't be clearer. Or more perfect."

A brief interlude sees me go to the toilet and Kim, or whatever her real name is, put a blanket over her baby sister and stroke her forehead with a damp towel. Her breathing's settled down slightly after a lengthy period of baby spastic jerks, her heart gnawing at her ribcage like a trapped piranha.

The bathroom is surprisingly tasteful, with chrome tap handles, a large slab of patterned blue ceramics and a couple of small, framed, hand-painted Egyptian postcards. The toilet seat is marble as is the toilet handle and there is a range of bathroom accessories that give the bathroom the hint of character. A silver beaker safely holds an electric toothbrush, various hair products and a cutthroat razor. I can see myself in the reflection of the blade as I try not to miss the bowl and I'm strangely oblong: a beige ghost with big oval eyes.

"You going to be okay?" I say relieved, emerging from the sliding door and careful not to speak too loudly.

"Should be fine. I'll stay here for a while and then get a cab or something. Try and get her home."

"Do you need some money? Or would you prefer me

to take you?"

"It's fine, just another normal night. We're used to it by now."

There's no let-up downstairs. The screaming has intensified to a level that sounds as though we're buried deep in some African rainforest, the reverberation off the walls making my teeth chatter and ears ring.

Mayhem is a tame word right about now.

A girl runs past me (who looks remarkably similar to Kitten) and I'm about to stop her when she dives into one of the indoor plunge pools, landing like a squid. She raises her head to reveal that she isn't Kitten and her nose is bleeding which turns out to be the funniest event ever to happen to her. Her hysteria is short-lived though when she looks down to see half the bone of her kneecap exposed sending her laughter into bouts of screams that seem to just blend into the rest of the madness.

While this is going on a young woman is being chased around the room by another young woman, both without a thread of clothing, the chaser holding a kid's water pistol, the scene not dissimilar to the large white penis scene in *A Clockwork Orange*. The fear is real yet aggravated, and the pistol is loaded and potent. In another room I see a man holding a pepper grinder over the open mouths of about a dozen people, their eyes tightly shut and tongues protruding like hungry hands. Another man is filling another pepper grinder with brightly coloured pills, orange and black I think, grabbing handfuls from a swivel stainless steel snack tray. The room flickers across the begging faces, the light and dark of a television screen flashing what must be porn over the inhabitants.

There is no normality.

There is no calm.

Just manic energy.

I pinch myself to see if this is all fabricated; to see if this is the humming in my head; to see if my quiet existence has somehow created this world that defecates itself right before my very eyes.

I see the pinch mark, pink and white, between the hairs on my arm, and still the same.

A dream world waiting to end.

A cold beer pressed against my forehead provides brief respite and I down it, scolding myself for being such a closed minded fuddy-duddy. Life's a short, once-in-a-lifetime experience that should, perhaps, be lived to the max taking no heed from the dangers of yesterday. Two women who can modestly be described as glamour models approach me and offer me 'some of the good stuff'. Now there's so much of the supposed 'good stuff' floating around that I hesitantly appeal for clarity on what exactly the 'good stuff' is. A small packet of white powder bound haphazardly with a grey elastic band is produced from God knows where and dangled in front of my face. Now under normal circumstances I would feel exceptionally privileged that two such magnificently manufactured creatures approached me with such an offer, but in this happyland

I put it down to the male female ratio and the fact that everyone is off their respective faces on something. And I'm a new face.

The girls lead me into a small, abandoned study and splash the off-white powder all over a dark oak table. They take turns to snort the stuff using a rolled up note without taking the time to separate and chop it into lines. It's as if they're taking drugs as a junk food, the abundance having little or no impact on presentation or conservation, the only important factor being consumption. After a few loud snorts the moment of truth arrives and I take the note and sniff a load into my brain taking care not to blow out and splash the stash all over the Persian carpet. For an instant the burning on the right side of my face makes me feel as though I've had a stroke and then the warmth kicks in. Or maybe I'm lying and nothing kicks in, only societal and Hollywood indoctrinations ensuring we all feel the same as flowerchildren while we embrace the 'good stuff'.

The real feeling emerges like a lonely pile when one of the girls presses her lips onto the table and moves towards me, her white lipstick ready to harpoon me. I'm not quite sure how or why it happens but this girl's lips are on top of mine and then I no longer have lips because they're so numb that I'm scared to talk in case I swallow her. The other one, I think, has me inside her: there's a sensation down near the captain, but for all I know it's my imagination. It has to be. I think I try to speak a few times before having the most wonderful drag of a cigarette in the history of mankind, every nerve and taste bud alive and erect in my being.

Then I'm in swimming trunks and can feel women hanging off me like hooked fishes and running their hands over my stomach muscles and nibbling my eyelashes and laughing way too loud next to my ear and splashing me.

And suddenly I understand how easy it is to run away from manic land to happy land.

It's an excuse.

An aphrodisiac to escape the pain and noise.

The paranoia suddenly grabs hold of my throat and begins squeezing, suffocating the air from my lungs as Bama enters my skull through the front entrance. I jump out of the pool much to everyone's hilarity and speed up the stairs to see if she's okay. The calming effect of the drug takes hold as I approach the door. It's slightly open now and everything around me unexpectedly acquires an unnerving haze. Something seems amiss or the drug is making me believe that something is amiss. I can taste the air and it tastes filthy and fetid and horrible. I can hear a consistent noise behind the door but it's still dark inside. This I know because all light at this stage sets my neurons on fire. I push hesitantly at the door and slip in sideways without noticing what is transpiring.

There's someone else in the room and I can see that it's a thin man. As my eyes fight to adjust and focus, the image clear then blurred, blurred then clear, I see two figures, one moving. One on top of another. Thrusting. Then he stops, sensing that someone else is in the room, so I crouch down behind a cabinet. And a voice.

"That you Bryan? Bryan? You wanna come join in here? This dummy bitch isn't even awake to enjoy me sticking my dick in her arse. I think it's the young blood keeping me lubricated here," he laughs and gives a few more thrusts. It's dark enough for me to get away with this, I think.

"Yeah Jamie, it's me Bryan. Get her ready, I'll be right in," I say, slipping into the bathroom without turning the light on. I see Jamie more clearly now as he turns an unconscious Bambi onto her back, her arms and legs as limp as a ten-year-old rag doll. He then begins punching her in her face in an effort to revive her and I can hear each sickening thud against her bones echo through my soul. He then shoves his fingers into her mouth and nose yelling, "Hurry the fuck up Bryan, I'm getting bored!" He looks as though he's trying rip off her tiny erect nipples and just as he's leaning down to what can only be bite one off I react.

I approach from behind and scoop his neck just inches from her bare chest between my forearm and bicep dragging him from the unconscious girl and towards the bathroom. He's quite strong for a boyband member and can't quite comprehend why his fellow band member is doing this. But I can smell the booze and drugs as my face is right beside his and he's giggling a bit, carelessly believing this to be just another chapter of a bad trip.

But it's not.

So he stops struggling.

And allows himself to be dragged to the toilet.

Jamie James.

The only one who can sort of sing.

The Mouth.

In the bathroom he opportunely passes out from the exertion around his neck and I take his pulse just to make sure that I haven't killed him.

Yet.

And there's a beauty about my situation now: I'm calm.

Everything is happening for a reason now.

There's a boyband member lying on a bathroom floor in front of me with a young girl's blood all over his penis and his fingers and the humming in my head disappears.

I'm now holding the cutthroat and it feels as though I was raised to yield one even though I've never actually used one.

Cutting into the flesh of a tongue is difficult because you have to hold the tongue with one hand and cut into the warm pink speckled texture with the other, almost like cutting into a fish from the side. But the tongue is not sufficiently erect to make a clean slice so I saw into the flesh, the blood squirting all over my hands and wrists. The pressure suddenly gives way as the blade skews off to the side, dissecting only a half-moon shaped sliver off the tongue. I've still got the bit that's connected tightly between my thumb and forefinger and the more I squeeze the more the bleeding stops as though I'm acting as a clamp.

I don't think I'm satisfied at only getting a tongue sliver so I reach onto his mouth and try to dry his tongue with my hand so it will be easier to hold. His tongue is conveniently long which suits my task, but the muscle is still too slippery now that it is bleeding profusely. My impatience gives way to a revelation as I pull the tongue out as far as possible and slam his jaw upwards with the heel of my hand. The teeth embed themselves way further up the tongue than I could have ever hoped to get, but still the majority remains attached. Another smack sees the capped teeth cut right through the tongue and more belligerent bleeding ensues, making the boyband member look as though he's a vampire demon vomiting blood. The tongue chunk clumsily lands on the bathroom floor and I'm expecting it to wriggle around like a fish on the shore. When it doesn't, just sitting there motionless; a bird dropping, I get slightly paranoid and pick it up, shoving it into my back zip-up pocket. I shove the smaller bit I sliced off earlier down Jamie's throat, pushing it down his trachea with two of my fingers, then jamming a toothbrush handle down with water, making sure his tongue stump doesn't get in the way.

Get the matter as far down as possible.

One of two things will hopefully happen if and when

he wakes up. Either he will involuntarily swallow the bit or choke and spew it out. Either way he will be missing a very important and potent weapon of his.

His quick tongue.

Now in three mutually exclusive segments.

The Mouth.

Getting the blood off my hands as well as the toothbrush and cutthroat is quite simple because the excessive amount has meant that it hasn't had time to dry, so its fluidity spirals down the drain and is gone. Jamie begins to stir and I can hear noises from Bama in the bed which sound like painful sobbing, so I make haste after a quick check to see that no blood has splashed anywhere on my face. Looking into the mirror with a tongueless boyband member on the floor below you, who has recently raped an unconscious teenage girl in a mansion that would put most Columbians to shame is a healing experience. I can see a different calm in my eyes, the light above the mirror making the green bits sparkle as never before. I step carefully over the now dark pool of blood and exit the room as though I was never there.

When I hear the inevitable scream from upstairs I'm fully clothed playing patty cake with two praying mantis-like females in a triangular bathtub with water jets bubbling in a hundred directions. I'm not in the tub because I'm getting rid of any traces of me being upstairs, oh no, I'm in there because I'm a crazy cat who loves jumping around and acting bizarrely along with all the other degenerates tripping of their faces. Everything that was upstairs with me is now soaked. Including Jamie's core bit of tongue that now flaps around inside my pocket, safely contained by a trusty steel zipper.

The commotion upstairs sends an unnatural silence across the house as everyone pricks their ears up as the tone goes from exhaustive joviality to anticipatory uncertainty. Bryan shoots down the spiral staircase and looks as though he's enjoying the moment of being able to shock everyone by telling them what's happened.

No shoot the messenger here, just hold your mouth and seek to comfort.

"There's been an accident upstairs," he says, shaking his head and looking downwards with an incredible level of copied concern. "We'll be calling the ambulance as soon as all this shit has been cleaned up, so please clear the fuck out as soon as possible."

"What's happened?" someone yells from a bar counter.

"It's Jamie. He's had an accident. He's bitten off his own tongue."

CHAPTER 33

BEAUTY IS IN THE EYE OF THE TOWELHOLDER

I'm so preoccupied with blowing saliva bubbles from my tongue in a long-jump style me-on-me Olympics that I nearly don't hear the door squeaking open followed by the click of the cubicle lock next to me. No sound emerges, not even the panicky metallic grasping of a belt buckle with the accompanying slap of thighs against the unsteady toilet seat. Just silence and what sounds like deliberate soft breathing.

I notice a small inscription on the loo roll holder beside me. I think it's been there for a while inscribed with a paperclip because the lines are exceedingly narrow and some of them taper off in fishing hook shapes. It reads *Fuck this place* which makes me think that inspiration levels here are just below subzero.

My visitor remains silent so I finish up with a couple of *just-to-make-absolutely-sure* wipes and flush, sincerely hoping that my excessive use of toilet paper will go slippy sliding down the porcelain shaft as opposed to sit in a mushy pulp for the remainder of the afternoon.

It's one of those lacklustre days that go so slowly you wish you'd fall asleep and wake up the next day so the regular monotony can be replaced by something slightly different. It's been just over a week since I made Jamie James bite his own tongue off. It's also been just over a week since I felt I was making a difference in this world; a difference among the movement.

But everything's tapered off again and I'm empty inside. The press and the band have had a field day from the publicity. A few evenings ago hundreds upon hundreds of teenage girls gathered with flowers in Hyde Park to mourn the loss of Jamie's tongue. Most were sobbing hysterically, clutching their lower jaws and weakly fighting back bouts of tears and emotion.

No more Coastal Love for now.

The UK tour cancelled.

And the band too took the story to the cleaners saying Jamie fell while helping a female friend into the bathroom, biting off his tongue as he hit the ground. Bryan even managed a few tears on national television saying, "He's like a brother, man, and we'll stand by him no matter what. Coastal Love needs to reflect on this horrible, horrible tragedy…

Sniff

…and regroup. For our fans. For the people who love us.

Sniff.

It's the least we can do."

Coastal Love is hosting a little known children's game show tonight and Bryan has invited me to attend and hang out with the band backstage. I'm not even sure if I can make it as I've promised Her that I'll look at new bathrooms but ultimately decide to attend based on cracking my monotonous egg into a thousand tiny pieces in an effort to make a sickly omelette.

My life as Manfred's right-hand-man; his bitch in essence adds to the boredom like a cruel wind in a barren desert. Even though lately he seems distracted, almost distant. Or like he's pretending to be distant. Or maybe it's just because he's not around much lately, our initiative complete. At first all that pushing finances around was an annoying diversion, now its absence is leaving an unnerving hole in my daily grind. Perhaps I should talk to Manfred but something is telling me not to. He might still be pissed about the coffee machine incident and still willing to use it against me to ensure my loyalty. What's the worst that can happen if I leave him to his own devices? I've always felt that Manfred would play an important role in my life and this seems the perfect taste from which to raise my arms, place them behind my neck and enjoy the cool liquid.

I'm alone in my office and feel alone in the building. It's quiet even for a Tuesday. A trip to the coffee machine for old time's sake sees me run into no one worthwhile. Not even the new girl with the undeviating smile is around to brighten my day.

Smile at me!

Threaten me!

Blackmail me!

Stimulate me!

Find me out!

Just something!

Bring purpose!

My little stint of irritation sees me spill coffee on my white shirt as I make my way back to my office. The brown liquid quickly disseminates through the fibres and I feel that slight violent ache that seems to rear its ugly head when trivial and stupid actions intervene to tighten the proverbial sphincter. It's as though the anger's returning again which is just what I thought I was trying to cure. It's as though life annoyingly holds all those little deterrents; those little probing occurrences that matter as much as a chipped nail in a holocaust. But they still exist and they make the humming in my head worse until sometimes I'm tempted to raise my hands to my ears and tear the hair from the side of my head. And I thought it was getting better. As though my anger was now the calm that had a purpose. As though it was channelled towards the real problem.

Channelled towards the holocaust.

Not the chipped nail.

So it worries me that nothing in me is responding. The post tongue extraction euphoria was something special. Something very special. But since then everything's reverted back to normal. It's as though I'm waiting. As though planning is too boring and the only substitute is fate. Which I have to wait for. Like a subservient spouse. So the interim equals a plethora of excessive boredom until the next fix comes and life hopefully becomes that bit clearer and people understand the picture in its entirety.

The message, I suppose, for society.

And young people.

Impressionable people.

The Face.

Bryan greets me at the ostentatiously decorated studio with the usual amount of false jubilation and fervour. He gives me the standard bear hug topped off by grabbing both my cheeks, shaking them and saying

"You" followed by a cupped tap on the back of my neck. I look back at him, pointing my hand in the shape of a gun saying "No, you" before exchanging a couple more minutes of pleasantries which revolve around Bryan.

Backstage I run into Jamie and the rest of the band who are fidgeting nervously in Brady's dressing room. They hardly notice me as I'm among a hundred other busybodies ranging from hair stylists to makeup artists to stagehands to costume advisers to refreshment assistants to forehead patting executives to arse wiping trainees. Someone mutters something about "Bryan's friend again" and I know it's not Jamie because he's not talking that extensively and when he does it sounds more like a rendition of the winning entry of the special Olympics opera. I think it's PJ Glow, the gay one with the long hair, but can't be sure because he's just spat in his hair stylist's face and thrown a curling tong across the room. I watch the embarrassed stylist try to calm the situation down after wiping the light yellow globules from her lips and eyes.

The Face. Spit from the Face. Not spit in the Face.

The commotion begins to wind itself up as the director yells, "On in thirty" and Floyd attempts a new spin on his toes which looks copied and Brady is admiring his pectorals in the rectangular mirror, each one jerking upwards as he tenses in spasmodic succession. Bryan comes and goes, checking his hair and makeup and getting an earful from PJ Glow who is actually glowing now, the anger illuminating his face like a red light bulb. The poor stylist looks terrified, glancing around the room for the support that will never exist.

"Get this bitch out of here now!" yells PJ. "I need someone who's done a little more than shave a sailor's arse hair for a living. Get me someone who knows hair! Fuck off back to hair school, you bitch! Fuck off! What do I always say? What? Say it with me – *old-fashioned hairspray*, not fucking gel spray. That's the only thing that works for me. Look at me – I look like a fucking bell!"

The stylist wisely says nothing, apologising profusely with humble bows and approaching PJ like a wounded dog. The rest of the dressing room take not an iota of notice at this hullabaloo as though it's just another day in the life of a vain boyband. PJ's campness becomes magnified, campnified if you will, as he descends into a rage: the rolling eyes, the click at the end of each sentence and the hands on the hips. He's grabbing at his hair now, scrunching it and dropping it in hopeless despair.

"Just fucking get out of the dressing room. I've had enough. Oh God, I'm on in twenty minutes and I look like this. Get out!" he finally yells, trying to kick the poor girl as she scrambles towards the yellow door. In the background the stamping of little feet on wooden floorboards signifies the arrival of the children who make up this week's game show contestants.

PJ begins smearing some hair product through his

ends and then massages a load of something else into his roots. He's trying to avoid his hands shaking from the severe time constraint: only fifteen minutes to do his hair. After half a dozen more products and ten more application methods he strolls over to the cupboard to retrieve a full bottle of good old-fashioned hairspray. The gold canister glints in the bright artificial light of the dressing room, the picture of a woman's full hair almost looking as though it's flowing. PJ looks at the can with a certain amount of satisfaction, almost as a soldier would look upon his weapon before going into battle. He shakes the can furiously and then begins to spray all around his mane, holding his other hand over his eyes without letting up on the constant jet stream. The miasma cloud sends most of the dressing room inhabitants coughing and edging away which sees a large gap form directly behind his chair.

The next few seconds were about as quick as a slow nod and about as deliberate. My movement into the gap behind PJ is hardly noticed as is the cheap red plastic lighter in the shape of a chilli concealed in my dry palm. I see his highlighted locks hanging down behind the back of his chair and he can't see me because his hand is up over his eyes. The first flick is too far away from the hair and nothing happens. But the second is timed to perfection because a split second later I'm on the other side of the room watching with the rest of the onlookers as PJ does the involuntary Lambada between all corners of the dressing room.

It's amazing the effect when a spark creates a tiny flame which is held just below a mass of hairspray-coated strands. It catches and shoots a spectacular orange ray up the length of the hair followed by a purple smoke as the hair begins to cook. The smell is instantaneous: burning hair, almost like burning rubber.

No one is sure what to do. There is no visible water in the area and no one thinks to smother the blaze, so PJ Glow's head burns and his scalp begins to bubble because he can't extinguish the peacock-like flame. Some droplets of liquid hairspray catch alight on his forehead which he tries to wipe away only making it worse by smearing the burning flesh across his forehead. And suddenly he's not so good looking because the hairspray is catching everywhere, his cheeks the next to burn. I'm not quite sure if his nose is spared but it seems intact when someone throws a towel over his head and pats the fire dead with cushions.

A pillow fight.

With the Face.

And for a change there's no noise. Everyone stares in disbelief, some with raised hands to mouths, some hiding behind others, afraid of the sight about to be revealed from the smouldering towel. He's not moving; motionless, with just his hand twitching and equally terrified to unravel the towel. One of the stagehands rushes in and begins tugging on the towel to relieve the reluctant prisoner, who lets out a yelp and a murmur which sounds like: "Stop! You're going to rip my fucking face off!" It seems as though the towel has fastened itself to PJ's skin, the burning hair the adhesive in this welded closed effect. Still the smoke uniformly rises from the lone figure. Still the onlookers look on in dismay and shock.

The ambulance eventually arrives and the children are sent home, their curiosity levels at fever pitch. PJ leaves on a stretcher, still wrapped in the pale pink towel and still silent in a desperate attempt to preserve his mouth which creates a bubble as he breathes into the towel and is wielded past me. There's a piece of burnt skin wrapped in blackened hair which I pluck deftly from the side of the stretcher, shoving it innocently into my pocket, hopeful that no one's spotted my collector's habit.

"Terrible tragedy," I say to Bryan who is standing beside me looking as though he's thinking about something else. "What do you think happened?"

"I think this is the perfect time."

"Perfect time for what?"

"You won't say anything."

"Of course not."

"It might just be the perfect time for a launch. The launch of Bryan K as a single artist. A solo career, Paton. A solo career."

CHAPTER 34

DON'T CROSS THE STREAMS

I watch as my urine stream zigzags along the vertical wall of the white urinal basin in the gent's toilet of a trendy bar in the city. There's only the slightest hint of yellow in my urine almost as though it's the ribbon on a parcel, giving it definition and form. There's no one next to me despite the bar area being uncomfortably full, which means I am able to let the stream flow without the added stress of approaching and not performing.

It's, I suppose, like not being able to get it up.

Stage fright.

It's the feeling of realising that you have to push

using your sphincter muscle. The one shot you've got is at that moment when it's supposed to flow. If you lose that, zip up and ship out before your prolonged stay is over, it just makes the self-induced humiliation worse. Not that anyone, I'm sure, gives a shit. It's not like they return to their friends and lovers and point you out across the smoky room as the guy who couldn't piss on cue. It is a nice feeling though, when those first few drops emerge like oil and one more push sees the stream gain momentum until your fish mouth of a hole spews forth in proud delight.

Someone entering the gents disturbs my concentration and I focus on trying to squirt an oblong piece of chewing gum, which I've dropped in the urinal, down the drain. It's one of those pressure situations because I only have a maximum of forty seconds of my wee left and the gum is dangerously close to being manoeuvred into the perfect position down the grate. Time is running out, I can feel it, and the heavy bald man trying to piss next to me makes it harder. He's too pissed to get stage fright and spouts forth with little regard for the imposed proximity. I move slightly to the left which means my gum trajectory is slightly disadvantaged. The thought of not succeeding is not an option here and I base the entire rest of my life's happiness on getting the white indented gum down the drain. It's almost there. Almost! But I'm almost out!

Bingo! It slips down like an expensive oyster just milliseconds before the stream's tension goes from a straight line to an oblong arc. The dickhead next to me staggers out without washing his hands which not only annoys me but also gives me a fantastic idea.

Staggering home that night after another uneventful night of meaningless chat and boring stories with so-called friends, I pass the beggar whose drinking habit I tried to curb. I begin to wonder whether I'm making any difference at all, and in despair drop a couple of twenty pound notes onto his lap saying, "Go get pissed," the man passing out without the slightest acknowledgement. I pass all my favourite fast food joints and resist them, which is worrying because I can feel my stomach is empty apart from beer and the odd bloody Mary. Swishing around in my gut like toxic urine.

Getting the key to fit the front door is a chore as the alcohol seeps into my brain and begins to make me question where I am. I recheck that I'm on the third floor of the correct apartment block and eventually slide the key down the lock's throat in triumph. I try to be really quiet as it must be at least three in the morning but only manage to rip the bathroom light cord which could be argued is not my fault. Drinking a jug of water only succeeds in bloating me further and still food remains a nauseating alternative. I strip off in the lounge and even manage to brush my teeth with my finger before making my way through to the bedroom.

There She is. As innocent as the first time I laid my eyes upon Her. Curled up delicately in a ball and clutching Her pet toy dog George. Her eyelashes are visible in the murky streetlight and seem to be painted down the top curve of Her cheekbone, almost stretching down towards Her collarbone. She's doesn't hear me lose hold of the door as it clicks shut. Her breathing seems harmonious, almost as though there's an old classical tune playing in Her dreams. I wonder what She is dreaming about. Am I still the one who steps into Her dream like an insistent salesperson? After all that's happened?

The curve of Her lower back glints from the tiny smear of sweat as She stirs, opens Her eyes for a moment and then turns from Her side onto Her back. She's perfectly naked and for once I do feel lucky having this creature as my own. For no apparent reason, perhaps the alcohol, I feel my throat swell and a bout of tears form at the bottom of my eyes. Instinct makes a futile attempt to hold them back but something just allows them to flow down my cheeks and onto the wooden floorboards. I sniff which gives Her a fright as She sits up in bed clutching the cover under Her chin.

"You okay, baby?" She mutters, half-comatosed.

"Come to bed." I wipe the tears from my face with my back turned and blow my nose with a tissue from the shelf. A welcomed breeze cools my forehead before I slump into Her warm embrace and enter a safer existence.

"Look after me," I say as alcohol induced sleep gets me into a half nelson and the heaviness of my eyelids wins the battle.   She says nothing, breathing more heavily now and letting off a little wind before kissing me on the forehead and saying, "Just be good to us."

CHAPTER 35

RED WINE, ORANGE SUNSETS, YELLOW CIGARETTES & A THIN BLUE LINE

"Have you told your wife?" I say.

"Not yet, but I'm making progress."

"Progress."

"Is there an echo in this room?"

Suddenly I respect Jonathan a little bit more after that

chopsy comment. He sees the approval in my eyes and I don't even have to tip my head and raise my eyebrows. There's a different man in front of me.

"You're going to counselling?"

"Yes. And to a good counsellor too."

"And she knows you like men?"

"Well not exactly. She knows I would entertain the thought of being with a man."

"You've got a lot of work to do."

"You see I do love her. And I love our children. And I love her for giving them to me. But I don't love her physically."

"She knows this and accepts it?"

"I don't think she fancies me too much either, to be honest. She's confessed to having an affair with her personal trainer for a year now which actually makes me feel relieved."

"Good for you."

"So we've agreed to see each other often, almost live together, but not sleep together. Neither of us wants that anymore. But we don't want a messy divorce or to jeopardise the children's futures."

"Everyone's happy."

"Well there are a few logistics to work through but we're on our way. You want credit for this don't you?"

"I'll settle for a beer in a straight pub."

Straight Pub – Early Evening

"Have you seen Manfred lately?" says Jonathan as he for once sits upright with shoulders back and opens his eyes wide.

"Not for a long while. You seen him?"

"I was convinced I saw his Mercedes following me home one night but it could've been my usual paranoia. It's dark…

"Blue with mag wheels, yes. He also has a BMW I think."

"So it was him. I also noticed something strange the other day. Again it could be paranoia, but when I got into work my office room felt hotter. In the morning it usually has that slight chill, but this was different, as though someone had been in there. The mailroom boy had been working around the floor from the early morning and claimed not to have seen anything. He's a little bitch though and will do anything for a tenner."

"I gathered."

Jonathan blushes and it's not one of his usual girly blushes with the index finger placed coyly on his pursed lips. It's as though he's genuinely ashamed of what he was; what he resorted to to express his frustration of being a gay man in a loving heterosexual relationship. He takes a moment and I truly see the length he's come in realising that the journey of life is the length of a string and the more of that string you double back on itself and waste, the less time you have to be happy. The credit I wish to take for this is not only arrogant but it's pompous. Jonathan's closet exit was mainly to serve the selfish fulfilment of my destiny. But thankfully he's an innocent bystander who's turned his situation into something better.

"So the bitch seems not to have seen anything, but something's amiss. I feel the handles of my desk drawers and they're a tickle off steel cold. So I check to see if anything's missing. Everything is okay apart from one thing which I'm not completely sure about. Remember the picture you gave me of that guy who we tried to rob. Well the guy I robbed and who you…"

"Yes of course. What about him?"

"Well I kind of kept the picture."

"I kept the picture. What are you talking about?"

"I'll be honest, I was taken by his boyish good-looks, so I downloaded a few pics from the net. Bryan K. That's his name. Part of Coastal Love."

I feel more irritation than anger emerge near my sternum and then subside as I look at Jonathan's earnest face, his concerned mouth taught as though waiting for reprimand. I refuse to be one of the masses who has made this poor man's life one of cowering and making apologies for acting upon his normal desires.

"It's okay, Jonathan. No problem."

"You're not pissed off with me?"

"Why would I be pissed with you? I've downloaded plenty of pictures of Laetitia Casta. I think she's the most beautiful woman in the world ever – that's not my fault. And it's not yours that you think Bryan K's worth downloading. The real issue is why you believe

Manfred nicked it."

"I'm a man who's in touch with the things around him. I'd say someone was in there and whoever was took the picture. It's the one thing in my desk drawers that doesn't make sense. The rest is either work related or if not, some explainable personal paperwork like my mortgage or insurance. That picture of Bryan K was taken that morning. Of that I'm more than guessing. I'm not even going to ask what's been going on there. I've seen the news. All that stuff about Coastal Love."

I watch more intently than usual. The sun sets deliberately. A sunset in London cannot be a cliché because it's such a rarity. When that bright orange ball cuts through the smog on a temperate autumn evening it's as though you're seeing the world from a flying carpet ordained for your nirvana. Although it's not good for you, I look directly into the gaseous ball a hundred million miles away and thank her for keeping the good things on this earth functioning and running as usual. And sometimes not running as usual, but that's okay too.

I take a moment to sit on a crumbling wall flanking an imitation main street and light a cigarette before flicking it from my hand without breathing in. Not sure why. A breath through my nostrils tastes horribly of red wine and I suddenly feel thirsty as the last of the golden sphere mesmerisingly disappears behind a row of horizon buildings. This life thing's good, isn't it? We moan but things could be worse.

There's a vibration in my pocket followed by the Pumpkin's 'Today' which jolts me out of my moment like waking from a solar dream. It's my mobile phone and it's ringing. I'm tempted to leave it but have another weak moment and check who it is. I see Caroline's lonely name flashing on the turquoise screen, beckoning me to pick it up and save her.

Be her saviour.

Be her help.

Make a difference.

Get rid of the humming.

Because only kindness, fate and mayhem seem to be the antidotes.

"Caroline," I answer, this time lighting a cigarette for real, the phone clamped between shoulder and ear. "How goes?"

There's only silence at the end of the line.

"You okay? Caroline? Caroline?"

"I'm okay," she sniffs as though emerging from a shadow in a dim alley.

"What's happened? Are you hurt? Is it the shoulder? Do you need me to come over?"

"No, I'm okay. It's … it's David."

"What's he done? He hasn't hurt you?"

"He's got no need for me anymore. Well that's what he said anyway – 'There's no place for you in my life anymore, fatarse. You've served your purpose and frankly you're a dead-end. So do me a favour: take your moon crater pockets of cellulite and your stupid fucking lawn decorating mutt and fuck off back to lard land.' That's what he said, Paton. That's what he said right to my face. And he'd even given me the key to his house, which we decided to leave in the pot plant on my front porch. Just in case. Just in case I needed to see him. Or in case he lost his keys. I've still got them. He gave me his keys. He even gave me his keys. That was when he told me he loved me."

Saturday afternoon: one of the most cherished and loved periods in any working person's life. There is no threat, on either side, of deadlines or stress. Sundays can be horrible, the imminent onslaught waiting just around the corner like a rapist.

I'm on the balcony in my underwear breathing in the disjointed sunlight and smiling.

Because it's Saturday afternoon.

She's back in bed reading after a morning of baby nibbling and deliberate stroking.

Like two lovers again. This time truly in love.

And happy.

The sun is not yet hot enough to sting my shoulders as it weaves behind a cloud that looks like a hummingbird, the rays illuminating the beak as the wings flap motionless on either side. The wooden bench I'm sitting on creaks a little as I lie slightly further back and cast my mind away from anything real.

I awake to the clink of ice in a tall dark green glass

and Her standing in a white dressing gown at the balcony entrance. She smiles; a quick smile, just long enough to show Her teeth and squint Her eyes away from the brightness. I take Her hand and beckon for Her to come and sit next to me, but She pulls sedately away and wraps herself tightly in Her gown.

That's a major difference between men and women. Men are always too hot and women always too cold.

She returns to Her book, this time in the lounge as I hear Her pop a serene CD on the player, the treble marginally too high.

The way She likes it though.

A small thing that I used to worry about.

But not anymore.

There are more important things to worry about in life.

In fact the worry has dropped off considerably, as has the deafening humming, as the conquest has moulded itself towards fruition.

There's suddenly a commotion in the lounge as I hear a glass being knocked down as She hastily makes Her way to the toilet. The sun disappears for good this time as a large minacious dark purple cloud jumps in front and shrouds the giver of light for what seems to be the rest of the glorious Saturday afternoon. I wander innocently through, adjusting my pack on the way, to find Her hunched over the toilet with the remains of three scrambled eggs, now even more scrambled, in the bowl with gastric juice and orange juice to taste. She's pale and looks up at me and nods.

"Are you sure?" I say.

"Not yet, but the gap is growing."

"When was it meant to happen?"

"Three days ago."

"Should be like clockwork if you're on the pill."

"I know."

"Let's get a kit to make sure."

Thirty-four minutes later I'm pacing outside the toilet door as She holds a small cream pen-like contraption under Her pee stream. I hear the constant dribble and the gap followed by the dribble. I ask how She is before continuing my pacing. She's doesn't reply.

In two minutes and seventeen seconds She comes out holding up the contraption. There's a bright blue line perfectly dissecting the small screen that sits in the middle of the devise like a swimming pool in an aerial photograph. I take it from Her and uselessly squint at it as She collapses on the bed, Her face buried in the pillow. I lie down next to Her and stroke Her hair as the curtain blows raggedly at our feet. She turns over to reveal a couple of smudged tears.

"What are we going to do?" She asks, taking my hand to Her face.

"What do you think?" I reply, my heart racing out of concern for Her wellbeing.

"I don't think I can get rid of it."

"Then let's not."

We look at each other intently for the first time ever. She puts Her arms around me and squeezes me tightly which makes us both cry together as the heavens simultaneously detonate outside and a streak of lightning sprays a burst of light through the window.

"You'll make the most beautiful mother," I say. "We're on a new slope and this one's not going down. I love you."

CHAPTER 36

APPLY WAX EVENLY AND CONSISTENTLY THROUGHOUT

There are eight tiny cotton wool swabs fitted between each of my toes as I wiggle them to hopelessly scratch the tickling irritation that has begun atop the soft white foot pillow. I'm not meant to be looking through the cucumbers over my eyes but can't resist as a large woman files my toenails.

"I'm sorry," I say, "but I've got sort of a ticklish thing with my feet."

"That's okay," says the woman looking at me over the top of her green-rimmed glasses and smiling. "Should I hold them a bit tighter?"

"You read my mind. That's exactly what I used to say as a kid when my mum clipped my toenails: 'Hold tighter, Mum, hold tighter!'"

We laugh together in a polite manner as she moves towards the crescent shaped formation of calluses that has formed along the inside of my right root. This is the first pedicure in my life and I have to admit I'm loving it. I can't say I'd ever want to be fiddling around with pieces of flesh that stay concealed in a grungy sock for most of the day, but hey, it's either for you or not.

Like most things.

This pedicurist feels like the ultimate-best-ever-connoisseur of the foot world as she kneads the bottom of my foot, but I can't make certain judgements like that because I'm a pedicure virgin.

A pergin.

The thought of being a father ambles into my thoughts as I forget that someone is fiddling with my feet and doze into semi-oblivion. Holding a tiny creature that I've created is not the worst thing that can happen to a young man. I always thought I'd react differently if it wasn't planned. I always thought maybe I'd want to get rid of it and preserve myself. But it's different when you've fallen back in love with someone who you can't remember how you fell in love with the first time. And plus, things are different now. They've changed faster than rapidly. There is no longer the smell of men's cologne around for one.

I'm alone in a bright white almost angelic room with soft pink floral curtains, glossy magazines and an aura that forces one to do anything but not relax. I hear a regular commotion coming from next door and figure it to be Bryan who's banging one of the young assistants. I hear her scream softly and I wince, hoping her bellows are in ecstasy and not pain. The constant thudding becomes more audible when she says, "Ow, that was my head," to which Bryan replies, "Shut up and take me you little bitch." My pedicurist does not even flinch as though this is more commonplace than a rude taxi driver in London.

Bryan called me on my mobile in between breakfast and lunch on a Sunday and, without any better alternatives, I accepted his offer of a trip down to the salon for 'whatever I wanted including a facial – getting or giving'. I accepted on the provision I could rip his trachea out with my bare hands and feed it to his adoring fans and he just laughed.

He just laughed.

So I settled for a massage and a pedicure.

When I arrived, Bryan and Brady were ogling a new receptionist with a packed bosom who seemed a bit old and wise to be swept away by their immature charms.

When the 'Do you know who the fuck I am?' didn't work, Brady resorted to lifting his shirt and flexing his abdominal muscles, asking her what she thought. Again her disinterest with these schoolyard bullies sent their determination into overdrive as they started manhandling her. It began as pinches on her person and then trying to rip open her white nurses top. When they finally did, to reveal a hanging bosom contained in a conservative bra, she swung at one of them, threatening to call the manager. They dared her and eventually ended up both having their way with her which was a weak assurance that she would keep her job.

While all this went on I watched like a chump, helpless and impotent, letting my gastric juices splash onto my oesophagus and my nails dig into my palms until they bled.

But now I'm calm because I have a plan.

And my toes are sparkling and comfortable.

Brady the Body.

I deftly move onto my massage after thanking the woman, who blushes and grins. The masseuse is another kettle of fish completely with a more than generous portion of forced up cleavage bubbling over her white top like the coming of a miniature tide. She asks me to take off my clothes and offers me a blowjob to warm me up. I refuse but thank her anyway. The dialogue goes something like this –

Masseuse: "Hi sir."

Me: "Paton."

Masseuse: "Would you like me to suck you off before we begin? To get you in the mood? To warm you up?"

Me: "No, that's very kind, but I'll stick to the massage. How long have you been doing this?"

Masseuse: "How long have I been a masseuse?"

Me: "No, how long have you been, uh, providing alternative services?"

Masseuse: "I'm not a hooker. I used to be. This sure beats big hairy old men strapping on a dry condom and asking me to talk dirty to them. Now I get guys like you coming in. You're a friend of Bryan's right?"

Me: "I suppose. Does he often bring friends because this doesn't exactly look like a place where a person pays for services? What's your name?"

Masseuse: "Holly."

Me: "Nice name."

Holly: "You don't pay directly for the services. I mean, you can, but it's not exactly the norm. It's all part of the package. A special service for special clients. There's an annual fee I think which is high because most of our clients are the rich and famous. So they come here and they get what they want from whom they want."

Me: "Do you know the band? Coastal Love?"

Holly: "I think I've slept with all of them. Well at least blown them all anyway. I know Brady the best, but I'm not his favourite. He likes Daniela, the one who waxes his back. I can always hear them down in room 3G. Even though the boss tells us to keep it down. But Daniela's a bit loud and Brady's a bit rough. He likes to slap the girls around a bit. Sometimes it's playful, other times more than playful."

Me: "Has he hurt you before?"

Holly: "Not badly. As I said, Daniela's his favourite. But she's sick today. I think it's flu or something. The new girl's doing the waxing today, the receptionist. I think her name is Felicia, but I can't be completely sure. Would you like Jasmine oil to open up your lungs?"

So as Holly goes to work on my back, kneading and pressing in all the right places and my face flattens against the soft towel, I begin to drift to a better place when a loud yelp emanates from down the corridor which makes me arc up with a jerk.

"Holly will you excuse me for a second," I say, slipping a towel around my waist. "If you don't have any more clients in the next half hour will you wait for me right here? I want to continue this."

"Sure, but can I quickly sneak outside for a smoke break? It won't take more than ten minutes."

"Perfect!"

"Where are you going?"

"I've got to make an emergency number two if you know what I mean."

Sure enough the noise is coming from 3G where supposedly Brady the Body is having his back waxed. The rest of the corridor is silent and the plush carpet absorbs my footsteps without announcing that I'm tiptoeing towards the room. I arrive at the door and lean forward to hear what's going on. The door is shut and the 3 is slightly higher than the G, the copper in no need of a coat of polish. The noise starts up again.

"Oh stop fucking crying will you," I hear Brady saying accompanied by a slight whimpering. "I've already saved you your job, now don't make me call the boss. He should have told you I like it this way. I'm sorry okay. I'm sorry. Just hurry the fuck up with the waxing. And where's my eye cream? I'm meant to have my facial skin and eyelid cleansing while you wax my back and chest. Stop fucking crying! Jesus! I wish you'd just fuck off and bring Daniela back. This is bullshit. I'm paying a lot for this service. Do you know how much I'm paying? Do you? Do you know how much I'm paying to receive shit treatment and a whining little bitch on the floor? Get the fuck up and get the wax going, come on."

"The wax is not at the right temperature," she whimpers. "I've got to heat it up a bit more. I thought we were doing the face and eyes first."

What follows is a persuasive thud that makes my teeth chatter and I force myself not to imagine what has just transpired in order to preserve my composure.

"Just get the fucking eye pads on me and fuck off until the wax is ready! And turn the wax as high as it can go – am I the fucking beautician?"

I hear her adjust the wax dial and scuttle towards the

door so I dive sideways, landing in an unprotected nook partly shadowed by a spiral staircase looming above. Felicity, or whatever her name is, emerges from the room with a dribble of blood from the corner of her mouth and clutching her top which is torn to shreds. Luckily she heads the other way, leaving the door ajar as she exits. I decide to enter.

The door squeaks enough to make Brady stir a little as I deftly pop my head around the smooth yellow painted edge. The room is sparse apart from a naked man and a bulbous pot of wax on a green shelf jutting from the wall above his head. He's on his back with his hands lifelessly at his sides with large circular cotton pads covering his eyes. He's not sleeping because he continually scratches the inside of his left nostril with his right hand. It is these sorts of details you notice when your heart is pounding inside your ribcage and your uvula is dry, pressed against the roof of your mouth like a pancake stuck on the kitchen ceiling after an adventurous flip.

I shouldn't really be looking but notice that his penis has an abnormally thin shaft with a disproportionate helmet resting innocuously on his lower stomach. It is one of the uglier penises (or is it peni?) I've seen in my life and notice its mushroom like qualities as I manoeuvre my entire body into the room and close the door to a fraction of being completely shut.

His breathing seems to slow and become more regimented. I watch him closely as I edge forward inch by inch. When I'm about a foot away I stand on an unsuspecting glossy magazine, which crackles under my foot and Brady contracts a little more violently than I would have hoped.

"Hurry up, you bitch," he mutters almost as though from the realms of a wet dream and raises his hand towards his eye patches. There is nowhere to hide; no corner to dive into or crowd to blend into; no drugs to blame anything on or brolly handle to rely on; no twenty pound note to burn or brothel to experiment with; no baseball bat or fragmented pen; no hopeless accomplice or devious plan.

Nothing.

Just me in a room alone with a boyband member.

At first it's in slow motion until he lifts the white object from each eye and focuses on me standing in the centre of the room with nothing on but a signed towel. I'm frozen; speechless; helpless as he sits up on his elbows and raises one nostril in absolute confusion. The large pot of wax on the shelf above his head lets out a pressure bubble which momentarily lifts the lid from the rim spouting a warm gush of wax smelling air. The outer rim is crusted with dark brown wax and traces of tiny black hairs.

A paste.

"Whatever the fuck you and Bryan have got going on mate, I don't want any part of it," he says fidgeting and looking for an escape route. "You can stay his bitch. I'm not into big men."

"I'm not here to sleep with you," I say. "I'm here to punish you for your cruel and undeserved assault on the modern world."

Pulling the pot onto his face is difficult because it's heavy and hot and because he tries to make a dash for the door. The force of the pot stops him like a bullet as the lid flies off and the hot molten lava pours down his face and into his mouth. I have to hold him down with both hands to make sure the wax floods into his mouth and burns the inside of his throat. Watching a man choking to death on wax can be enlightening but not if your raison d'être is to ensure the death has something to do with the body. It turns out to be a great means of incapacitating the victim because he is unable to scream, the only sound now emerging from his throat, as I pull out the cooled hardened wax, a mere kitten's meow.

He's in so much shock that I can easily hold him down with one hand. His head is bleeding from the pot's decisive blow and the profusely pumping wound begins making a mess as the bed sheets can no longer soak up the liquid and it begins to spill over the side like a brown and red suffocating waterfall.

I know my time is limited before Daniela's protégé returns so I discard roasting his body in the accompanying sunbed and make quick work of finding a towel and lifting the large sizzling pot before dumping in onto Brady's stomach. The sheer weight of the object, even with half the wax spilled out, pins him like a butterfly to polystyrene, his fragile body folding upwards like the closing of a book. Laying the pot on its side provides the right touch as the metal burns through the skin of his stomach and seems to attach itself to his perfectly sculpted abdominals. It must be true what they say about the human body switching off before true pain sets in, because he jerks and sputters for about a minute as the wax flows out over his pecs and abdomen and the pot continues to singe its way through his flesh, the tiny bubbles making him look like Bubblewrapman. His eyes are now wide open and his whimpers rendered even more pathetic.

Brady the Body.

Lying atop a high wooden framed parlour bed.
Lying in a pool of wax and blood and his own shit.
The fear of death now real and an unhappy ending.
With a large metallic pot which has now burnt a hole right through him, the cavity a colourful mixture of muscle tissue and hairy wax.
I think I can even see his spine for a second, but it could just be a slimy bit of sinew.
A doctor would know.
With his insides on show I'm able to easily peel a piece of stomach tissue for my collection. It crackles as it peels down, the white sinew flicking splinters upwards in a sort of domino effect. Removing it is more difficult and it takes a number of tugs before I pull the piece free, holding it up triumphantly, keenly aware that

the smell of burnt flesh now fills the room and coats my exposed flesh like perfume.

Still the vacant aliveless expression directs a stare towards the happy little boyband stage in the sky.

Being alone in a room with a dead guy is weird. And I'm not overly keen to stay but something makes me take a step back from my masterpiece and admire. The accident value of this scene is priceless: all I have to do is break the shelf which is easy when armed with an elbow and fifty litres of adrenaline.

A broken shelf.

A hot pot of wax which has slammed onto his head and rolled down his front settling at his gut to burn a hole in it, leaving a trail of wax to cover the real point of entry.

His body covered in gently simmering wax.

His throat burnt out, muffling his pleas for help.

The pot holding him down.

Priceless.

Better than any normal salon visit.

Brady the Body.

My obsessive compulsive nature sees me wipe wherever my bare fingers might have touched before slipping out the room and sliding into home plate a couple of seconds before Holly returns, stinking of stale smoke and cheap, recently applied lipstick. Hopefully drowning out my stench.

"You had two cigarettes, didn't you, you naughty little minx?" I say. "Those things will kill you if you're not careful."

"Why are you sweating?" she replies.

"You know," I say, lacking a real response and turning to face her, my left fist clenched containing the only part of Brady that no longer exists outside his extermination chamber.

"Do you want me to now? I really wouldn't mind with you. I suppose I kind of want to," she giggles, undoing my towel and playing with a strand of hair as she lowers her head.

I succinctly refasten the towel. "The only thing I want you to do is stop smoking and fix this knot in my shoulder. It's been troubling me all week," I say as a scream echoes satisfyingly from down the corridor to greet both our bemused faces.

CHAPTER 37
MEN'S COLOGNE

A concerned face can never be overdone. When I answered the policewoman's questions I nodded with a wrinkled brow and an expression splattered with brusque concern. There was no hand raised to the mouth, the fingers straight and touching the lips; no 'Oh my God', just a helpful and attentive performance.

"If there's anything else I can do please don't hesitate to call on me."

Who knows if they suspect foul play. For me none of it was either foul nor play. Well, maybe a bit of play. A death in a boyband is nothing like a death in a family.

Bryan rushed off to make sure he looked good before the reporters, armed to the hilt with over-focussed camera lenses, arrived. I caught him practising crying, actually forcing the tears from his nictitating membranes like toothpaste from a tube. And mouthing "Brady, a true friend. Sorely missed. Already." And clutching his fist over his heart, not dissimilar to the way he would assemble harmony on a Coastal Love music video.

The ambulance arrived with sirens wailing, forcing through the reporters already gathered like a protesting mob on the lush footpath dissected lawn of the salon. I cannot rule out the possibility that Bryan tipped them off as another attempt to raise his profile and launch the highly and eagerly awaited solo career.

I'm blinded by the bevy of flash photography that erupts as the body is wheeled from the depths of the clean white building. Perhaps it's my imagination but I'm sure I can smell wax when he's carried past me mixed with the delicate yet poignant aroma of melted flesh.

Pockets of reporters disperse themselves around patrons and staff. I'm ignored for most of the time until a scrunch-faced woman with glasses that are too big for her triangular head asks me if I knew the victim to which I reply that I didn't. She's about halfway to asking me whether I heard or saw anything when she scuttles off towards a crying nurse.

I left further details with a policeman with a raspy

voice and a scar on his upper lip, feebly covered by a ginger moustache that seemed to grow around the scar in whirls. He took everything down with incredible care and precision and said he'd be in touch for further information.

At this exact moment I'm sitting with a wet underarm, the person responsible excreting tears and mucus onto my shirt as she enjoys the warmth of my arm around her and my head cocked onto the top of hers. I contemplate suffocating her as I put in another memorable squeeze to console her, not because of any ill feeling, quite the contrary: because I want to end her misery. Everything about this woman's life has and will be miserable. It's as though she has no hope and there's nothing I can do about it.

My presence in her life only seems to make things worse. There's never been anyone like me paying her this kind of attention and I think it confuses and frustrates her. She loves my presence in her life and because of my attention and unwavering kindness she loves my nature.

My being.

My being there with her now.

Letting her sob in patches into my armpit.

While I hold her and think about ending her life.

It would be quite easy I think. I'd take her further into my chest as I'm doing right now, patting her head and stroking the side of her face more and more gently as she slowly lulls into an emotional daze. I'd then either snap her neck back by grabbing under her solid chin and lifting upwards or I'd push her nose and mouth steadily flat against my chest until she began to struggle and flap her arms and all the life was squashed out of her.

Caroline sits up quickly which foils my supposed plan and goes against the deliberate nature of the scene. Her eyes are now properly swollen which only serves to further aggravate her narrow eyebrows and hide the bit of colour which her pimple-like grey eyes bring to her face. She's intermittently blinking in front of my face, dispelling more tears down her plump cheeks, some running into bits of matted, frizzy hair and absorbing immediately.

She nestles this time onto my lap, the silence still filling the room and the spitting rain allegorically mirroring the circumstances within. She loves me this woman and it kills me that I can't for just one second drop everything and take her in my arms, make love to her and try to fabricate a break from the tedium and unremarkableness endemic in her depressing life. I would but for a few criteria.

I'm going to be a father.

It would complicate this situation into something a soap opera would be scared to approach.

And I don't find one tiny bit of her attractive in *that* sort of way.

You know – *that* sort of way, where every second not

writhing naked with the person is like an eternity in hell. That sort of way only comes when you fall in love; when Her physical prowess and personality join together in your mind like a two-piece puzzle, the snap echoing through your brain.

I couldn't look past the double love handles.

Or the treble chin.

Or the quadruple breasts.

Or the quintuple bags under the eyes.

But in some strange, unerotic way I do love this woman and wish I could replace her life somehow.

Perhaps by murdering her.

Killing her to save her.

Killing Caroline to save Caroline.

On the way home I notice a burn mark on my forearm, which, after closer inspection, smells of wax. I wonder how long these scars take to heal and make a mental note to wear long sleeve shirts for the next couple of days. The activity on the street is characteristic of a Sunday: impersonal and sparse. I pass a group of kids with water pistols and an old woman rummaging through a trashcan, sucking the remains of a random straw. I see a poster for Coastal Love and actually have to stop.

While I'm standing outside my car another car slides past, spraying a fine film of water on my car and bellowing my favourite bandnameless song, the noise faint then momentarily loud and then faint as the car turns into another narrow street. I check on the radio and still can't find the song.

It must have been a CD.

The poster stares back at me, all their faces attempting to evoke some form of admiration. No one is around so I fish out a sharp object from the glove compartment, which turns out to be a rusted old screwdriver. With my left hand pressed against the top corner for leverage, I slowly and jaggedly scrape a cross over Brady's midriff, cutting through his exposed stomach and into the bright red shirt that hangs aimlessly on either side of his torso. I then scratch away Jamie's mouth to reveal another poster beneath, advertising some kind of moisturising facial soap. PJ's hair and face are the next to go leaving two remaining affiliates until my symphony is complete. I neaten up my edges and the effect is phenomenal: Brady (no longer) the Body; Jamie (no longer) the Mouth and PJ (no longer) the Face.

Coastal Love.

No longer.

When I enter my home a facet of the old days comes back to haunt me literally like a bad stench. She is home and I smell men's cologne all over Her as I hug Her. This eats me now, more than it used to. I put it down to imagination when I didn't smell it for a while but now it's all different. I'm to be the father of Her child and She still stinks of it. Just like She always has. Maybe I've been numb for a while and lured into a false sense of euphoric love, and maybe witnessing the boyband being knocked off like skittles has refocused my senses. Either way it's there: cheap men's cologne, sticking to Her skin like a rash.

She senses I know something as I pull away from the embrace and breathe the foul aroma deeply in. I'm not trying to give it away but I think She guesses as I turn my head to hide the annoying tears creeping into my eyes. I feel no longer like I know where I'm going, but rather I've suckered myself into something far bigger than I could have imagined. I almost hear the clap of the bear trap around my ankle as I realise I've let my guard down. Let myself be hurt.

The confused look on Her face as I leave the room to answer the phone is begging me to talk about my issue. But I cannot. It's not inside me to be humiliated and watch Her lie to preserve the family. I cannot face that so swallow hard before picking up the malignant telephone receiver and resign myself to the fact that I've made my own bed and thus rendered helpless to do anything but lie in it.

CHAPTER 38

JOIN THE DOTTED LINES

I get a surprise visit from Kitten at work, who has had a breast reduction and walks into my office confident, hair tied back, with glasses and a designer suit. My mouth turns down on both sides as I nod in complete approval and she performs a pirouette to show off the new her, mouthing, "The new me" before presenting both cheeks and plonking herself in one of the dark blue leather seats across from me.

"You can't smoke in here," I say as she pulls one from a silver case to light it. "So make sure you blow the smoke away from that sensor." I point to the far corner of the office. "How've you been?"

"If I say 'couldn't be better' I'd be lying. Things have been tough but slowly they're coming together. With a little help from the blood links."

"I don't follow."

"I took your advice, you see. I let go of the bullshit dream. I stopped letting myself be abused. No more Kitten and her breasts and her better than average blowjobs. Introducing: Grenada Gant. So I began working in a small boutique as a shop assistant and, after realising how much debt I was in, went back to sucking dick for a living, only this time it was the owner of the boutique rather than a director or producer. This kept me alive for a while and blackmailing him also paid a couple of bills until it all went a bit pear-shaped and his wife found out and divorced him and the cash dried up. I was desperate. Then a miracle happened. A small miracle. My mother died leaving me a small farm which turned out to be worth all my debts and a small boutique now called *Kittens*."

"You're lying to me."

"I'm not. Here's my card. I even have a steady boyfriend now and he's not a member of a band. He's an accountant. My accountant."

"So you don't miss the life? Miss the fast times?"

"Reporters still hassle me here and there, but no, this is the life I'm loving now. Even thinking of a few kids, but I'll have to bottle feed – these babies are shot to hell after all the work," she says motioning towards her modest chest and hint of cleavage while the mention of children sends my stomach into knots and makes my toes curl.

We head out to lunch at a cute deli just off Gloucester Road and Kitten orders a few bottles of wine which write off the rest of the afternoon in work terms sending my listening skills back into impending overdrive. We talk about her mostly and a bit about Coastal Love whom Kitten, sorry Grenada Gant (or double G), feels amazingly sorry for.

"It's all over the papers," she says. "People are saying they're jinxed. Jinxed to fail. That it's a sign for all boybands. That they're coming to an end; going out of fashion."

"I certainly hope so," I mumble under my wine.

"Pardon?"

"Is that right? So they're what? Bringing this on themselves you think?"

"Maybe someone put a curse on them. Someone like you, you little sorcerer," she says, pinching my rutilant cheeks from across the table. "Or Harry Potter. Look at this picture." She pulls a newspaper from her bag. "Some kids had a bit of fun scraping away bits of the band from a poster and it's made the front page. Look. It says that 'Jamie had the voice and he bit off his own tongue. PJ was the looks of the band and burnt off his face. Brady had the physique which saw a bowl of hot melting wax burn through his stomach. The big question now remains: who will be next?' These tabloids will string anything together to make a good story. What do you think?"

"I think if I was Floyd, I'd be making sure my feet are carefully looked after."

CHAPTER 39

I see
Manfred

I see Manfred for the first time in months and he shifts past me sideways, a long thin smile spread across his face like a wound. He's working the room, shaking hands with lots of pug-faced, swollen, influential men who nod and hold out their sweaty sausage-dog fingers waiting for the comforting grip of a hand.

Manfred doesn't seem to be smiling at me. He seems to be smiling towards me. His manner is, for the first time, unnerving because he's been avoiding me so effectively and his calm demeanour shows no sign of the panic-stricken man whose head was exploring the inner depths of the coffee machine.

I firmly believe I have most people in my life sussed. They are, after all, creatures of habit and follow a routine that drip feeds from their characters and serves to mould and construct a predictable animal.

A male lion walks nonchalantly downwind while the female executes the prey.

A male leopard mates and then selfishly returns to eat the young, his only deterrent an overprotective and thankfully often elusive female.

These creatures follow an opposite but distinct pattern.

One embraces family.

The other doesn't: the loner.

This behaviour ceased evolving a long time ago.

Now Manfred behaves like a lion on a lone crusade or a leopard raising cubs: he's calm, collected, confident and most disturbingly, careful. Since our relationship began he's always been the one to approach me. I've been the receiver, never initiating interaction or action. I don't do those sorts of things. I'm passive. I wait. So as I shift around the work cocktail party atop the second tallest point in London, Manfred deftly avoids me. And it's not as though I'm approaching him. I'm moving between platters, perhaps making myself available for him to bump into me and initiate something. At least then I can respond. Anything would do. Even a polite exchange would give me a little clue as to what he's up to.

All the way up at the top of Tower 42, we celebrate reaching our third consecutive profit target. If group communications are to be believed, we exceed the target by four million pounds which serves up a splatter of red wine stained grins, expensive cigars, and so much back slapping that I'm sure most will need wrist physiotherapy.

Before I swallow a circular piece of expensive cracker with bright orange salmon curled dexterously into a spiral, the gaps punched full of caviar, I take a millisecond to get unnerved when my eyes focus on Manfred talking to a group of woman executives in front of me. He doesn't look at me once and has the fighting females in a frenzied fit as he articulates a colourful story. Something is wrong for sure: it's almost as though he's gone through a complete transformation.

I think back to the Manfred yelling and screaming with his head stuck in a coffee machine. I think of the Manfred returning with the incident as his weak stick to beat me with while I followed his command; did the job at hand to the best of my ability. I think of the insignificant Manfred, the ultimate corporate cog good only for approving my salary and enforcing how my life should be about a higher purpose. I think of Manfred and this all seems out of place. With consistent determination Manfred Dill has always been obvious and blatant. Focussed on his one goal.

Obvious and blatant.

A colleague momentarily interrupts my train of

thought making a weak attempt to chat about the football last weekend which matters little to me. I focus on his young lips moving but take in almost nothing of the dialogue, just smiling, nodding and laughing on his similar cue. I cannot extricate Manfred from my conscious and for the first time in a long while I'm scared. I'm scared of what I don't know. I'm scared of not being able to control my own fate. I'm scared of the past frivolity of Manfred Dill and all his idle and insignificant actions. I'm scared of the bigger picture that now presents itself as an organised package in front of me, ready to strangle at the given moment or slice at the opportune time.

I am a pig waiting to be slaughtered.

I am a pig who knows he's next when he hears the screams of his fellow pigs in the execution chamber.

I am a pig waiting for the sensation of a metallic bolt being plunged through my brain so that I jolt and look around for a couple of seconds before falling limp and being packaged for consumption.

Manfred's consumption.

"Paton? What do you think? Paton? Are you alright?" I hear from a place far far away and excuse myself to splash water on my face in the bathroom. Luckily there's no one inside and I lock the door and stare into the mirror with my straightened elbows propping me up on the sink like an inebriated man. There are a few naked unwrapped soaps, the froth still tepid from a fresh lathering only moments prior.

Perhaps Manfred's.

My paranoia sees me stumble back to the gathering and down a few glasses of red wine, continually wiping my clammy and pale forehead with my forearm as Manfred calmly flits around, purposefully unaware that I fear him and what he's up to.

"What is your name, sir?" I hear behind me and turn to face a small waitress with a smooth forehead and oversized incisors. "Are you Mr Lafayette? James Lafayette?"

"No," I say, struggling to focus on her shiny forehead. "I'm Paton. Paton Stipps. But I- I know James. Is there anything I can help you with?"

"Do you know Mr Manfred Dill?" she says as the mere mention of the words send pins up my back and creates indigestion in my gut. Her quizzical expression must be addressed.

"Yes I know M-, um him."

A waiter shouts at the small student woman who glances anxiously around and then quickly back to me in desperation.

"I wonder if you could do me a small favour. There were two messages left at reception for your colleagues. I wonder if you could hand them on."

"Certainly," I say as she hands me two folded pieces of paper and scuttles off to grab a bottle of wine and keep the fluid flowing.

Manfred is about a long jump distance from me and the curiosity brings me back to a degree of composure and calmness. There are two pieces of folded paper in my paw, cocked towards my wrist in disguise. James is on the other end of the tower so I make my way to him with a slight detour for a top up of wine. He's grateful and says something about having to get home or he'll have no balls: his wife's been with the kids the whole day.

Manfred's back is towards me and I seem isolated so I turn around and open the folded paper, cupping the edges so as not to reveal the white of the material. It reads: 'Manfred Dill, your car is ready for collection' and is signed by the downstairs carwash.

Executive Cleaners.

That was exciting.

I reread the note just to make sure it's not an encrypted Nazi message coding the activities around the proposed assassination of the Queen Mother. I really am a pathetic fart as my eyes skim pitiably over the text: first right to left and then left to right. I chuckle to myself until my eye does settle on something familiar.

Something strangely familiar.

Something unnervingly familiar.

Something fuelled by my paranoia that, briefly subdued, now bubbles through my being awakening every living-breathing cell in my entire body.

His name: Manfred Dill.

Manfred Dill.

Manfred Dill.

Running away.

In the toilet.

Stalking me.

Watching my every move.

My every blink.

Moving towards a vehicle.

The handwriting is flat and leans to the left hand side of the page. There are capital letters interspersed between lower case letters in a spastic, random yet significant way. The 'M' is a capital. So is the 'R', both 'Ds' and the second to last 'L':

ManfReD DiLl.

But most importantly the 'R'.

The spacing of the letters leaves a gap between the 'f' and the 'R' and the leaning effect means both names almost appear as one, the two Ds reaching out towards each other like parted lovers. In under forty seconds the paper is crumpled in my fist and I'm down the 42 storey elevator and outside in the not-quite-fresh air with a wild excitement in my eyes as I hail a cab and head for Sidcup, flicking my mobile open.

"Hello."

"Hi Caroline, it's Paton. Are you busy right now?"

"No I'm not. Well, you are always welcome, I mean I'd never–"

"Caroline, listen carefully. I want you to start telling me everything about Dave. Dave Reddill."

CHAPTER 40

COVERUNDER

She is out shopping for any type of food that will stay down when the buzzer to our apartments sounds. I don't have a peephole so don't know who to expect when I open the door. A man and a woman stand confidently in front of me, my attention shifting straight towards the man's tie which is so mid-eighties that I expect him to be wearing leg-warmers too. The dark blue and light blue and white diagonal lines clenched together in a small knot below his Adam's apple send me into a kind of trance and I fail to see the woman reach into her pocket.

"Detective Constable Garden. And this is Detective Constable Venables," she says, flashing the appropriate identification in front of my vision. "Are you Paton

Stipps?"

"Yes," I say a bit too quickly following with the standard response, "How can I help you officers?"

"We would like to ask you a few questions," they continue the lines. "May we come in?"

The kettle boils and I pour the boiling water in towards the mocha java filter coffee: a bit much for cops, but hey, how often does this sort of thing happen in a lifetime? The finely ground coffee particles quickly absorb the water as the jug fills up, leaving a thick layer of brown grime which is shoved to the bottom by the plunger. I hear the two chatting but cannot make out the conversation which makes me hurry a bit and spill some milk on the sink.

"…feeling pain. It's here on the side of my chest. Too many…"

"Here we go," I interrupt. "Coffee. Help yourselves to milk and sugar." I motion towards the tray, ceramic milk jug and African sugar bowl with accompanying zebra handled spoon. They note the effort and nod in appreciation. I'm trying really hard not to do anything too obvious so calmly sit down and wait, saying nothing and merely staring directly, in a friendly way, towards my two guests. When they've completed the pedantic procession of coffee additions they both sit back in perfect unison and stare back. Still I say nothing. Just smiling. They start.

"You're probably wondering why we've come," says the woman: Garden.

Still silence.

"Well," she continues, "we're questioning people in connection with the death of Brady Mullet."

Two things grab me about the sentence and almost blow my cover – one, the words 'in connection with' which deserves the reply, 'Let's get outta here', the most overused movie line in history and two, Mullet! Pause for a minute. What a schoolboy affliction! You couldn't make that shit up. Still I say nothing as the back of my mouth dries up and my breathing becomes uncomfortable.

"I believe you are friends with his fellow band member Vernon Killick and were present when he died?"

"Which part do you want me to answer?" I finally say, regretting the overly confrontational tone as the words escape from my mouth.

"Do you know Vernon Killick, Mr Stipps?" says the man, adjusting his tie and my eyes.

"I don't believe I do, Officer."

"A K A Bryan K?" The letters spat at me from across my mail-ordered coffee table.

"A K A?" I say in an increasingly bad attempt to buy more time and clear my thoughts, potentially further aggravating the belligerent cloud now forming.

"Also Known As!" The woman this time.

"Ohhhh, okay. Yes I do know Bryan."

"Do you have relations with him?"

"Relations?"

"Are you friendly with him, Mr Stipps?" The woman again.

"I don't mean to be funny, but do you guys have the correct paperwork to be here? Do you have an order or a warrant?"

"We don't need one to question you," says Venables.

"No, don't get me wrong. I'd answer your questions regardless. I'm just curious as to your procedures that's all. Carry on. What else do you need to know?"

"Are you friendly with Vernon Killick, also known as Bryan K of the rock band Coastal Love?"

A rock band! I feel insulted and almost tempted to educate these two as to the true meaning of a rock band. Comparing Coastal Love to Pearl Jam is like comparing a rectal exam to a foot massage. All sorts of thoughts belch into my mind as their blatant ignorance fills me with anger and aggression. I could kill them. They don't look armed. I could pretend to get something from the kitchen and come back with a carving knife longer than either of their long faces and slice them up for their calling Coastal Love – a fucking boyband – a rock band! I'm just at the part when I'm slicing off Garden's nose and feeding it to Venables when one of their mobiles rings, snapping me out of my fantasy and forcing me to cooperate. 'This isn't a game,' I tell myself a few times until the phone call ends and the questioning resumes.

"I am friendly with Bryan K, yes."

"How did you meet Kill-, K?" says Garden as Venables excuses himself from the apartment to make a call.

"I foiled an attempted robbery. Just off–"

"Kings Road. Yes. We've got your description of the man."

"Did you get him?"

"No, we haven't yet."

"Probably not top of your list eh?"

"We treat every case with all available resources."

"Well he didn't get anything did he? So it's not really a true crime."

"How do you know he didn't get anything?"

"Because Bryan didn't report anything missing. We're friends, remember. I saved his book."

"And you reported a break-in a few months ago?"

"That's right. Two men broke into my house. The assigned detective's name was Smith or–"

"Smyth. You put those two boys in hospital for a long time."

"They weren't boys and I was protecting my girlfriend. They invaded my privacy and were hostile towards me. It's all in my statement."

"One of the men shits in his pants every time the door opens and the other stutters to the extent that he sounds like an old scooter. Did they deserve that?"

"I was defending myself and my girlfriend. No one forced them to break in. Do you think they'll do it again?"

"And where were you on the evening of Thursday the thirteenth of May this year?"

"I'm not sure. Can I fetch my palmtop?"

"No never mind, it's just that someone close to your description was spotted leaving a bus after an assault on four teens."

"Will this take a lot longer? I've got to be somewhere."

"And you are friends with Brady Mullet?"

"No I was not friends with Brady Mullet."

"So you didn't like him?"

"No I liked him just fine. I just wouldn't say we were friends. More an acquaintance. A friend of Bryan's."

"So Bryan and Mr Mullet were friends?"

"Yes, well they worked together, didn't they?"

"How many times had you been in contact with Mr Mullet?"

"Mr Mullet and I were not well acquainted. If I spoke to him a dozen times it was a lot. I saw him most of the times Bryan and I spent together."

"Were you present the day of his death?"

"You know I was."

"Did you hear or see anything strange that day? Anything out of the ordinary? Anything that wouldn't typify a day in the life of Paton Stipps?"

"Well I had a pedicure and a foot massage which were both a first."

"Did you have sex with anyone that day?"

"I beg your pardon."

"Did you pay anyone at the establishment for sex that day?"

"No."

"Did you know about the goings on at the parlour?"

"I gathered, yes."

"Yet you remained?"

"I wanted my feet done."

"Did you leave the building at any time?"

"Not during my stay, no."

"Did you see anyone leave during your stay?"

"I can't remember."

"Did your masseuse leave during your time there?"

"I think she might have. For a cigarette."

"So you were alone during that time. Did you leave the room?"

"No."

"Are you sure?"

"Positive."

"Where were you when the body was discovered?"

"Well I heard the scream during my massage."

"And were you the first to the body?"

"No."

"What did you see?"

"I saw Brady with a large pot on him and his eyes were open. And there was wax everywhere."

"How did you know it was wax?"

"I could smell it."

"So you know what wax smells like?"

"Yes."

"Like what?"

"Like wax."

"Were you in the room where he died?"

"I told you I went in to see what the commotion was."

"You did not tell me."

"I went in and consoled one of the nurses who was crying."

"Did you touch anything?"

"I can't remember. Probably."

"Thank you for your time, Mr Stipps, we'll be in touch."

CHAPTER 41

THE CLOT THICKENS

"Hey maaaaaaaaaaaaaaaaaaaaaaaaaaaan!" The American accent rings out like an alarm bell in the busy street. An old man crouched over a walking stick with a messy combover has nudged Floyd in his helpless haste to catch a bus. "Man, people are so rude, I mean, think of the damage this dumb-ass old dude could have done. My shoulder coulda been busted." I turn to look at the benign scuttling crab of a geriatric and wonder to myself how much force it would really take to bust a shoulder. I wonder what would happen if a shoulder of a full-grown man was placed between a large hydraulic industrial vice. How long would it take for the bones to crackle and crunch like cereal? How long would it take for the skin to squirt an uneven mixture of crumbled bone, blood and tissue? It would be quite an effect whatever the mechanics.

Floyd wears a dark green beanie to hide his identity and bright orange dark glasses that are too big for his face to draw attention to his identity. Of all the things in the world, I'm shopping with him. Root canal work was a doddle compared to this. Bryan conned me into it, which is even more annoying, saying that Floyd was struggling with Brady's death, meanwhile Floyd can't even remember who Brady is.

I'm more aware of my surroundings now. The visit from the policepeople excited yet unnerved me slightly. Being tall can have its disadvantages as we scrum through the seething masses in search of baggy clothes. Floyd is the only American in the band and is desperate to embrace the rapper hidden deep beneath his lack of talent and weak chin. For the first couple of hours he tries on over two dozen dungarees and twenty beanies and still hasn't been recognised.

"What do you think of this one, man?" he says to me, emerging from locker room number one hundred and five with a grubby denim outfit that should never have left the realm of the painter. He looks exactly as he did in the other twenty-three with the exception perhaps of an inconspicuous patch of a gangsta hidden on one of the numerous pockets.

"Very nice," I reply. "That's the one."

"Do ya think? I mean man, what is really good for me is that I show the British people that I'm black."

"Floyd you are whiter than a translucent jellyfish."

"Trans what man? Oh yeah those white trains. Yeah. But I gotta be a brutha," he says, punching his chest with the side of his fist and straightening his arm. A young girl, not older than twelve, spots him from across the other side of the store and bolts across to get an autograph.

"Who do ya want me to make it out to?"

"Rebecca."

"Okay just one second. Okay."

He trots over to where I'm sitting and asks, "Hey man, how do you spell Rebecca?"

"R – H – B – R – E – C - K – R – E - A," I spell out for him feeling vaguely guilty that the little girl's bubble is about to splatter. He mouths what he writes: "Dear Rhbreckrea, Floyd loves you, man. Always. Your Homeboy. Floyd." Her face is stoic yet confused as Floyd holds his fist out towards her after handing the note back to her. She accommodates and presses her diminutive fist onto his. Her group of friends are waiting in excited anticipation as she saunters back, slipping the note into the back of her jeans and shoving it right down where no one will find it.

"These girls, man," he says to me, putting on a pink beanie, leaning back and crossing his arms over his chest in front of the mirror. "They're so funny, man.

All of em." He then follows his pose with a twirl on his toes, ending up facing the mirror again and leaving me wishing I wasn't near him. The shop assistant giggles and goes into the back to share her vision with a colleague.

"I'm working on this new dance move, man," he says now aggravating my embarrassment by running through his demo right there in the shop. "It's called Floyd's Flip. I named it myself, man." And now he's gyrating on the spot as though he's connected to a wire and his arms are flailing and legs crossing and hips pulsing and wrists making circular motions. He's slowing down and I hope he's nearing the end of his routine when he unsuspectingly breaks into rap. All I can hear is something about a *mutha fucka* and *my brutha* and *dem bitches* and *honeys* and it sounds so bad that I contemplate murdering him right there in broad daylight, coming out of hiding to embrace my eradication of the most repellent boyband in the known universe.

No I'm not having a bad dream when he asks me to join in and I refuse until he invites people in the shop to judge his performance. They are all laughing at him and my sympathy remains at subzero because in his immense stupidity he truly believes he is redefining cool, right there on this breezy Saturday morning in Oxford Street. He's now holding a hanger and using it as a microphone as the crowd urges him into his oblivion of self-humiliation and when he finally (thank

God) ends with a twirl on his head followed by the splits, the crowd erupts in hysterical applause with Floyd the Feet bowing and loving the moment.

CHAPTER 42
GREAT EXPECTATIONS

Bryan's apartment has more books in it than a library. I'm marvelling at the plethora of impressive titles that enshrine me with a repertory of colour and expression. On every wall in every room are shelves, jam packed with hardcover, paperback, short, tall, fat, thin, square books, between which an eyelash would struggle to fit. Unbelievably I notice the book I saved: *The Dice Man*, squelched between *To Kill a Mockingbird* and *The Catcher in the Rye*, as Bryan dumps his coat and picks up the telephone.

"What kind of woman do you want?" he says

catching me completely unaware.

"Medium rare with pepper sauce," I reply not quite sure how to proceed from here.

"I'm sick of these little underage bitches sucking me off, so I thought we'd pay for a bit of action. Top dollar of course. So what's your preference?"

"One without a disease."

"White, black, Asian, Hispanic, Eastern European, short, tall, slim, athletic, big breasts – real and false – shaved minge, hairy as Led Zeppelin – beetle bonnet – you know, big arse, small arse, anal, come in the face, swallow, two girls, three girls, girl and guy, dark, blonde, red, pink, underage, overage, fucking anything man. It's on their website."

"I'll tell you what. I've got a bit of a thing for slapping a large wobbly arse. But it has to be fucking huge. Monumentally huge. So big that she needs to be pushed up the stairs. And ugly too. I want the ugliest fattest oldest dirtiest smelliest most decrepit whore in London. Can you find her for me?"

"You're shitting me."

"I'm not. Can't you organise that?"

"I can fucking organise anything," he says, flipping to another page of his diary. "You are one sick mother fucker, you know that, Paton."

I'm still marvelling at the literary collection that decorates the lounge when Bryan joins me for a cocktail. He negotiates the ingredients clumsily but emerges after a brief stint in front of the glass cabinet to join me on the brown leather couches.

"Sorted. My girl will be here after ten pm. Your swamp donkey will be here after eleven when she's finished gargling the public toilet water she just had the squitts in."

"I didn't know you were such a reader. There are some really great books in here. Who's your favourite author?"

"Probably Jilly Cooper – her covers are the best."

"Jilly Cooper – can't say I'm familiar. What's she written?"

"Can't remember. I don't ever read the books."

"You don't read the books?"

"No. I mean I read the back cover. That's why I buy them. To read the back cover. I was always a comic fan and figured books would look better than comics, so I buy them, read the back and then pop them onto a shelf. For safekeeping. In case I do actually read one one day."

There's a large white sculpture in each of the four corners of the open plan lounge. The cone-shaped chandelier that cascades above us sprays light in all directions turning the smooth white surface of the sculptures into real live animals. The elephant starts to trumpet and the dog runs to hide under the Persian rug. The tiger growls and leaps over my head while the flamingo blows smoke rings from its arsehole. It could be the light or perhaps the cocaine splattered all over my olfactory canals and in my brain.

I stagger through to the kitchen while Bryan puts on a home video of him whipping two teenage girls. Drinking water doesn't help. Still my godlike presence remains and still I feel out of control. But hey it's a night in; a night for friends and pillow fights and midnight feasts and secrets. Big secrets. The kitchen is colourful, the black and cream cupboards precariously waiting to be opened and explored. I'm not particularly hungry but manage to force down a left over pork pie that sits nonchalantly in Bryan's light grey retro refrigerator.

On my way back to the lounge I take a wrong turn and end up standing in complete darkness in one of the rooms and almost urinate on the white duvet cover. I rest for a while and seem to wake up on the toilet with an imaginary turd hanging from my bottom. There's another cutthroat razor above my head and at first it feels as though it's oozing hot wax all over me until I fight through the flames and make it back to the lounge where the porno belts out at me like a circus act.

Suddenly there are lips pressing firmly on mine and I'm watching a tall, red-haired woman with an elongated neck kiss me on the mouth on a video screen. I don't want this to happen and roll off the brown leather couch and onto the soft carpet which cannot meet my mental request and engulf me and take me away to a peaceful place. Despite my protests the redhead takes direction from the cameraman who sets up a tripod while the girl raises her red dress and sits firmly on my face, half suffocating, half breaking my nose. The only thing I can smell is warmth as I feel a rough mouth close over my penis and I'm asleep in my bed as a child in a small town sucking my thumb and fiddling with a figurine.

He-man.

Or a Thundercat.

I have the Power!

Thunder Thunder Thunder Cats Whoaaaaaaaaaa.

Then I'm awake and the camera is directly in front of me on a tripod and I don't feel better because the image projecting on the screen is me lying flat on the floor while Bryan forces his mouth onto me and the redhead performs the same action upon him. In my delirium he moves up to force his mouth against mine telling me to relax and run with it while he straddles my shoulders and shoves himself into my mouth while ordering the redhead to occupy herself while she watches. This could all be a horrible dream and I paralytically pray it is as I'm dragged towards the wanton depths of human existence, joining the teen masses who have all blown a boyband member.

The next minute there's blood all over my hands and small clumps of hair under my fingernails and I can hear screams from somewhere as I hunch over the toilet and vomit the undigested remains of a pork pie.

By the time I answer a knock at the door I've cleaned the blood from my hands and fished out the bits of pork pie caught in between my teeth. The woman on the other end elicits another spurt of bile into my mouth which I promptly swallow and smile without showing my teeth, trying not to focus in on the hairy wart that erupts from the tip of her nose like a cactus branch.

Her breath smells of cheap whiskey, smoked cigarettes and I gag as I tell her I will require her services in the very near future, but not tonight. I take her details trying to keep my wrist from shaking scribbles all across the post-it note and pay her double what she was due to earn making sure she'll pitch up on request for the next round of fun.

She smiles and runs a badly painted nail down my bare chest which makes me flinch and then try to cover up by ushering her politely away. Her smile reveals all four of her front teeth missing, the gums coated with grimy saliva like lubed rubber. She licks her gums while her mouth is open telling me something about 'a better feeling blowjob' then turns to waddle down the crazy paved footpath. Her fat rolls spill over her wide flaked white belt that looks as though it's tucked just under her enormous breasts that hang freely at her waist. The tight red dress she's belched into depicts each and every multi-sized loaf and the pockets of moist cellulite decorate her behind and upper thighs like polka dots. She waves and blows me a kiss before squeezing through the gate and pulling the dress from in between two tummy rolls.

The door shuts and the interior once again presses

down on me. Everything is silent in Bryan's apartment and still the literature stares down on me, the only dog-ears existing on the back page.

CHAPTER 43

A CLEARER PICTURE

Caroline likes to save money wherever she can. Her collection of grocery store coupons rivals that of a stamp collector. And she uses them. Even if there is no way whatsoever that she'll use the product, she will still buy it in order to get the discount.

She's a discount junkie.

Purple and blue pack of fifty cardboard party plates.

Pineapple cottage cheese – buy one get 50p off the next.

Garden spade - £2 off.

4 miles of super durable cling film.

Set of 24 metallic candle extinguishers.

I'm tapping my finger on the photo development counter of the chemist directly above the jumbo display print which shows an eighties style female with a golden retriever licking her face. The attendant stares vacantly back at me chewing gum with her mouth open and rolling her eyes as her assistant fishes around the counter below her for the prints. Caroline stands beside me looking up nervously but glad to be spending all this additional time with me.

I went round to her house exactly five days ago. I know this because this is how long the cheapest version of photographic development takes:

£2.99 in 6 days.

£3.99 in 4 days.

£4.99 in 2 days.

£6.99 in 1 hour.

Caroline picks 6 days.

There is no rush.

They're just photos.

Of her.

And Dave Reddill.

AKA Manfred Dill.

Caroline's description of Dave matches Manfred but for a few minor details. It was upsetting for her to describe him but she managed it when I told her it was important to me. She had no pictures of him except for the spool she handed in the previous day. It would take another five days. And here we are. Waiting. Waiting and wondering.

Caroline's confusion on the subject remains. Making her describe Dave Reddill in every conceivable detail (down to his penis which is still etched in my memory from the day I bumped into him at the gym) and dig through her entire flat to find something of his or at least a picture further intensifies the confusion. But nothing. So I rely on the description which is not enough. Accusations of this nature need proof and nothing provides better proof that a picture. One that takes six days to develop. Worth waiting for.

When the attendant finally digs out the pack he's more overjoyed than I am while the checkout girl doesn't alter her expression, tapping the keys of the till with practised precision. The gum still gets chewed.

"That'll be two pounds ninety-nine pence sir," she says as I place three pound coins that I've had ready for five days in her hand. I don't even hear the thank you as I grab Caroline by the wrist, bolt out the shop and head for the fast food dungeon across the road. Caroline orders a fresh portion of e-coli while I rip open the pack of photographs and begin flipping through.

Most of the early ones are of her dog which is both endearing and a bit sad. The first picture of Dave Reddill only reveals his palm, shielding his face from the camera. The next one's of Caroline looking disorientated after undoubtedly being relieved of the camera. Then there he is. A profile view but enough and all my fears receive a large but very definite tick.

Caroline's bemusement at the situation is further exacerbated when I rush off leaving her a masticating mess with tray in hand and fries in mouth. This puzzle is now confidently unsettling me, Manfred's unremitting involvement in my life slightly more serious than his idle threats. Is this revenge for the coffee machine? Does he want to hurt those around me to help the folds of scarred skin all over his ear heal? Does it have something to do with the trades, account transfers and client payments or has the coffee created an inner dementia where all he wants to do is get close to me? My major concern is that he's trying to get more than he already has on me. When he came back from hospital I felt there was something foreboding but that it would amount to nought but bought support for his promotion. I was never overly concerned, blinded by my quest. But now his dating, mating and extricating of Caroline leads me to believe that Manfred is not perhaps as stupid as he behaves. Still I believe my role to be passive: lie in wait in the shadows like a predator until Manfred hatches his maniacal plan. And plus I have more pressing business to attend to. Business that must be addressed very soon.

I seem to fluctuate on the topic of Manfred Dill. His extracurricular dealings can, as have been recently displayed, set my pulse throbbing and shatter my nerves. And at other times it's as though he's an annoying horsefly, punch drunk from being indoors too long, buzzing around my brain, waiting to be flattened at my discretion.

The key to my apartment won't fit inside the keyhole and only after a couple of frustrating pokes do I realise that I've mixed up my keys with Bryan's keys. She opens the door before I can rectify my error and kisses me on the cheek spanking me with a fresh dose of cheap men's cologne. It's stronger than ever this time which makes my coccyx ache and fails to deter Her chipper mood. She tries to make me feel Her belly which She claims is swelling. I don't have time and can't find what I'm looking for.

"Where is my toolkit?" I yell with my head buried in the hallway cupboard. "What?" I yell again, banging my head on the toiletry shelf above and bringing the entire shelf clattering down around me. She laughs at me sitting amidst a haphazard decoration of glass and plastic and tin. She starts helping me pick it all up which ends up swelling the volume levels of my irritation and then my hand comes to rest on a bottle of men's cologne. Cheap men's cologne. A brand name I can't remember. Her face notices my sudden lack of movement as I contemplate this boringly rectangular object in my hand. There's no shock, no nothing in Her eyes.

"What?" She says, looking bewildered.

"What's this?" I say, removing a lens case from inside my shirt and holding the cologne bottle up.

"It's my perfume."

"You've got men's cologne?"

"I like the smell. It's different."

"You wear men's cologne?"

"Well yes, but it does have subtle tones of lavender and peach. It's very androgynous really. Don't you like the smell?"

"I'm not sure," I say, getting out from the cupboard and dusting the remaining toiletries from me like beach sand. "Where are my tools?"

"I lent them to a colleague; at work. Remember I asked you a couple of months ago? Bill Bronson, Head of Finance? He and his wife were redoing their place?"

I vaguely recollect nodding to something of that effect while engrossed in a late night horror film, but hide my annoyance by mumbling to myself as I try to find a substitute. To say that my life is very full at present would probably render it the most understated thought that has crept into my skull since birth.

When I leave I think She's crying so I run all the way back up the stairs and kiss Her on Her belly which immediately floods Her face with happiness and glee, and fills me with, I am not afraid to admit, warmth.

CHAPTER 44

THE SHOW MUST GO ON

"So, you fancy yourself as a bit of a mover?" I say, pressing a series of drawing pins capaciously into his feet. He can't move too much because I've tied the extension cord about as tight as possible, and expresses his discomfort by wiggling his toes and screaming through the red bandana tied around his mouth. The drawing pins glide easily into the arch of his foot, the soft skin considerately parting and making way for the sharp gold metal points. The blood disappointingly doesn't squirt out but rather forms in a big globule before limply dribbling down each foot. The heel is harder to press drawing pins into and seems infinitely more painful. I've already tried unsuccessfully to saw off his toes with a blunt kitchen knife and only ended up meshing the fine black hairs on his toes into a rash-like paste. Bryan watches with fear splashed across his brow, his eyes trembling and naked body shivering.

"I have to, Bryan; it's the only way," I tell him. "I have to complete the prophecy and I've had very little time to express myself lately."

When I left home earlier that day I returned to Bryan's apartment to clean up the remainder of the mess that had presented itself to me. I had always planned to take it slowly towards the end and perhaps give the remaining uninflected members a chance to redeem themselves but they had both failed.

Dismally.

And as with the other three, the opportunities jumped out and bit me, making me completely and utterly convinced that this is the way it was meant to be. As I drove towards Bryan's apartment I watched the weather change four times in the space of an hour, each phase a metaphysical contrast on the previous. I watched as the rain flicked down on my windshield hardly worthy of the wipers, and then how the grey wind swept a host of orange leaves across the narrow street. I watched how the sunlight replaced itself with darkness, each ray exterminated like the repair of a holy bucket.

So when I arrived at Bryan's apartment the day was dark with early night-time hues, the transition earlier than normal. The door handle was cool when I entered and the hallway was quiet.

And I was calm.

Calm now that I know my fatherhood duties become more and more imminent and that my gift to future generations is to expose these phonies for what they really are; inform and educate the world. Tell them. Tell the youth. Make the world a better place for the unborn.

The dead girl was still in the bath. I'm not sure why I put ice in the bath that night, perhaps to prevent the body from rotting even though it wasn't that humid. Or perhaps to prevent any stench. But there she lies, her once vacant stare now enshrouded by dead eyelids and thick black fake eyelashes which I considerately left in place. The blood around her legs and the splatters speckling her entire body are dried but remain shiny from the half melted ice that surrounds her in the deep tub.

Bryan was half dozing when I got there so I woke him with a nice cup of filter coffee and a fresh cheese and onion bagel. He ate like a man possessed in between gulping apologies that fell on deaf ears. I kept telling him, he had to see the show; he had to be alive to witness history. Then his mood changed and it was back to hurling abuse just as the robber did when he realised the sucking-up approach was a dud. So I regagged his mouth to shut out the noise and checked his circulation under the tightly wound tape. His hands and feet looked a healthy colour and he didn't mention them in his desperate fit so I assumed they were receiving enough blood.

I checked his phone messages and there was one from Floyd who said he'd be coming around to pick up the dungarees Bryan said he could borrow. His timing could not have been more nerve-wracking as, if he was to be believed, he would have already been there. A couple of seconds after wheeling Bryan into a more prominent position in the lounge and locking the bathroom door, there was a loud knock at the door accompanied by the muffled beat of rap through the headphones of a Walkman. After another knock he let himself in because I had taken the latch off the front door and circumspectly peered around the hallway glass wall to find me smiling with open arms.

He wasn't sure why I was there. In fact I wasn't that sure why I was there and thought about finding the dungarees and sending him on his merry way. But hey, how often does one get two boyband members in a quiet apartment with a bevy of utensils and objects? When he walked ahead of me, swinging his limp arm from side to side in an attempt to emulate his African American heroes, I waited for him to enter the lounge and find Bryan, gagged, bleeding and bound.

It was a most confusing and exciting time for us all. When Bryan laid eyes on Floyd they lit up as though salvation was near, the joy manifesting in the form of inch-by-inch rabbit jumps towards the door. Floyd, after spouting a few 'maaaans' and 'muthafuckas', ended up running behind Bryan's chair, the terror just too much for him. For the first time he lost his ghetto accent to reveal a high-pitched whimper, which was not only barely audible but exceptionally disjointed. I hadn't yet made any sort of sudden movement and walked calmly over to Floyd whose confusion erupted in a menagerie of tears and screams. With Bryan acting as a twitching pole I chased Floyd around Bryan as though we were two kids playing catch. I eventually had to dive over Bryan to secure Floyd and calm him down. Floyd bit me on the shoulder once and left a now swollen gouge which has severely hampered my recent efforts. He also urinated and defecated in his pants which I made him change before tying him up with an electric extension cord. Oh yes, and I made him put on the highly sought after dungarees which he did so reluctantly. Once he was tied up and his gangsta demeanour safely flushed down the toilet along with his soiled underwear, I assured him that he would die and that it would be painful but that Bryan would get it far worse and that he would truly be famous after this. He was contributing to mankind after all. He would be remembered as the Feet and Bryan the Cock.

CHAPTER 45

A SURPRISE PACKAGE

While I'm in the middle of my work there appears an annoying text message on my mobile phone, which reads: 'Your phone is about to ring – I suggest you answer it.' The tone is so ultimatum-like that I feel sorely tempted not to take the call. And plus I've successfully removed an entire foot with a sharper kitchen knife and a screwdriver to pry between the bones when the vibration begins followed by the ring tone. The caller is not identified so I carefully answer it, expecting the worst.

"He doesn't know," says a woman's voice; Her

voice; the mother of my child's voice. "It's all covered up, don't worry. We can continue as normal. Don't you want to know that I'm pregnant?" And then the dead tone reverberating through my brain like a shockwave. I'm tempted to exert some pent up aggression out on one of my prisoners which I avoid by justifying the torture as a specific, deliberate and patient act rather than an angry one. Plus, Floyd has not moved since I twisted his foot free from his leg and asked him to 'rap' into the bloody end.

The recording of Her voice, probably over the telephone, has achieved its objective because I'm pacing up and down the book-filled lounge, wondering and waiting. Then another message appears stating merely an address which is a well-known coffee shop in Knightsbridge. I'm out the door without checking how securely my prisoners are fastened to their chairs and without cancelling Bryan's hot date.

The trip there is tedious and I can feel the nervous palpitations of my heart against my sternum. I've got a freshly cleaned hammer in my jacket pocket for protection which, only hours earlier I was using the back of to try and rip Floyd's toes from his feet. After a number of twists I tried to bend them off, similar to pulling a bent nail from a piece of solid wood. When that didn't work I used the hammer to bash a hole in both his kneecaps, which helpfully contributed to his 'drawing pin jive' which wasn't that dissimilar to his display in the clothes store.

I run my fingers along the cool metal: my phallic protector.

The coffee shop is full of tourists. There are too many bags littering the floor and a chorus of foreign accents and laughter. No one looks familiar so I unobtrusively saunter over to the counter and order a double espresso then proceed to one of the two unoccupied tables which is luckily in the corner right next to the bright orange print of an oversized orange.

The first sip settles in my stomach when two men walk in, one familiar, and join me at the table without ordering a coffee. Before lighting a brown cigarillo, Manfred offers me one which I refuse by shaking my head, never taking my eyes off his. I knew it was him but don't say this, quickly surveying the larger man who accompanies him, his thick neck rolls like mounted dough below his bald head. The hammer is still sturdily by my side, a more than apt substitute for my trusty brolly handle.

"This thing was always bigger than you and your little games, Paton," says Manfred eventually. "This is Koki, he's a, shall we say, private investigator-cum-gun for hire."

Koki nods and then settles back into his chair to stare at me from beneath his dark glasses. All I can think about is engraving his bald head with the hammer and then shoving it down Manfred's windpipe, hooking his lungs and ripping them free from his body leaving a giggling mess writhing on the dark red coffee shop floor.

"You and I were always going to cross paths, Paton. It was meant to be. You were sent to help me. You were a Godsend, sent from above to make sure I stay out of trouble and you stay in trouble. So I thank you, my dear friend. I thank you for your stupidity and for your convictions, no matter how sick and twisted. I suppose that's why Koki is sitting next me, just to make sure that you don't feel the urge to pour a bunch of wax down my throat."

The mention of wax immediately sends shivers down my spine and I'm already on the back foot, although I didn't really expect anything different. Manfred's hands are still, unlike mine which I have to clasp together to avoid knocking on the table. I still haven't spoken.

"I'm here to blackmail you, Paton. There I said it. Now you know. It's all out. On the table. I know what your first question is: how? Am I right? Of course I'm fucking right, you mute! Are you going to sit there like a fucking dummy your whole life?"

"No, just for the afternoon."

"Still the comic. It's all a big joke isn't it. It always has been. I needed an erratic loser, you see. Someone no one would take seriously until it was too late. Someone who really didn't give enough of a shit to notice. Someone no one would miss. Someone stupid enough to do something so blatant that blaming them for it is easier than putting the winning medal around an athlete's neck. But the beauty of this is really how wonderfully you fell into place.

"You were a rather tough nut to crack in the beginning though. At first I thought let's see if we can get Paton Stipps to do something a bit rash; for a bit of leverage. Provoke you to attack me or something. Lash out. At least for this first part of the ploy because good old fashioned command control management wasn't moving this forward quickly enough. Shoving my head into a fucking coffee machine was, in hindsight, suitable for keeping the impetus of you doing exactly what I told you up but clearly not enough to ensure your silence. What I truly love about you is how you just kept doing it: transfer the money, leave the signatories blank, ignore company procedures. You never thought anything was up? Or perhaps you did but were a slight bit distracted to notice.

"So I needed to try a couple of other things to get better leverage; to get my hooks into the private life of Paton Stipps. With your help I was in so deep by then there really couldn't be anyone else but you. So I started dating the girl I thought you were fucking: the fat ugly bitch who was about the most frigid and repulsive lay I've ever had the displeasure of participating in. Stupid bitch. She lapped it up like the dirty pussy that she is. She couldn't believe someone was paying her so much attention: buying her flowers, sending her little romantic text messages, fucking her all night long. Puke, puke, puke! And she too came up with nothing. I mean it's not that I really thought you'd ever fuck something as fat and ugly as that, it's just I thought she might lead me to greener pastures.

"So I suppose it's fitting that your little gay buddy, who you seemed to be spending a lot of time with, provided the real clue to the secret life of Paton Stipps. And oh what a secret life it is, Paton, what with your little obsession with boybands."

I can hear him relay the events of past moments before me but it comes across in slow motion as though he's mouthing the words without actually saying anything. The meaning is glaringly clear though. I have become Manfred's obsession just like the boyband is mine. He has me in his sweaty little clutches. Somewhere, somehow, I've gone wrong and it's going to cost me dearly. And I'm about to find out. And still I finger the hammer that potently sleeps in my jacket pocket.

"Cigarillo? No? So enter Koki: the hired help. And not cheap at that. It's fucking hard to find this sort of help if you don't know where to look. You don't fucking go digging through the yellow pages, that's for fucking sure. You dig these fuckers out of the pit of society you do. They exist elsewhere."

Koki stirs uncomfortably without dropping his menacing aura and without altering his expression.

Not even a raised eyebrow.

Or a clenched jaw.

"Thank God there are a couple of Dills who were on

the bad end of the gene pool, because without them our dear friend Koki would not have entered our lives and provided such a rich tapestry of ammunition.

"So I dump your bitch hog friend when I realise I might have to chew my arm off first before I fuck her again and I realise that she's no good to me anymore. Koki bugs your home phone line and begins following you based on my suspicion of another woman. This would have proved the perfect ammunition, you see: blackmailing you to your girlfriend for sticking it in somewhere else. But that didn't work either and I was beginning to lose all hope when bam-a-lam – a double whammy jumps into my lap."

Without receiving a signal Koki takes from his person a dull yellow non-descript envelop and empties the contents onto the table, the loud clatter not deterring any of the manic patrons. The rubble includes a pile of black and white photographs, Jonathan's downloaded picture of Bryan and a small grey Dictaphone complete with miniature tape inside. Manfred proudly surveys his arsenal, the corner of his mouth turning up in proud affection. He lights his fifth cigarillo.

"Pick one Paton, go on," he says waiting for me.

"Why don't you pick for me," I say.

"Don't you want to know what all this is for first? Aren't you curious as to why I've spent most of my recent waking adulthood trying to pin something on you? Isn't there a slight pang of curiosity in that body of yours which aches to know why? Why. Because it doesn't matter if you know now. From now on whatever you know about me or my dealings will follow you to the grave."

Another gauche silence.

"Money Paton, money. That's what it always comes down to: money. You see our little investment firm has their grubby little fingers in a lot of dirty pies which means a lot of useful information falls on not-so-deaf ears. But because we aim to be such an upstanding organisation, we are prevented from acting personally on any such information. What's the fucking use of that? We can't trade if we are regularly getting the shit-hottest stock tips around? We can't sell debt if we know the bond's dipping credit rating before the market does? It doesn't make sense. Someone has to stand up and break the mould. Someone has to say, 'Screw the rules' and do a bit of cheeky inside dealing. Someone has to break the law and that someone is you. Well your name anyway. My fortune and your name. So when you can't explain to the authorities where all the millions of pounds you made from your insider dealing accounts are, you'll be locked up. But trust me, taking the wrap for that will sure beat taking penalty shots from the resident head nigger in the maximum security prison when you're serving life for murder.

"You know we know that you killed that celebrity. But what you don't know is how we can prove it. Koki followed you for a long time before striking gold, and even then it was difficult. He followed you home and to work and to your boyband boyfriend and to your fat friend and to the fucking toilet and eventually you end up in a high-class brothel and you dump a load of wax on some dumb celebrity. So while Koki's snooping around the salon he stumbles onto the video surveillance unit tucked neatly away in a small room at the back. Conveniently there's no one in there so Koki gets comfortable to keep an eye on you. So while he's there his naturally low attention span begins to shine through and he pops in one of the videotapes lying around. As it turns out, these cute little entrepreneur hookers all dressed in virginal white have been running a blackmail business on the side, recording prominent members of our esteemed community fuck their brains out. So Koki pops a tape in and pushes record, and lights, camera, action: Paton Stipps kills someone. It's all there. Keep the tape. We've made copies."

The sweat, which has now dribbled from my palms down my wrists to collect at the front of my elbow, cools my skin. All I can do is sit and listen, helpless in my own controlled environment; powerless and unable to slash two people open in public with a hammer. The silence now becomes deafening as the surrounding noise becomes distant and the people all begin moving with slow shuttered motion leaving trails of previous actions behind them.

It's a dream. I'm dreaming, that's it. This is all a bad dream and when I wake up, I'll be late and a big fat arse will be waiting to block me on my way to work.

I wake with a start and still Koki scratches his nose without touching it and Manfred smirks in front of me, waiting for my move. I'm not sure why but I try to stand up and then sit straight back down. I decide to talk.

"So I'm done for," I say. "That's it. The end of my life. And you did it. You succeeded where others might not have. Well done. So what happens now? What happens now?"

"Nothing my dear boy, nothing. You sit and wait for the cops to knock on your door and take you away for insider trading. It'll happen sooner or later. Then they'll ask you for the money. This is where you have the real decision: refuse to tell them and you'll get ten years tops. Tell them about me and the tape comes out with all mayhem breaking loose. Ten years will seem like a midnight piss compared to the media circus that will follow. You said you wanted to change the world and you certainly did: my world."

Manfred adjusts his tie beckoning towards his impending exit. Koki stirs and stands upright, his large mass shadowing my seated body like a mountain. With Manfred's red carpet ready he stands up to leave, dusting off imaginary dust from his jacket and once again straightening his tie.

"Oh yes, and the Dictaphone is an additional gift. A compilation. Call it a reality present; a perk of the phone bugging trade. It's just so you don't go through life hankering after some stupid bastard, and I mean bastard in the purest sense of the word."

And then like a ghost he disappears and the density of the coffee shop remains while I reach out a shaking hand to find the play button on the Dictaphone. First static and then the following exchange –

"Hi, it's me. Can you talk?" says a muffled woman's voice.

"Yes, Sheila's out, but I told you not to call me at home. What the fuck are you doing calling me at…" a man's voice is cut short.

"I'm pregnant," says the woman again.

Then static again which lasts for an eternity then the exchange again, this time the voices more audible and the background interference significantly less. Another conversation altogether.

"He doesn't know," says a woman's voice; Her voice; the mother of my child's voice. "It's all covered up, don't worry. We can continue as normal. Don't you want to know that I'm pregnant?"

"We spoke about this already." The same man's voice.

"You are the father for fuck's sake! You know that!"

"Yes I know, just calm down."

"Bill, if you leave me hanging, I will tell your wife."

"Calm down! We spoke. We can continue as normal, okay. How did you convince him?"

"I made sure there was no doubt that he was the father."

"So you…"

"I had no choice. I even fucking bought a bottle of

your shit cologne and emptied half out. He always smells it on me and if he finds out he'll leave and I'll be alone with a married man's bastard inside me. What he doesn't know won't kill him. Now I just have to make sure he finds the cologne and believes that I wear it. So change your brand or stop fucking bathing in it!"

I can feel the hammer still dormant in my pocket and the extent of my aggression centres on my own stupidity.

CHAPTER 46

BLED OUT

Nothing makes sense for a while. Floyd bled to death from the numerous holes punctured in his leg. I throw him, his leg (severed between the knee and the ankle) and his ankle (with drawing pins still decorating the sole of his foot) into the tub with the dead girl who is still as fresh as fruit salad.

Floyd the Feet.

No longer.

I settle next to Bryan to watch the recorded scene and try to make sense of everything that I have brought on myself over previous months. Despite Manfred's threats and the carnage around me my mind still wanders back to Her like an abused child seeking shelter with violent parents. Things were just beginning to make sense too: the humming in my head had started to die down and mornings had become happy times without inside-out umbrellas, fat arses or obnoxious kids on buses. Now the humming drills pores throughout my skull and there seems little passion left in my work.

I contemplate killing Bryan quickly, just because I've lost the urge to tie up my final boyband gift to the world. Bryan now refuses to talk or eat as the tape rewinds and static is replaced by a perfect test pattern.

"Looks as though you taped over something important," I say in a pathetic attempt to evoke conversation with a gagged boyband member.

The last of his kind.

The last with his prized asset.

Dangling innocently between his legs.

The only one left with the power.

The tape spurs forward reluctantly to reveal Jamie doing a few press-ups before what looks like an outdoor shoot. There is a barbershop in the background. Brady is next to him applying his clumps of gold chains as though they were healing mud. PJ sits with his legs crossed in a make-up chair inaudibly unhappy with the application of his eyeliner. Floyd's practising dance moves in between signing autographs and doing mini-rap songs for adoring teenage fans. The camera is placed on a bench and from behind it Bryan reveals himself and rushes over to a group of teenage girls who are beside themselves with him. The camera picks up

the detail of their obsession: they're crying, reaching out as though he were Christ, trying to get just one little touch from this eager, truly pitiable boy aside me, with a hooker's blood splashed all over his face. He signs a few of their t-shirts and hands them what looks like a business card. While he's signing one particularly innocent looking girl's shirt she takes his hand and places it inside her shirt on her small, humped breast. He leaves it there, only smirking and squeezing until she recoils slightly. Then he rushes back to pick up the camera mouthing, "They love the Bryan K," on his way.

I forward through the dance routine and more autograph signings and general juvenile behaviour including riding around on a toy tricycle, group hugs, attempted tough looks, various exercises and the lifting of shirts for adoring fans.

"Which song is this?" I ask Bryan, taking off his gag and pretending to know Coastal Love's greatest hits. He doesn't answer, staring blankly at the screen as more static follows and the music video of the shoot suddenly bursts forth from the flat screen as the polished final product.

The setting looks awkwardly familiar although I'm viewing it from the wrong angle. I should be lower and sweating. As the first lyrics splash across my face a joy then a pain forms inside my head that drowns out the humming and makes me want to push a knife through my Adam's apple. I try to unblock my ears by swallowing but nothing seems to happen and when I close my eyes I see Her smiling face with a dead foetus in Her arms, the blood and white mucus torrenting down Her arms and breasts and stomach.

I'm not allowed in this world. It's just too much for me. I will struggle to find happiness again among the rubble of boyband bodies, insider-dealing sentences, videotapes, faked sex, old half-smoked cigarettes and favourite songs.

Coastal Love sings the song I've been after for months.

The one that remains at the top of the charts.

The one that ricochets through my mind now and still sounds good despite the source.

I think Bryan notices my distress because he looks nervously over as I sob openly into my hands until they're covered like old food in the fridge, only this time with bucket tears slopping now onto the floor.

"Tell me you didn't write that," I cry, unable to look in Bryan K's direction.

"It's a remake," he says. "A cover version. Can't believe it did so well. Kids lap these things up don't they?"

Then the video is interrupted by the foul shenanigans that transpired the other evening and I watch, determined to refocus my efforts and find a reason to complete my prophecy. I watch as Bryan performs oral sex on me and then me on him, my hallucinatory state further amplified by the lucid picture. The girl is reasonably passive at this stage, following Bryan's directorial commands and sitting on me. What follows is me passing out from the drugs, for all of a sudden my body goes limp and, even after a few playful slaps in my face with his penis, I am out for the count. The girl, now uncertain, stands up looking wearily at the camera then at my lifeless form on the carpet.

"What the fuck are you stopping for?" yells Bryan, grabbing her by the back of her hair and shoving her face into my crotch. "Wake him!" Bryan then disappears while the redhead nervously tries to arouse me with her mouth. The camera moves slightly to focus clearly on her face with her eyes closed, engulfing me in her mouth. Then suddenly her eyes bolt open in fear and pain as something happens behind her off camera. Then a belt is flung around her neck and she's clawing at it, her nails snapping as she tries to pull the taut leather free, her skin bunching in diminutive folds and her windpipe swelling under her chin.

When she's almost lost consciousness Bryan releases the belt and again dashes behind the camera to pan out, revealing a wooden handled kitchen knife protruding from her arse. He returns to her and enters her from behind, the fusion of juices and blood heightening his pleasure as the mixture splashes up all over his face. Somewhere in the middle of this I see myself wake up and pull the knife from the girl which makes me vomit immediately. Bryan falls back from inside her and laughs as he brings himself to ejaculate, his manhood now shining with the girl's blood, the colour an almost identical match to her hair which now drapes in opposite directions across her lifeless shoulders. I grab the girl in my arms trying to talk her into living as she limply hangs from my body, a river of brown blood escaping from between her legs.

"Is this all you are pissed off about?" he says in the present. "Or is it that you wanted to suck my cock? She was just a dirty little whore, man. A dirty whore who didn't know how to follow directions. They should learn with me."

"So you killed her?"

"Didn't she deserve to die? Will anyone miss her?"

"Probably *no* to both of those."

"Why are you doing this to me?"

"I have to set an example for the world to follow."

"They won't follow this deranged shit. The world loves me. The world fucking loves me. Thousands around the world will mourn when I'm gone. I'm bigger than the twin towers for Christ's sake – at least they can be rebuilt."

"Why do you choose to live this lie?"

"It took me nineteen years to get laid. Girls at school used to laugh at me and tease me because my ears stuck out or because I was short or because my hair was too curly. Now who's laughing? Call it retribution. Call it what you like. Whatever the case, it sure beats making apologies your whole life. Like you. You'll be making apologies for the rest of your life when you end up rotting in some shit prison with rats and grime and shit."

"You're probably right there," I say, picking up my car keys.

My journey home is wrought with anxiety. Again I need something and again I'd rather She wasn't there. I just need to slip in and slip out without being noticed like an odourless fart in a cinema. I'm not quite sure how I'll react when I see Her. I'm not quite sure what I'll do when I lay my eyes upon Her sordid face and Her infested womb. Perhaps I'll cut the bastard from Her and feed it to Her. And it won't be punishment for Her but rather for me for allowing queer emotions to dominate rational thought and basic survival. But I would lie if I say I wasn't angry because now my forehead is numb and raw from bashing it on the steering wheel in resentment.

The windows are shut which is a great sign because usually they sit wide open while She is inside, rollercoastering and filtering used air. The place I've been going to and from for so many years now seems almost foreign to me as though it's a distant memory or some early chapter in a book. Up until now it has been my safe haven, away from the madness of the outside world, sheltering and protecting me and providing me with a constant. I've always been able to run there. Solving the world's problems; teaching kids manners; dissolving false publicity ideals; setting failures on the road to success; helping people discover their true selves – all external. All away from this place that was my home. And now nowhere to go but back to the blood-stained apartment where my prisoner awaits to receive his sentence.

The thought of completing the lesson immediately fills me with peace and calm.

The fresh smell of food cooking glides my way as I enter. She appears wearing an apron and armed with a wooden spoon and grater. Her cordial smile bites right through the middle of me like an angry bullet, tearing my insides out and rendering organs useless in their plight. She knows something is wrong because She immediately drops the utensils and rushes over to hold me. I feel Her small body against mine as my arms hang rubbery by my side and She tries to nestle into my heart like a worm.

"Love me," She keeps repeating. "Our love can mend it."

I feel Her hands holding onto my shoulder blades, crossed over one another and holding on like a rock climber knowing that if She lets go She will fall to Her death. It's very easy to kill Her now. I mean the logistics are easy, but the energy that remains in my body cannot, no will not, take this life that deserves better than me.

For one brief second I lean down and kiss Her jagged parting for the last time. I escape from Her grasp and then find my package which is exactly where I left it in the back of the freezer, wrapped in a brown packet behind the opened frozen peas. I look across at Her cooking and walk out secure in the knowledge that She will be eating that on Her own tonight.

When I reach the entrance hall She's huddled in a corner sobbing hysterically and cussing to herself.

"Why did you let me go?" She asks hugging Her knees like a child. I open my mouth to reply but nothing comes out like the last bit of air left in a deflated tyre.

"It's not too late," She screams.

"I can't," I say, choking on the words. "It's too late for me. It must be this way. There's too much that will haunt us. Goodbye. Goodbye Janine."

And as my steps echo down the stairwell I hear Her frenzied screams turn to eternal sadness. The silence that now seals the building mirrors the three souls that will be forever alone.

CHAPTER 47
THE END OF THE WORLD AS WE KNOW IT

Caroline doesn't lie because Manfred's key is tucked safely behind the hanging green pot plant that dangles above her porch, twisting awkwardly in the gusty gale. I make one call on my mobile before heading back to Bryan's to finish this thing.

When I get there she's waiting in the same red dress she was squeezed into the night I had to turn her away. I usher her inside trying not to touch her and avoid any prying eyes from the outside. As she walks through the door her worn heel collapses and she hits the floor like falling granite.

"Are you okay?" I ask, grabbing her arm and pulling her to her feet, the loose skin of her arm sliding between my fingers as my hand slips from her elbow to her wrist.

"Yes I'm fine," she says, readjusting her crotch. "Just need a new pair of heels I will."

"That's fine, this will cover more than that." I hand her a wad of cash in a disorganised bundle.

"This is a load of cash it is. What exactly am I being paid to do in here?"

"Well let's say that this won't be your normal sort of job. And what happens in here will need to stay between us."

She laughs so that the wart on her nose bobbles like a worm in the sand and her wedding cake appearance seems to convulse in waves of spasm.

"Mister, do you think a girl like me is hired to do 'normal sorts of jobs'? Do you think men pay me to turn them on? For this kind of cash I'll perform whatever you want, however you want, whenever you want and to whomever you want. This is what I do it is."

"The first time you ever had sex, what was it like?" I ask Bryan, cleaning him up with a warm cloth while the fat lass dirties herself in the bathroom.

"I had to pay for it," he says, nibbling on the

chocolate bar I've thrown in his lap and sipping the gin and tonic I've lovingly poured for him. "A friend paid for it. She was fit as well. Only she laughed when I could only last a few seconds. Bitch."

"And since then it's been hot hot hot. Only hot bitches for our Mr Bryan K."

"Well I can't deny I was a late blossomer. And yes I have fucked some of the cutest little pussies around the world. But that starts to get boring after a while. It was never enough to get blown by some little underage bitch until she choked on my come. I needed more."

"I have just the thing for you. Now you behave while I tie you in a different position and get the camera."

Bryan is tied in a ritualistic X when the hefty hooker enters. The manoeuvring of the ropes is exceptionally skilful even if I do say so myself. His wrists are taught above his head in a 'stick em up' pose and his legs are spread. Each bookshelf has acquired some of the rope tension and thankfully Bryan's excessive reading habit ensures that the shelves are pillar steady. The camera is running when she runs over to him, drops her parachute like panties, squats over his face and explodes. The spray of shit everywhere is like bursting a balloon filled with runny chocolate. Bryan is now gasping for air, spitting bits out of his mouth and scarcely able to comprehend what has just happened. Before he can gain his breath she sits straight down, her huge mass leaving a cracking sound: probably Bryan's altered again nose.

Then in a strangely corporeal way she begins sliding her exposed cavities all over his face, backwards and forwards, rubbing most of her insides all over what I imagine to be Bryan's exasperated expression.

While she does this she leans forward, undoes Bryan's trousers and begins giving him oral pleasure. Surprisingly he achieves wood relatively quickly, which sees her begin spitting snot all over his crotch. She's squeezing his balls inordinately tightly and I'm about to stop her, in fear of bursting one, when one of Bryan's far away looks in the video jumps into my head and I think fuck it, let him try that look now. His fans would love that.

"Can we turn him over?" she asks trying to get at his anus with her brightly painted chipped nails. I tell her it's too difficult with the ropes and that he'd prefer it if she entered from a difficult angle. That it would give him more pleasure, I tell her. Bryan's screams are amplified when she lifts her abdomen mass from his face, the trail of thick moisture and faeces creating a web-like effect between the two lovers.

She then eases her mass down his body and onto his erection which is slowly beginning to wane. His screams and cursing arouses her even more and she begins riding him violently and decisively. She leans back and changes his erection from the front to the back, then leans even further to cup his mouth. This is like some great anti-porno where the woman has all the power: her thrusts more penetrative than any man;

retribution for her abused sisters. It's so brutal I think she might slam the two of them through the floor and downstairs. I see her expression change and again she straddles his face to climax. Her orgasm would rival a rhinoceros, the sheer volume of liquid raining down on Bryan's muddy face enough to drown the man. The splash partially cleans his face and he can again see which means he pukes all over his chest. He then tries to spit his vomit at her to get her off which only sees her backhand him a few times into submission.

The camera picks up her quest to invade him where he invaded the redhead with the knife. The precision of her nails scraping open his hairy chocolate starfish makes me shudder because it's quite obvious she's trying to get her whole fist inside. I leave the camera and move around to the front, the graphic display way exceeding what I expected. When Bryan eventually spouts forth, the woman does have her fist, bunched in a globular ball, inside his bleeding rectal cavity which seems to heighten the pleasure and the pain. The grand finale; the pièce de résistance in the Hulk's *Ode to Bryan K* consists of her feeding him back his own semen by taking him in her mouth, then spitting the load into his throat and holding his mouth shut until he swallows.

Bryan the Cock.

HOW TO MURDER A BOYBAND

Breaking and entering in London can't be that difficult. There aren't many burglar bars. There aren't many high walls decorated with barbed wire. And there certainly aren't many dogs. These are the criteria I'm counting on as I drive towards Manfred's house armed with my trusty hammer and an A-Z.

While I'm stopped at a traffic light I reread the note I've scribbled. It gets more and more perfect every time

I read it. I fold it along the same line I folded it previously and pop it back into the envelope. The contents, all carefully wrapped in separate freezer bags, shift as the note dissects them and nestles into its home before the envelope is licked and sealed. Manfred Dill is written in capitals on the outside in a thick black marker pen. Even the curvature of the letters shows an element of distress. Just the way I've planned it. As though I never wanted to commit these atrocious acts of violence.

Minutes before I reach Manfred's abode I dial 999 and say the following, "I can't handle it anymore. He made me do it." The operator tries to calm me because I'm now sobbing into the receiver. She's trying to get my name and address but I'm not quite done yet.

"He forced me he did. Manfred Dill. And now I'll have to live with the guilt of knowing what I've done for the rest of my life. Get Venables or Garden. The officers. They'll know. They'll know I did it. Coastal Love. The end of the boyband. Forever. I never wanted to. He made me. He promoted me and blackmailed me. Made me perform all these horrible acts on those poor boys just because of some hidden vendetta. Meaningless really. The blackmail too. Something about insider trading. Said he'd go to the cops and tell them everything about my insider trading: buying stocks using inside company information. I only did it because he told me to. Said we'd make money from all this. Said it was legal. And now he has it all and I have nothing. Only a heavy conscience. All because he hated boybands. All because he hated boybands. All because he hated…"

I cut the line there and try to get out of character. The lights near the front part of the house are on and there are two vehicles outside: a dark blue Mercedes and a white BMW. The neatly manicured lawn outside is sparse but for a few ferns and well-watered pot plants. After I've sidled up to the front of the house with my lights off, I exit the car and slip around the side of the house where there are no lights on. The wind whistles between my ears and my jacket collar, chilling my hands as I carry the return package.

The kitchen sash window is ajar and I decide to use Caroline's back door key when the window creaks loudly as I try to shift it upwards. At the back of the house the air seems colder, almost more foreboding as I almost knock over a vase full of seashells resting precariously on an oval garden table. No noise comes from inside the house.

Manfred hasn't changed the locks since he broke Caroline's heart because the key slips into the lock as it has done a million times before. I open the door as slowly as I can, praying there won't be a large fellow named Koki waiting for me on the other side with a sawn-off baseball bat. The tepid air from the hallway welcomingly sprays my face as I shut the door behind me and make my way down the long corridor.

Still no sound bellows from within; no game show

cheers from a television set; no boisterous laughter or smoky air; no kettle boiling or cup chinking; nothing.

Nothing but the dim shade of light angled off walls and peering at me from the end of the never-ending corridor. I place two fingers on the side of my neck to check my pulse and it seems normalish I suppose.

When I reach the end of the corridor I peer around the corner picturing my nose appearing in slow motion to the recipients on either side. But disappointingly there's no one. Just a closed door to the left and the remainder of the corridor leading to the kitchen on the right. Something catches my eye just to my right and after quietly swinging around I find myself staring at a reflection in a large, silver-rimmed mirror. I try to figure out what is going on in my face; what is going on in my existence, looking thoroughly into my own eyes watching the blinks and waiting for me to do something, when the back door opens behind me. Suddenly light sprays in every direction and I hop left, pressing my back against the door. I hear keys thrown on a glass table, the clatter reverberating towards me like a hungry cricket. And the footsteps, casually approaching the end of the corridor, the heel-toe tap so distinctly familiar I crouch, ready to pounce somewhere.

Then another noise, this time behind me from the other side of the closed door. A flush. The sound of water taking away waste as the door opens without the customary washing of hands. And the odour reaches me first before the doorframe is filled by a large and surprised expression.

With large unwashed hands.

Now clenched in fists.

One step towards me accompanied by a yell to the approaching homeowner.

As far as reactions go this has to be one of the more decisive. I feel my thigh lift as I kick forward and catch the man perfectly in between his legs. My shin slices upwards and finds gold as Koki drops onto one knee before the same leg smashes into his face sending him reeling backwards into the smelly toilet.

Before I can turn around I feel a large ceramic crash on my head and the warmth of blood as it seeps through my hair and mingles with my scalp. Manfred is armed with half a statue in front of me, the jagged edge now thrust into my stomach which tears me open. Manfred's eyes burn in front of me as he twists the statue, grating through my flesh, bits snapping off to dwell inside me. I feel my head jump at him propelling down on top of his nose, which only sees me further impaled on the half-eaten statue, the pain searing through each exposed vessel. My legs are abruptly weak and I feel my head aching when a large forearm curls around my neck, suffocating me. I'm a human pincushion for a while as Manfred pokes holes in me with the sharp, blood-moistened statue.

I'm now horizontal and I'm not sure how much time has transpired. I'm lying on top of a plastic sheet on the floor and I see two figures pondering over something a couple of feet away. The pain in my abdomen stings through towards my toe tips and fingertips and I feel like I need a glass of filtered water. Or a fresh orange juice. I can't lift my head which is probably a good thing because I'm convinced my insides are hanging on either side of me like electrical wires.

Darkness again but I can hear talking. It sounds like Bryan K and the rest of Coastal Love practising their assault on an unsuspecting world. I see their faces clearly in my head now: each pose a dreamy look into the camera, each one killing a note and mouthing the words as though their agony is like mine. Their eyes are all bright and alive; their jaws clenched, their gazes distant, their tracksuits shining white complete with silver linings and dark blue glitter lines. They're all singing and then suddenly one thanks God and breaks into evangelical prayer. Bryan now cries for himself, the choking tears so fake that he pretends to blow his nose on his sleeve. They're a boyband; a different species; one created in a Petri dish in a cruel laboratory; one grown and nurtured to act pathetically and programmed to be idiots. In their genetic makeup. Made to believe they're cool. When they're not. Not their fault.

I'm cold and seconds feel like hours. I want to ask for help when Koki slaps me awake, still panting from the exertion near the toilet that occurred only moments before. He sits me up on a chair after placing the plastic down first so that my blood won't stain the furniture.

Manfred puts himself in front of me and his mouth moves but I can't hear him. He waves the package in front of me and brushes it across my face, his crooked teeth reflecting the bright living room light into my eyes.

I'm dozing off when Koki again slaps me awake so that I'm staring at Manfred holding a freezer bag containing a big toe in front of his face, his expression now one of absolute confusion. He reads the label on the bag to me, his tone questioning, "Floyd the Feet?" Then he pulls from the package another bag, this one a partially frozen piece of tongue: "Jamie the Mouth?" Then a videotape labelled 'The End Of The World As We Know It' which he tosses to Koki, instructing him to put it on. He continues rummaging through nevertheless pulling a bag labelled 'PJ the Face' containing a sliver of skin haphazardly wrapped in matted hair, the end crinkled and burnt. Then a peel of sinew, the edges black with dried blood and traces of wax still present labelled 'Brady the Body'.

The tape starts rolling and immediately Manfred's attention is away from the package as the three hundred pound leading actress appears in the frame. The angle of my body is such that to turn and face the television set would be too painful so I watch Manfred's face, his contortions an accurate depiction of the performance. Then the final bag is hoisted out of the package like a trophy: a severed penis, average in size, lifeless, at the bottom of the bag, the label 'Bryan the Cock' like a museum exhibit descriptor.   And Manfred, slowly connecting the dots, then lifting the note out of the bag and turning the video off.

I watch, breathing in short final bursts, as his eyes dart around the page, Koki on the other side of the room waiting in poised anticipation. I breathe in and smile as a commotion ensues outside and the front door is kicked in. Manfred and Koki look up in that direction in perfect unison as my laughter turns to coughing and then choking. Manfred's hands suddenly go in opposite directions tearing the page in two and he shoves the one bit in his mouth as the police point weapons at each man and demand he spit the evidence out. Manfred's glance at me as the police rush to all three of us is stern and beaten, his surprise at the text now replaced by hopeless bereavement. Bereavement at his forthcoming loss.

The pain now takes me on a longer journey as the paramedics wheel me away and put me in an ambulance, the flimsy blanket not enough to keep the chilly air from attaching to my aching bones. I'm clutching the blanket as the siren begins and two fastidious hands begin fiddling inside my wounds. When I wake again I'm still in the vehicle as the siren continues and I'm sliding from side to side as sudden turns are made. There are the same two pleasant faces fussing over me in paroxysmal jerks, reaching from me to the side of the ambulance and back again. One of them strokes my forehead for a second and then continues trying to save me.

There's now a new feeling inside me. One without

fear or resentment. One without loathing or prejudice. One that warms me and refuses to let go. I'm not a father yet, this much I know but I feel as though I have created something truly wonderful. There are a whole bunch of clear plastic wires hanging above me swaying as the journey continues. A monitor beeps I think. My throat is aching, numb and raw and the nicest face mouths something to me as I blink and try to smile. I feel myself cry for no reason other than there's a beautiful face in front of me. Someone working furiously to bring me back and reintroduce me to the life I have resented and taken for granted for so long. Her smile moves from my vision

Boyband slain in New York hotel room

US based boyband LoveBoyz tragically lost their lives in a midnight chainsaw romp in New York yesterday evening. The Los Angeles based God-loving band were on their summer tour when Jim Phillips, a twenty-four-year-old delivery boy, entered their hotel room at around 11:15 pm with a chainsaw concealed beneath his overcoat. Sources say the band were indulging in illegal substances with a large number of minors which meant Phillips was easily able to gain access to the band's room under the false pretence of being a member of their church congregation. Hotel staff are not claiming responsibility stating that the band clearly issued authorisation from the room. Hotel residents claimed the noise from the slaughter was not dissimilar to a 'horror movie', the band's screams heard some three floors above. Detective Kirk Coolidge of the New York Police Department was put on record saying that there was no connection between Phillips and the murder of British based boyband Coastal Love. Manfred Dill still maintains his innocence as he serves out his life sentence in Dartmoor Prison. Other sources claim an underground cult has been growing in popularity and recognition, started by the events that shook the pop world almost a year ago. The cult is said to aim to exterminate all boyband members in bands around the world and it is claimed that bands around the world have been altering their images in line with this new fear-based phenomenon. LoveBoyz, like the members of Coastal Love, will be severely missed by loyal fans around the globe. Their music touched the lives of many and will be remembered for their carefully choreographed stage acts, the miming scandal a few months ago and the admission by members of the band to having been involved in tame levels of paedophilia. Still LoveBoyz set new records for singles sales topping the US charts a record 28 times. A tribute to the band is rumoured to already be underway and will be held in Central Park hosted by main rivals Boys Will Be Boys. Let's hope organisers are able to step up security efforts on a day that will surely be memorable.

BV - #0070 - 180225 - C0 - 197/132/20 - PB - 9781912964994 - Matt Lamination